Acknowledgement

I would like to thank my awesome editor at Triplicity, Ashley Hutchison, for being patient with me. I know Tajel and Arianna weren't easy to deal with neither. Also to those who continuously told me to quit my day job and publish a book. I did it!

I0536375

Dedication

For the many women and men who serve our community as First Responders! And the ones who served alongside me in our boxed in ambulance, letting me stay glued to my laptop between every call. Thank you! Lastly, to my EMT Instructor who kept on me! I wouldn't have been able to write a book like this if not for your awesome teachings.

I Belong
with Her

by

DOMINA
ALEXANDRA

2018

I Belong with Her © 2018 Domina Alexandra
Triplicity Publishing, LLC

ISBN-13: 978-0999737057
ISBN-10: 0999737058

This is a work of fiction. Names, characters, places, and incidents are the product of the author's imagination and are used fictitiously. Any resemblance to actual persons, living or dead, business establishments, events of any kind, or locales is entirely coincidental.

Printed in the United States of America
First Edition – 2018
Cover Design: Triplicity Publishing, LLC
Editor: Ashley Hutchison - Triplicity Publishing, LLC

Prologue
Arianna

"I am so freaking glad you finally moved your ass out here!" Danielle leaped into my arms for the one-hundredth time, squeaking excitedly in my ear.

Her blissful joy was contagious. I smiled, happy to be here too.

"God, you're going to love Oregon. And the gay community in Portland—"

I covered Danielle's mouth. It took her approximately two years to talk me into moving out here and after my last blow up with my family, I needed this change. I lived a very private life, not in the closet mind you, only private about my affairs. She snickered under her breath, nearly dropping her shot glass. People stared pryingly.

Danielle lifted her shot glass. "We're celebrating. *Chica*, you are in a gay bar right now. Get over yourself. No one cares, except perhaps ..." her eyes wandered around the bar, "a lesbian."

I looked around the bar. It was dimly lit with a counter that stretched parallel to the wall and was about fifteen feet long. There were several barstools scattered about near the counter, and a few small tables were situated next to the windows that overlooked the patio. Left of the counter was an anteroom that housed some pool tables and booths.

I shook my head and took one of the seats across from Danielle. "I came here to start a new life. That means my new job, nothing more."

"And what? No women to keep you warm and safe after one of your rough shifts?" Danielle stood abruptly.

"Where are you going?"

"Can I grab another shot since I'll be drinking for the both of us?" Danielle frowned, but there was no hint of anger on her face. "We are supposed to be celebrating your arrival, Arianna. Let loose for just a few hours."

"Sorry I asked." I chuckled and stuck my tongue out.

Danielle snorted exaggeratedly. "Damn right—you better be. I'm giving up pussy for a night. Entertain me."

I grunted in disbelief as she made her way to the bar. I was uptight, but that was my normal. I had a lot on my plate and there was simply no time to loosen up. I nibbled on the inside of my cheek while waiting for Danielle to return. But of course, she was busy flirting with the bartender, so I knew I could be waiting for a while. My phone vibrated in my pocket. I pulled it out and took a quick glance, noticing it was a text from my mother. I wasn't in the mood for her disapproving observations, so I put the phone away. My family was not thrilled about me moving to Oregon, but I could worry about that and my future on Monday. Right now, I should relax and drink. I could have one drink. That wouldn't hurt.

"You go to bars just to sit and think?"

It was a woman's voice and I didn't think she was talking to me until she decided to take a seat. As I looked up to see who was speaking, the first thing I noticed was the curve of her breasts hidden beneath her black, V-neck tank top. Her figure was slender, but I couldn't see every aspect of her shape since it was hidden underneath a thin layer of covering, not that I wanted to. God, but I did want to. I tried to avoid her eyes, afraid she would detect my roving gaze. *Get a fucking grip, Arianna.*

Let's try this again. This time I made it past her breasts to her mouth, which was formed into a smirk, telling me that she knew I was checking her out. Eventually, my eyes met her deep-set ones. The gray in them reminded me of this old sweater my nana knitted for me when I was a little girl—it stood out from the rest of the sweaters I had in my closet as a child. *What was she doing sitting next to me?*

"Can I buy you a drink?" She grinned, the white in her teeth adding extra effect to the fluttering in my chest.

She had a few tattoos on both of her toned biceps. I was sure many women melted at the sight of her because she exuded confidence as bright as a light bulb. I was pathetic. *Damn, she has dimples, too.* I wanted to walk away, but for some reason, I could not walk away, and I could not speak. It was as if my tongue had been swallowed. I knew I was blushing.

She studied me for a few seconds before looking over my shoulder. "My apologies. I didn't know she was taken."

I could tell that it was Danielle behind me whom she was speaking to by the sound of her laugh. "Oh no, I'm just her best friend. Nothing more. You can have her."

Was she seriously going to embarrass me? I wanted to say something, but the idea of this woman having me—my panties were already wet from the idea. Thank God, she had no supernatural ability to sense what was going on inside my pants.

The woman rose from her seat to allow Danielle to sit. "So, about that drink? Can I buy you one, or do I have to earn that somehow?"

The way she spoke made me realize that I could easily indulge myself for a night with such an intriguingly beautiful woman. *What was the harm in that? Just one night. Fuck. Could God go to sleep for just one night and not watch?* I didn't need the Mighty Lord telling my folks. Danielle, failing at nonchalance, was mouthing for me to take this woman up on her offer.

I finally worked up enough courage to say, "Yes."

"Great. I'll be back." Her dimples were back on display for me, this time Danielle bit her lip at the sight of them. "What would you like?"

"Gin and tonic," I replied, trying to act casual.

The woman smiled and headed over to the bar.

As soon as she was out of earshot, Danielle squealed. "Oh, my God. She could just wink at me and I'd cum right now!"

I smacked Danielle on her arm.

"Shut up!" I glanced over at the beautiful woman who was getting my drink. "I don't know about this. I should just stick with my plan."

"Don't you dare talk yourself out of this," Danielle argued. "You need at least one memorable night before you stick with your horrible plan to be celibate."

I frowned, but she was smiling at me. Danielle's eyes widened, indicating to me that the woman was coming back to our table. She placed my drink inches from my hand, which was resting on the table. I looked up, smiling politely. *Okay, Arianna. Just one night of fun.*

"Thanks," I said.

She nodded.

Danielle took this opportunity to leave me alone with this woman, saying that she had to meet up with her girlfriend. She didn't have a girlfriend. She had a girl she was more than friendly with, but that wasn't the same as having a girlfriend. Huge difference. I felt myself panicking, I was terrified of being left alone with her. My heart throbbed in my chest. *Okay, I can do this.*

"You're not from around here, are you?" she asked curiously. Her eyes scanned my body for a time before returning to meet my gaze.

I wasn't offended by her confidence. I shook my head. "Just moved here."

"Ah," she said as if that explained what she was thinking. "You do look a little tanner than all of us out here."

"That obvious?" I asked, smiling shyly.

She laughed and immediately, I wanted to pounce on her. "Just a little."

I swallowed, again turning my head away from the smile she kept giving me. I decided to finally take a sip of my drink. It was like she knew how gorgeous she was. I ended up finishing my first drink quickly and before I knew it, I was on my third round. I was done after that. My head felt cloudy and from the way the woman across me was moving, she didn't appear to be much better off than me.

She laughed hysterically as if I had made a funny joke. "You want to get out of here?"

I think I said *yes*, but I wasn't certain. I kept reminding myself that I wanted to sleep with her. It was just one night, and I wouldn't have to see her again. We found ourselves in a cab heading straight to her apartment. The moment we walked through her doorway, our lips smashed against one another's. All I could think about was seeing her naked. I know she had to look good underneath her clothing. When a woman looked as good as the one I was with, what could you do? Her hands explored my body and I moaned as her lips established a base on my neck. I closed my eyes thinking of her lips and once I opened my eyes again, it was morning.

Chapter One
Tajel

"Why are you busting my chops?" I spoke between partially gritted teeth. *Choose your words carefully.* "I made a great call. My partner and I just don't work well together."

Chief stood apart from his oversized chair, running his hands through his scruffy beard. His eyes scrutinized me, and I knew what that look meant. He was planning to tell me something that I wasn't going to like.

"Chief—"

"Tajel, don't." He shook his head, warning me to stay silent. "Jason doesn't want to be partnered with you anymore."

"I'm not surprised by that," I snorted. I took a seat and began unraveling my ponytail, letting my curly, black hair fall.

"Straighten up," he ordered.

I sat erect in the chair as he fell into in his own. Chief shuffled through a bunch of papers that were scattered across his dark, oak wood desk. I watched him anxiously, wondering what he was about to tell me.

"It has become apparent that the crew here either hates or adores you. I get why many love you, but I also get why many don't." There was a knock at the door. "Come in."

Chief narrowed his eyes at me. I didn't bother turning around. I wasn't in the mood to meet another new partner.

In fact, I was already thinking about how our partnership would end: he would either not approve of my lifestyle as a gay woman, he would try flirting with me until I wanted to blow his balls off, or he would be totally accepting, and we'd actually become friends. I did have quite a few of those here at the station, but I still wasn't going to take shit from anyone.

"Tajel," he kept his eyes hooked on me, "please stand and meet your new partner."

I sighed loudly and stood. *Let's see how long he'll last.* I was dumbfounded when I turned to see who was standing in front of me. My eyes widened, and I looked at the floor while sucking in my breath. *Shit. I did not see this coming.*

There was no way in hell this was going to work. "Chief—"

"Keep quiet, Pierce," Chief said. *Great. He's calling me by my last name.* Chief ignored the expression on my face. "Tajel, meet your new partner, Arianna Castaldi."

I looked up to find that Arianna was just as horrified as me.

"Castaldi, would you give us a moment please?" Chief asked politely.

She nodded, walking out quickly. I turned to Chief knowing he was going to chastise me before I even had my first shift with this Castaldi woman. *Here we go.*

"I don't want to hear any complaints coming from her or anyone else, Tajel. I've given you chance after chance. You fuck up and I'll suspend you, which is long overdue," he bellowed.

That's harsh. "She's a fucking woman?" Maybe that was a bit condescending and egotistical considering I was a woman, too. "You know what I mean."

"Tajel, you've never been partnered with another woman. This is the only option I have."

"What if she hates gay people?" I asked. I was trying to get out of pairing with her without telling him I knew her in a not-so-professional-way. "Plus, she might get weirded out or think I'm coming on to her."

Chief walked around his desk, never taking his eyes off me. "Then I guess you better not come on to her." His eyes softened. "You're one of my best paramedics and my niece. Try to make this work."

I was about to say something else but kept my mouth shut instead. "Yes, Chief-slash-uncle."

"Good." He smiled, and I sighed, glad that this argument was over. "Get out there and show her around."

*

Arianna

I can't believe this. Of all the people who could have been my partner, it had to be the woman from the bar. God was punishing me. I never had one-night stands, and here in this new state, I end up having one with a woman who was going to be my partner. I bit my lip, attempting to hold in my frustration.

"You must be the transfer?" A masculine voice made me turn. He offered me his hand. "I'm Rogan."

I nodded and took his hand.

He whistled for someone a few feet away who was getting a cup of coffee. "That's my partner, Felipe."

Felipe barely acknowledged me and then went back to making his coffee.

9

"You're from California, right?" Rogan asked. *Damn, they were up-to-date on who I was.* "This is Portland, and a small station."

"Yes, I'm from Cali. I'm Arianna Castaldi."

"Well, welcome."

We heard shouts coming from the office down the hall where Chief and my new partner were. I sighed. This was going to be bad.

Rogan chewed on his bottom lip. "It's got to be Tajel in there."

Felipe leaned against the wall. "Oh, it is." He looked at me curiously. "Have you been assigned a partner yet?"

I lightly inhaled. "She's in there."

"No shit?" Rogan asked, nearly as surprised as I was. He noticed my worried and advised, "Tajel's her own person, and follows her own codes, but truth is, if you follow her lead you'll be just fine."

Then we aren't going to be just fine. I liked to lead as well.

"Until you don't do things her way or you challenge her decisions." Felipe added with a mocking smile.

Just fucking great.

The door to Chief's office opened and out walked Tajel with a smirk plastered on her face as if she believed no one heard her being yelled at. She appeared unruffled and her arrogance reminded me of the first night we met.

"Piss Chief off again?" Felipe asked.

Tajel's eyes swerved to meet mine and I couldn't tell what she was thinking. "Just talking about the situation that happened last week."

I suddenly felt out of place. I rubbed the back of my neck to make myself appear mentally occupied. The station wasn't wide, but it was narrow and long. Chief's office was across from the kitchen where we were all standing opposite the breakroom. It was the largest part of the station, second only to the ambulance bay. Tables were set up in a classroom pattern. Two couches and a flat screen were on the far end of the breakroom.

"Ready to go?" Tajel asked, looking as if she was inspecting me.

I told her I was ready, and we headed to the ambulance bay, which contained five rigs. I passed each one, impressed by their size. The box-shaped rigs were painted red and had enormous bold stickers that read: Portland Fire Paramedics. Lined against the wall were shelves stocked with supplies for our rigs and the station.

"You like them?" she asked.

I hadn't realized that it had been quiet for some time. Watching Tajel admire the rigs, it was hard to stifle a smile. She obviously loved her job.

"Definitely."

After a moment, I thought about what I should say next. I certainly didn't want the awkwardness to last much longer.

"Look—"

"You don't need to say anything. I know."

"We do need to talk about that night," I insisted.

Her face lost its color. She clearly wasn't expecting me to bring up our night together.

She pointed at the rig I was standing next to. "I thought you were about to compliment my rig. Our rig. It's the best looking one."

I turned to where she was pointing. Medic 112. Somehow, it did look better than the others. I sighed and faced her again. I couldn't just pretend that night didn't happen.

Tajel began speaking while I made sure no one was around to listen, "It's no big deal. We…"

"I'm not gay," I blurted hastily. The last thing I needed was gossip going around the station. "I was drinking, and I was only there because my friend is a lesbian."

When I returned her gaze, I realized she had found my words amusing. She took a step closer. I was sure my heart had stopped, and it was hard to keep my feet planted in place. I reminded myself of my plans: no women and no more Tajel. I then took a step away from her, balling my hand into a fist.

"Does my mistake amuse you?" I was becoming seriously aggravated by my own awkwardness.

The look in Tajel's eyes told me I had fucked up. Her expression hardened, and she stared at me as if she was imagining throwing daggers at my face.

"Don't fucking worry. I won't be touching you again." Tajel kept enough distance between us, but I could feel the anger radiating from her like the heat from a campfire.

Damn. I preferred the arrogant asshole. Not this version.

Tajel walked around me, making sure she maintained distance as if I was contaminated with some infectious disease. She climbed inside the ambulance, slamming the door. I looked around, unsure of my next move.

"Get in," she bellowed loudly enough for a few of my new coworkers to come into the bay, curious as to what was going on.

"How the hell did you get her mad so quickly?" Felipe wondered, a little amused.

"Shut up, Felipe!" Tajel snapped. She shot me a look that said, 'get in or I'm leaving you.'

I reluctantly got into the passenger seat of the rig. I preferred to avoid a confrontation with Tajel. She started the rig, keeping her gaze straight ahead.

She waited a few seconds before muttering, "Did you not wear seatbelts in LA?"

I fumbled around for the seatbelt, feeling foolish for letting her fluster me. *What did I say to piss her off?* The way she was gripping the steering wheel, I could tell Tajel was picturing strangling me.

"I'm ready," I told her coolly.

Tajel did not answer, only drove out of the bay. Maybe I should have asked where we were going. My first day of work was tomorrow night, so I didn't understand the need for us to leave the station. I worried that she was taking me to an early grave. This was Oregon, a place where it was only too easy to hide a body. *Fuck.* I had to make this right. Soon.

Chapter Two
Arianna

I tossed my coat onto the couch, dropping down next to it on the cushions. Opening the beer I took from the fridge, I groaned.

"Bad day?" Danielle asked, entering the living room and taking a seat next to me.

I exhaled, fighting the impulse to head back to the station to punch Tajel. *Fuck.* Even though I was upset with Tajel, I knew that I was partly to blame for her behavior toward me.

I decided to tell Danielle what happened at the station today. "You remember that woman I had a one-night stand with?"

Her eyebrows arched, and she grinned. "Yeah."

"She's also my new partner," I said matter-of-factly with a hint of distress.

She seemed unfazed. "And what's wrong with that?"

"Everything!" I yelled.

"Okay grouchy, what happened?"

"I don't know," was my response. Tajel was nice to me at first, despite how it ended.

"Did she act as if that night was a mistake or ignore you?" Danielle asked.

Realizing my mistake, I hung my head. *Fuck.* "No, but I did. Everything was fine. Next thing I know, I panicked and told her I'm not gay."

"First of all, you are very gay." She paused for a moment, and I could tell she was choosing her next words carefully. "Secondly, you are just going to have to find a way to make things better between you two that doesn't involve you lying about who you are."

"How am I supposed to do that?" I took a sip of my beer. "She absolutely hates me now."

Danielle snatched the beer from my hand. "She just fucked you a few days ago."

Wow. Really? She had to say it like that.

"A one-time thing, Danielle." I rolled my eyes, waiting for her to take a few sips so I could reclaim my beer. "Besides, I don't even remember that night."

"Shit." Danielle's sarcasm was obvious. "My body would have remembered everywhere her tongue landed."

I slapped Danielle's arm playfully. "You are so fucking nasty."

"And horny from this conversation." Danielle gave me a pouty expression, wiggling her eyebrows. "Want to, you know? Like we use to?"

I scoffed, not surprised by her invitation. "We were 15 and testing the waters."

"And God, it tasted so damn good. I've never left women since." Danielle chuckled. "I'm very glad we are best friends. I would never trade that for anyone, nor your pussy."

Good God. I stood to leave. "Good night, *chica*."

"Hey!" Danielle yelled, still holding my beer. "Seriously, find a way to make it work and tell her you're sorry. And maybe having her as a good fuck buddy wouldn't hurt. I'm sure that you two alone in that big ambulance with those soft seats in the back—"

"Goodnight, Danielle!" I screeched, my skin flushing.

I slammed my bedroom door, ending the conversation.

*

Tajel

"Are you looking forward to having a new partner?"

The sound of my uncle's voice broke the silence. I was playing with my spaghetti, moving the noodles around with my fork absentmindedly.

"Tajel?"

"Yes, uncle-slash-Chief. It's so cool to have a new partner." I didn't try to hide my sarcasm.

Having an uncle who was also my boss was double the punishment. When I came over for dinner on Saturdays, he'd always chastise me for something that happened at work. Whatever happened to work being separate from our personal lives?

"Roosevelt, don't bother her with work. No wonder I had to pull her arm to come tonight." Thank the dear old Lord for Aunt Laura. She always had my back when it came to my uncle hassling me.

He was undeterred.

"Something happen between you two?" When I didn't respond, my uncle tossed his fork onto his plate, causing a harsh, clinking sound. "Damn it, Tajel!"

"I didn't say anything happened. Even if it did it's between my partner and me." I'd never lied to him before, so I wouldn't now.

He grunted and went back to eating.

I grinned when some sauce dripped onto his beard. "You should really learn how to shave."

"You should really learn how to play nice with your partners."

I refused to be baited by that line. "I'll make a deal with you: if I get her to not want to quit or leave me as a partner, maybe even get her to like me, you let me join your SWAT team."

"Tajel, we've had this conversation."

I shrugged. "And we're having it again. I am not a little kid anymore. I can handle it."

"You say that now," he retorted.

"Honey, she's one of your best paramedics and it's not because she's your niece. It's because you taught her everything you know, and she has the passion to continue to grow. You can make this deal." My aunt winked at me.

"Fine." His eyes narrowed, and he pointed his index finger at me threateningly. "You screw this up, and I don't want to ever hear about this again."

"Fine, fine." I smiled inwardly, knowing this was a win. Finally, I was getting somewhere. "But, when I do join your SWAT team, I want you to give me a nice badge."

"Don't fuck up and I'll even wear a shirt that says whatever you want on it."

My eyes lit up from the many ideas that began swirling around in my head.

After dinner was over, I kissed my aunt on her cheek to thank her while we were standing by the front door of her house. She retrieved my jacket from the hall closet and handed it to me.

Her fingers combed through my hair. "He only wants the best for you."

"More like wrapped in a thick safety blanket, surrounded by an army."

My aunt giggled and zipped up my jacket. Since the moment I came to live with them at 14, my aunt had always been my nurturing confidant. She was someone that I could rely on to comfort me whenever I needed her.

"I want the best for you too."

"I know. You tell me all the time," I teased.

"Please, honey."

Here we go. I knew where this conversation was going.

"You know what I'm about to say?" my aunt asked, pursing her lips.

"I always do." I then repeated what she said to me whenever I visited, "To open up my heart and let that special woman, wherever she's at, inside."

I touched my chest knowing she would have done that as well.

"Okay," my aunt said exasperatedly. She gave me a kiss. "Get home safe, smart ass."

I smiled as I turned and headed to my car.

*

Arianna

Okay. Make this a good night. Make this a great night. I sang those words in my head all day after waking up from some much-needed sleep. It was evening when I pulled up to the station. I was scheduled to work at seven, but I decided to arrive an hour early. Some may call me an overachiever. I was. This was my first day and I wanted to impress my boss. Besides that, I wanted to find a way to make things right with my new partner. *She can't hate me forever, can she?* I walked inside, already wearing my freshly pressed, Class A uniform.

"Ah, the new meat has arrived." Felipe stood, smirking. "Ready for your first shift?"

"This must be entertaining for you," I remarked. I knew I had caught him off-guard. I patted his arm with a grin. "Don't worry. I can handle Tajel. You guys can stop worrying."

"Humph. Didn't sound like that the last time."

"That was a simple misunderstanding. I know what it's like to work around a bunch of men, so I'll say this once: I am not some kitten you can play with. I can hold my own. And if my name turns up in rumors around the station, you'll be seeing a side of me you don't want to see." I made sure to soften my warning with a smile, so he wouldn't think that I was trying to be a bitch.

It took Felipe a couple of seconds to recover from the surprise of my threat, but when he did he grinned and said, "I like you."

I returned his smile. "Good."

I waved to Rogan who had been standing quietly next to Felipe during our conversation, and then decided to take my overnight bag into my sleeping quarters. But as soon as I opened the door, I startled by the sight of Tajel without a shirt on. I froze. The only thing covering her breasts was a sports bra. My mouth watered, and my body flushed. I quickly turned around, slamming the door shut behind me.

Felipe was staring at me, confused by my sudden reappearance. "You okay?"

I cleared my throat and nodded. *Damn. Why is she so fucking hot?* Taking a deep breath, I decided not to make an even bigger scene. The strap of my duffel bag was still over my shoulder, so if I didn't go in that would only draw suspicion. *Please be clothed.*

I opened the door again, this time finding Tajel sitting on her bed wearing a tank top. She was tying her boots. I studied the feather tattoos on both her arms. Each had its own unique design. I couldn't help but notice her breasts bundled up in a tank top that didn't leave much to the imagination. *Stop staring.* Tajel cleared her throat and it took me a few seconds longer than it should have to look at her eyes instead of her breasts. I realized I was caught admiring her, and my face flushed again. I immediately turned away.

"Sorry about before, I'm used to being the only woman in this station."

For a second, I thought Tajel was apologizing for the other day. Instead, she was referring to being shirtless only a few minutes ago. I'm sure if Danielle was here, she would tell Tajel that putting a shirt on would be a crime.

"Oh, no sweat," I said, not without some difficulty.

I didn't hear her response because my heartbeat was pulsating in my ears.

"Hey, about the other day... I'm sorry." I turned around to find that she had already left the room. *Shit.*

Well, that went well. I put my bag away and threw my cover onto the bed incessantly thinking about how stupidly I've behaved since I arrived at the station. I promptly left the room, taking only my lunch bag. Once outside my quarters I searched around for Tajel, only to find Felipe pointing outside. He plainly knew I was looking for my new partner.

"She took the rig outside to be washed."

In this fucking weather? Thank God, I did not say that aloud. *Okay. I can handle this. I just need to suck it up. Go out there. Help.* As if that would make anything better at this point.

"Thanks."

"Sure," Felipe said, watching as I left.

I would survive this shift and all the other ones to come. I needed to make this work. No way in hell would I ask my new boss to find me a different partner. *Suck it up.*

Chapter Three
Tajel

I hid my smile for a few seconds, watching Arianna struggle to put on an additional pair of gloves. But when I saw her come out with a bucket of soapy water, I burst into laughter. The rain was coming down hard and as much as I would like to see her suffer a little bit, I wasn't going to be that cruel.

"What the hell are you doing?" I couldn't very well make her think I liked her already, so my tone was a bit hostile.

After her comment yesterday, my desire to see her naked had diminished somewhat. I hated when anyone, especially a woman, dismissed me rudely or made insensitive comments.

Arianna frowned. "I'm helping you wash the rig."

"Who told you that I was washing the rig?" As soon as I asked the question, I knew it was Felipe. "Never mind. It's too cold and raining too hard for us to wash it. I like my fingers to stay attached."

Arianna mumbled something under her breath. Probably cursing Felipe's name. Climbing into the rig, I closed the door behind me, shutting out the cold. Through the window, I observed Arianna standing still, as if waiting for some instruction from me. After a moment, she walked to the passenger side door, opened it, and climbed in. She was shivering violently so I turned the heat up another notch.

"Put your hands close to the vent," I urged. I watched her bottom lip quiver. "Your hands."

I grabbed her icy hands and pulled them toward the direction of the vent. She snatched them away and I found myself biting back my words. *Bitch. I am trying to be nice. I should have let your ass wash the rig.*

Perhaps it wouldn't be so easy to get her to like me. I didn't really know how I felt about her, especially now. I was no actress. I knew nothing about pretending. She was pissing me off and I wasn't afraid to let her see that.

"Where are we going?" Arianna asked.

"I'm hungry," I replied curtly

We left the station and sat in awkward silence for the entire drive.

When we arrived at Stumptown Coffee Roasters, I asked purely out of politeness, "Are you coming in?"

Arianna shook her head, so I shrugged and hopped out of the rig. I walked into the coffee shop, stomping my boots on the indoor mat to warm my feet.

"Hey, Tajel! How are you doing?" It was my best friend, Sasha, who was calling out to me.

I scoffed. "I'm great, considering."

"Damn, Tajel you look really good in that uniform, as always." Gina walked over to me, placing her used tray onto the counter. She always spoke as if she was purring.

I slept with her once and she never let me forget it. If I took her to the restroom right now, she would let me do whatever I wanted to her. I smiled charmingly, but I honestly wasn't interested in anything serious.

"Have you forgotten how good I look without the uniform?" I teased. I still liked to provoke a reaction from her.

She blushed, and I was certain that her face wasn't the only place blood was flowing to at this moment.

"Maybe a little," she purred.

"Then I should call you after my shift. I don't want you to forget."

"You do that." She nipped on her bottom lip, her eyes full of desire as she left Sasha and me alone, walking out into the chilly night.

I turned to find myself face-to-face with Sasha.

She appeared unamused. "You're ridiculous. She's only going to get more attached."

"Why not? I'm single, and it would be just a fuck buddy experience."

Sasha laughed heartily, and then changed the subject, "How is that new partner of yours?"

I was annoyed she brought up Arianna.

"Just sparkly. With a lot of attitude." I waved her off when she narrowed her eyes at me. "When I get an attitude toward someone, they always deserve it."

"Right." Sasha sarcastic tone was unmistakable. "But, you failed to mention your new partner was a woman and that she is hot."

I turned to see what she was talking about and saw Arianna entering the coffee shop. *Fuck. Why are you making an appearance now?* Arianna wrapped her arms around herself, doing her best to fight off the cold. My gray eyes found her brown ones, and she walked over to Sasha and me.

"Wait, isn't that the woman—"

"Shut up!" I hissed.

"We are going to talk about this tomorrow."

As Arianna approached, Sasha shut her mouth, but only for a second.

If her grin didn't make it obvious to Arianna that we were talking about her, it was Sasha's next words that made it plain, "Finally! It's nice to meet the first woman—"

I cleared my throat and gave her a stern look. When Arianna faced me, Sasha gave me a cheesy grin while mouthing that she was sorry. *Oh, you will be later.*

"Are you going to take much longer?" Arianna's impatience pervaded her words.

Play nice, Tajel.

"Sasha, this is my current partner," I introduced.

I was beginning to think I wouldn't be able to handle having her as my partner, which was bizarre, since it was usually the other way around. *Why did I make this deal with my uncle to make this woman like me? To join his team. Right. Get back on track.*

Arianna ignored the implication that she wouldn't last long and introduced herself to Sasha, "Hi, I'm Arianna."

"How is your first shift going?" Sasha was trying to keep the conversation going even though she knew I was ready to leave.

"Medic 112."

I pulled the radio from my waist strap, clicking the button. "Com 2, this is Medic 112…go." I turned to Sasha. "Talk later."

I headed for the rig hoping Arianna would follow. I looked back for her as the dispatcher began speaking again, "Medic 112, you have a cardiac arrest on 8150 SE 23rd Ave. Fifty-year-old male. What's your location?"

I already had my key in the ignition when Arianna climbed in and closed her door. "Com 2, Medic 112 responding Code 3 from 3rd Ave and Ash Street."

"Medic 112, copy you en route."

My hands tightened around the steering wheel as my endorphins exploded. I turned on the sirens, and the sounds wailed through the streets as the red lights lit up the buildings and their windows. I pressed the gas forcefully. Arianna pulled out the map.

"No need. I know where we're going."

"Repeat patient?" she asked.

I nodded. "Have you learned these streets yet?"

"I studied Oregon maps for months before arriving."

Okay. Maybe I'm a little impressed by that.

"This patient has a history of multiple myocardial infarction, hypertension, diabetes, and congestive heart failure." We were a few minutes away now. "His wife is going to be in the way, so you should—"

"I've dealt with hovering wives and family before," she snapped.

Jeez. Do you have to remind me that you're a bitch? I chose to bite my tongue. "Com 2, Medic 112 on-scene."

I never waited for dispatch to copy me. I jumped out the rig as soon as we arrived, rushing around to the back to open the door to retrieve my medic jump bag. Arianna was behind me, so I moved to the side to let her grab the Lifepak cardiac monitor. I then reached for the gurney. Once it was out, Arianna placed the Lifepak on it and took the jump bag from my shoulder, tossing it on top of the gurney beside the Lifepak. I reached for the airway bag and then we were ready to go.

We raced to the apartment and I didn't bother knocking on the door. I walked right in. It wasn't as if this place and this patient were unfamiliar to me.

"Jane? It's Tajel."

"Oh, Lord! We're back here!"

I followed Jane's voice, completely focused on what I needed to do as I headed to the back room to find the patient lying on the floor. I knew at that moment this call would be very grim, but I pushed through my doubts and fear, ready to do all I could to keep him with his wife.

*

Arianna

As we walked into the patient's house it became clear that Tajel knew these people personally. She fell to her knees next to the unconscious man, feeling for his pulse and calling to him. I went to the opposite end of the patient and pulled out a bag valve mask (BVM) from our airway bag and connected it to an oxygen tank. I turned on the Lifepak.

"Did he fall?" Tajel asked.

The wife shook her head. "I laid him there."

Tajel muttered under her breath as she began CPR, counting loudly. The wife paced, crying hysterically and loudly enough to disturb anyone unused to this situation. I wasn't. I tracked her count while getting ready to attach the defibrillator pads over his chest. Once Tajel counted to thirty, I held the BVM over the patient's nose and mouth, pressing down and squeezing twice when she was done counting. As I squeezed, Tajel grabbed the shears and cut his shirt open to expose his chest. I finished another squeeze as Tajel returned to performing CPR. I then placed one of the defibrillator pads on his upper right chest and one between his armpit, a few inches below the nipple, along with a pulse oximeter to check his saturations.

Immediately, I turned on the automated external defibrillator (AED) and it began reading his heart waves and alerted us of the need for shock. We complied. I then pulled out the electrocardiograms, placing four of the electrode patches over both ends of his upper chest and abdomen. I wanted to get a cardiac rhythm. After two minutes, the AED reanalyzed, finding no rhythm to shock so we reverted back to CPR.

"Damn it. I am going to start an intraosseous access over his tibia," Tajel explained as she drilled the needle into the front lower part of our patient's leg.

"Where's the fire crew?" I asked, my arms becoming exhausted.

"I'm giving him epinephrine."

Tajel concentrated on what she was doing, but she heard my question.

"I think I heard that they were delayed by a train." Tajel checked his vitals after a minute. "He has a pulse. Weak, but there."

We kept everything attached to him. The fire department arrived in time and brought the gurney closer to us when they came into the room.

I asked the wife, "Did you give him any nitroglycerin?"

She was in such a state of panic that she was unable to answer right away, so I asked again, this time more firmly. She shook her head and I moved over to his feet as Tajel finished giving him oxygen by mask since his oxygen level read 89%.

"What can we do to help?" the captain asked.

"Help us get him on the gurney," Tajel directed.

She scooped him up from under his armpits while I took his legs. We lifted him just high enough to carry him over to gurney. The fire crew assisted, collecting our Lifepak from the floor. When the patient was on the gurney, we strapped him to it. The captain ordered his crew to retrieve our airway and jump bag.

"We are taking him to Providence Portland Medical Center," Tajel told the wife.

"Please Tajel, keep him alive."

"We'll see you there, Jane," was her response.

We rolled him out of the apartment and to the back of our rig, raising the gurney and putting him inside. I instantly I proceeded to hook an additional set of cables into the cardiac monitor for a 12 lead ECG.

Tajel spoke up, "I'm going to put in a 20-gauge catheter. I need a saline drip."

As I waited for the cardiac monitor to read his heart rhythm, I put on the blood pressure cuff and pulse oximeter, waiting for it to take his vitals.

"He has a fast heart rate and blood pressure is high."

As the cardiac monitor recorded his heart rhythm I pressed the print button to review the report. I followed her hands as they steadily guided the needle into his vein, her facial expression was serious and focused. Watching Tajel, I could tell this was all she lived for. It was a feeling I could relate to. Then the needle was in, so I started the drip.

"Ready?" Tajel asked.

I nodded, and Tajel hopped out of the back, closing the doors behind her as she moved to the front of the ambulance. I could hear her communicating with dispatch on the radio, so I used my back-port radio to call the receiving hospital to give a full report on our patient. It took us about five minutes to arrive, and before I could finish placing the monitor on the back of the gurney, the back doors of the rig were opened. Tajel had a way of moving swiftly without seeming panicked. I scrambled out and we removed our patient from the back of the rig, rolling him into the emergency room. A doctor and a few nurses greeted us with several questions about our assessment.

Tajel and I placed him on their emergency gurney and the doctor and nurses began working on the patient. We got out of the way, knowing that they could take care of him at this point. I finally noticed a crack in Tajel's rough exterior in the tight creases around her eyes when we made it back to the rig. She started cleaning the back, wiping everything down as I finished the paperwork in the front seat. I had somehow forgotten the rain and the cold during the chaos. It was my first call in Oregon and I was already pumped for more.

When I was finished, I leaned back against the seat and shut my eyes. After every call my heart felt ready to explode with adrenaline. I had to admit, Tajel was good at her job, and we worked well together. Now all I wanted to do was to kick myself for being so rude to her earlier.

She was so different from other women, particularly the ones I had dated before. Tajel was an arrogant woman, but on the job, she was nothing but passionate, focused, and competent. Humble, even. I hated that she could provoke reactions out of me that made me uncomfortable. Seeing her this way, I didn't really know what to think of her.

I heard the wife of our patient suddenly approach the rig and fall into Tajel's arms sobbing. I knew what that meant.

Chapter Four
Arianna

The rest of our shift was somewhat mellow, especially since every one of our patients after our first recovered well in the hospital. I've had my share of dying patients and each loss was difficult to bear. My first patient in Oregon died due to cardiac arrest. It was a hard fact to swallow. Tajel drove us in silence back to station for our fifth and last time of the day. A whole 24-hour shift and it was already over.

"I'm sorry." Tajel waited for the light to turn green but stayed silent. I was not deterred. I wanted to apologize so I continued, "I know I was a bitch earlier—"

"Seriously? This is the wrong time to make this about you being a bitch."

Tajel's words stung but she was right. I was feeling guilty for being abrasive and wanted to make myself feel better. I thought about saying more to break the painful silence but chose not to. It was wiser to be mute. We pulled into the station and Tajel turned off the rig after parking. We sat together for a few minutes.

I wasn't sure if I should get out or remain in my seat, but for some reason I chose the latter.

"Great job on your first day here."

Before I could respond to her unexpected approval of my competence, Tajel was out of the rig and headed inside. There was no way I could approach her now when she was surrounded by our coworkers. *Fuck.* I truly screwed up this time. I thought I would fix things and instead, I only made things worse than before. I can't explain what came over me. When I saw her at the beginning of our shift without a shirt on, it flustered me. I had never allowed a woman to get under my skin. *Shit*.

Leaning my head against the dashboard, I took in a long breath and reevaluated my position as Tajel's partner. I lifted my head at the sound of someone knocking on my window. It was Chief.

"Sir," I greeted him.

His eyes studied me for some time before smiling. His beard was trimmed very close to his skin, a sharp contrast from the thick beard I saw the other day. His blue eyes held some concern and there were thin creases around his eyelids. He wasn't a very tall man, but his rigid demeanor certainly made him appear that way. I'd be a fool to mistake him for weak.

"How was your first shift? Any issues?"

He was fishing for information. If I said *yes* to his question, I had a feeling he would think it was Tajel's fault, which it wasn't. If I said *no*, somehow, I don't think he'd believe me.

"Having a new partner is never easy in the beginning, Chief. Yet, we worked well together, and I look forward to our next shift."

He was clearly taken aback, but I meant what I said, which surprised even myself. I honestly did not want to be thought of by Tajel as a bitch.

After a few seconds, he said, obviously relieved, "Good to hear. You have great night."

"Thank you, Chief."

*

"So, your first shift did not go as successfully as you hoped." Danielle was trying to make me feel better. She wasn't quite there yet. "Let's go out and shoot some pool. That'll relax you."

I stretched out on the couch. This woman was unbelievable. "You do know I just worked a 24-hour shift, right?"

Danielle shrugged. "I also know you had a good amount of sleep during that time, and it wasn't that busy of a shift."

"I need to stop texting you while I'm at work."

"Pool? Bar?" It sounded like a request, but I knew better.

I groaned loudly.

Danielle clapped her hands together in excitement.

"Great! Get dressed." As she ran to her room she added, "And try to look like you haven't just worked a long shift."

*

Tajel

Sasha bought another round of drinks for us even though I barely had time to down my last shot. We were on our third round of pool. I held the stick close to my body, lining up my next shot. My phone buzzed. When I opened it to the text messages, I wasn't shocked to see that it was from Gina, letting me know she was ten minutes away. Smirking, I slid my phone back in my pocket and prepared for my next shot.

"Isn't that your new partner?" Sasha asked.

Her question caught me by surprise and I struck the white ball prematurely, missing my target. When I looked up, sure enough, there was Arianna standing near the front entrance of the bar next to her friend. *Shit. Shit. Shit. Not tonight.*

"Fuck...you have to introduce me to her friend," Sasha pleaded.

Hell no. I came here to release the tension that Arianna caused. I did not need this. But before I knew it, Sasha was greeting Arianna and her friend, basically dragging them in our direction. Did she forget that I had an open invitation of full on sex-in-a-dress coming in the next several minutes? I did not need this. As Arianna approached, I could see she was not happy with Sasha's forceful arrangement either.

"Sasha, I'm sure they came here to be by themselves," I said, trying not to sound frustrated.

"Actually," Arianna's friend started, "we could use the company."

"Then its settled." Sasha pointed to Arianna's friend who introduced herself as Danielle. "Would you like a shot?"

"Most definitely," Danielle responded with a flirtatious smile. "I'll join you."

Arianna and I were left alone. I wished I'd invited Gina to my place instead of meeting here. Ignoring Arianna was the easiest route but then again, I would have to see her at work. *You can be mature about this, Tajel.* I could.

"Thought you'd be at home sleeping?"

"You don't have to talk to me. It's not like either of us wanted to be in this position." Arianna looked around the bar, trying her best to avoid making eye contact with me.

This woman was making it impossible for me to be nice to her.

"Fuck, I'm sorry," Arianna said, pinching the bridge of her nose. "I am usually politer than this."

"No, you're right." *No point in sugarcoating anything now.* "We're clearly not made to be friends."

Trying to talk to this woman was proving to be more difficult than I thought. Arianna looked hurt by my remark, but I blew it off. No way she cared enough to be my friend anyway. Sasha and Danielle returned with shots, and I snatched one from Sasha's hand, downing it faster than anyone else.

"You two been here long?" Danielle asked.

"About thirty minutes," Sasha answered, her gaze fixed on Danielle.

I rolled my eyes. I could see where this was going.

"Tajel." The purring sound reminded me that I had been waiting on Gina. *Finally.*

I turned on the charm, like turning on car lights at first sign of darkness. "Hey, you're looking appetizing."

Her hand slipped down to my ass as we hugged, and I knew she was making a statement. Seeing two women near me, I'm sure jealousy took over. She was like a cat.

"Do we have to stay here?" she whined, putting her arm around my waist.

I gave Sasha an apologetic look. Somehow, I knew she wanted me to stay but it wasn't going to happen. If Arianna was going to be around, then I wouldn't be. As I thought of Arianna my eyes shifted to her, but she was facing away from me, so I could not see her reaction to Gina's sudden presence. Not that I needed to.

"I got to go," I announced. Gina was already pulling me out of the bar, but I managed to shout good night to everyone.

I should have at least been polite and stayed for a few more minutes, but it was too late now. For some reason, not seeing Arianna's face before I bolted was bugging me.

"Hey baby, are you ready for me?" Gina leaned me against my car, putting her hands on my waist as she traced kisses down my neck.

Though it was cold outside, my body temperature was rising. I shuddered from the sensation of her lips on my skin. I grabbed her chin and I brought my lips to hers. Gina kissed me deeply, sliding her tongue into my mouth as if to devour me from the inside out. Our kiss was sloppy and lustful to the point that I wanted to remove her clothes without hesitation. We hadn't even left the bar yet.

"Let's go," I whispered in her ear before nipping on her earlobe.

"Yes."

I opened the car door for her and she slipped into the passenger seat. I quickly made my way over to the driver side. Once I was in the car I turned on the ignition immediately, so I could get the heater working. Looking out the window, I saw Arianna walking to her car alone. My friend and hers probably hit it off and she left not wanting to feel like the third wheel.

She was clearly upset, and I was tempted to go say something to her.

"What are you waiting for?"

At the sound of Gina's voice, I remembered I wasn't by myself, so I drove away. I wasn't quite sure why I cared about Arianna's feelings, but I needed to put her behind me. I wanted to enjoy every part of Gina.

Chapter Five
Tajel

"Tajel." My uncle stood in one of the doorways of the station along with the field supervisor. "Come here."

I never wanted my coworkers to know that Chief was my uncle. Professionalism was important to me. "Yes, Chief?"

My eyes steadied on my uncle, and I nodded to my field supervisor out of respect. My personal relationship with him was nonexistent, and our professional relationship wasn't much better. He was a prick. Prick, pervert, asshole, and a prejudiced fucker.

"Manny was just asking if there was anything you think Arianna needed help with in adjusting to Oregon? I know myself what it's like to move to a new state."

Chief moved here when I was a kid from Texas. Huge difference in cultures, but especially in the weather.

There was no way I would let Arianna be forced to suffer Manny and his offensive personality. "Actually, she's a quick study. She'll be fine without your assistance."

Manny glared at me, but plastered a fake smile on his face to please Chief. "If you're sure."

"Positive." I wasn't smiling.

This guy could make every straight woman in the world reconsider her sexual orientation.

I walked away with Chief following closely behind. "I hear your last shift with Ms. Castaldi went better than all of your other partner experiences combined."

I couldn't help the annoyed expression that appeared on my face. I had no desire to continue to talk about Arianna, but I knew he wouldn't stop.

"Castaldi told me how she enjoyed working beside you. That you two actually work well together." He wanted more details from me, but I wasn't prepared to give any.

To say I was surprised at what Chief said was putting it lightly.

"Was she wrong?" he asked, confused by my expression.

"Uh, no." I immediately thought better and added, "It went very well."

It was true. She never stepped on my toes nor I on hers. All I ever wanted was a partner I could be in perfect sync with, and she was the first to not make me want to push her out of the way and do her job as well as my own.

"Good to hear." He patted my back. "Keep it up and you'll get what you want."

I smiled, remembering our deal. "I need to get ready for my next shift."

We said our goodbyes, and I headed for the sleeping quarters I would now be sharing with Arianna. When I opened the door, I found Arianna already inside putting her bag on her bed.

"Hey," I said casually.

"Hi." She grabbed her jacket and headed to the door. "I'll get out your way."

"This is your room too."

I was starting to confuse myself. I thought after last night I would avoid Arianna. Now, I was trying to initiate small talk.

"Just, uh…" *Say something, dork.* "You don't have to leave on my account."

For the first time since the night I met her, Arianna gave me a sincere smile. It was unguarded and not strained. But after a few heartbeats, her expression went blank. It was almost as if she made it her duty to not smile. Why was it so hard for Arianna to express herself?

She bit the inside of her cheek. "Oh, I should—I have dinner warming up in the kitchen."

I stepped aside, giving her enough space to pass. She was out of the room in a matter of seconds. *Women.* I was aware that I was a woman as well. I was reminded of that actuality every time I took off my clothes. I loved being a woman, and I loved other women, but I liked to categorize myself differently.

After I changed into my uniform I headed out into the break room, which we paramedics consider to be our living room. Arianna was eating what looked like vegetable stew while sitting on the couch. From what I could see, our station duties were done, and our rig was ready for a call.

"Did you do everything?" I asked, a bit amazed by her work ethic.

"I got here much earlier than I intended," Arianna responded. "Do you mind that I did them without you?"

"I would be lying if I said I did mind."

Her eyes lit up for a second and then she looked away.

"You should really see yourself in the mirror when you look like that." *What am I talking about*? I hope she didn't think I was trying to flirt with her.

"Do I look like a bitch most of the time?" she asked.

I took a moment to think about my answer, knowing that I could make our partnership better or worse with whatever I said. "Today's a new day."

She stared at me, probably deciding how to respond to my remark. I hadn't quite answered her question, but the sentiment behind the comment was obvious. "That's fair."

I wanted to tell her that I knew what she said to Chief. Maybe I also wanted to thank her for not causing me any trouble.

Before I could tell her though, dispatch came on the intercom, "Medic 112, call coming out of a private residence. Possible drug overdose."

Dispatch provided the address and we sprinted to our rig. Arianna left her food sealed on the table. She was as fast and alert as me, taking the map from its compartment and quickly searching for the address.

"Com 2, Medic 112 en route from station."

Arianna began directing me to the scene and I followed her instructions, never doubting her. Unfortunately, I had that experience more times than I wanted to count with previous partners who had no sense of direction whatsoever. More than enough tragedies resulted from their ineptitude.

We made it to the scene in six minutes. I alerted dispatch to our arrival and hopped out of the rig in unison with Arianna. She grabbed our medic jump bag and I headed to the back to open the doors. Our Lifepak and the airway bag were already on the gurney.

"I'll check his level of consciousness and vitals while you find out what this guy took."

"Great, I love investigations," Arianna said with genuine excitement in her voice.

We rolled the gurney up to the door of our patient's home and knocked.

A few seconds passed, and then a girl of probably 12 or 13 opened the door.

"It's my dad," she said, barely able to get the words out.

The girl motioned for Arianna and me to come through the doorway, and we wasted no time doing just that. We found the girl's father unconscious in the bathroom with no visible indication of a drug overdose in the room, such as an empty bottle of pills or needles.

"Engine 12 from Medic 112, we are in the back of the house."

"Copy, pulling up," was the response.

I called out to the patient, monitoring him for any sign of breathing. He began to gasp deeply every six to ten seconds.

I felt for his carotid pulse and announced, "His heartrate's low, with nine breaths a minute. Inadequate chest rise and fall."

I put a BVM over his mouth and nose, assisting him with each breath. Arianna asked the young girl for information about her father's history while putting him on the monitor. The girl didn't know anything.

The fire crew came in. One of them jumped into the action. "You guys figure out what he took?"

"There's scarring on his arms," Arianna pointed out.

"His pupils are pinpoints and are weakly responsive," I said. "He must have taken an opiate. He's pale. Deep, gasping respirations every several seconds."

Arianna sat down beside me with a pill bottle in hand. "He's taking Abacavir."

"Okay." When I was done checking his blood pressure I told her, "He has low blood pressure. We have to move him carefully."

There was no way I would risk moving this patient quickly only to get stuck with a dirty needle that we hadn't yet found, especially now that I knew our patient was HIV positive, due to his use of Abacavir. Arianna and a few members of the fire crew lifted his arms gingerly. I was still assisting our patient with breathing. Arianna said she would roll him to her side first. His skin was soaked with sweat. She helped some of the fire paramedics roll him over toward her. As expected, we found the needle lying on the floor under his body.

The fire paramedic cautiously reached under him to collect the used needle.

"Heroin," I said without judgment. It was more of confirmation of what we already knew.

We loaded our patient onto the stretcher and then carried him to the gurney we had left in the front of the apartment, before rolling him to our rig.

"Do you have someone you can stay with?"

As soon as I asked, the girl's neighbor emerged from her own apartment.

"I'll watch over her," the woman reassured us.

We gave the woman our thanks and placed the girl's father in the back of the ambulance. Arianna began setting up an I.V. bag. I watched her while continuing to assist the patient's breathing. The fire paramedic applied a tourniquet to his upper arm to search for a good vein.

"Can you hand me a smaller needle? A 20-gauge is too big for this guy," he asked me.

I reached into our jump bag with my free hand and then passed a smaller needle over to him. I dug through our medicine case and pulled out the medicine I wanted to use to counteract the heroin coursing through our patient.

"It's in," I told him.

We moved quickly, and in tandem. Arianna caught me staring at her, and I forced my focus to return to the task at hand.

"I'm going to give him Narcan through the nasal cavity," Arianna informed.

A few minutes after administering Narcan, his eyes shot open. He groaned, staring around at Arianna and me completely dazed.

"Mr. Davis, I'm Tajel and this is my partner, Arianna. We're the paramedics."

It took him a minute to find the words, probably because he seemed frightened of the current circumstances.

"Where's..." he grunted. "Where's my daughter?"

"At your neighbor's house," Arianna reassured him.

She proceeded to ask him a few questions and I headed to the front, ready to get us to the nearest hospital.

"We can handle it from here," I told the fire paramedic.

It took us almost ten minutes to make it to the nearest hospital and by the time we were inside the emergency room, you would never have guessed he was unconscious from an overdose of heroin just 20 minutes ago.

"I'm glad that turned out okay," Arianna said, letting out a deep breath.

I started the rig. "Yeah, but it kills me to see a parent put themselves in that position only to let their kids find them like that."

I never made a habit out of judging my patients, but it was hard to ignore when the bad choices people made like this generally had heartbreaking consequences. Arianna was quiet. I looked over to her and I felt that I should say something, but she seemed to be deep in thought, so I decided to leave it alone. I didn't wait for a response clearing us for departure. It didn't matter anyway because we were soon contacted for another call.

*

Arianna

We made it back to station exhausted from working nearly 18 hours of call after call. Did people decide that today was the day to get hurt or sick? I was tired and hungry, and not sure of what to do first, so I decided to let my body guide me. Tajel sighed, leaning her head against the steering wheel. I knew she was feeling the same way.

"I can't decide what I want to do first," Tajel groaned, "but I'm really craving a tuna melt with avocados."

"That does sound good," I agreed.

"If only I had brought one," she groaned again.

With unenergetic motions, she got out of the rig and made her way to our sleeping quarters. We were thinking the same thing. She had lured me into the same direction. I didn't bother to take off my boots. I was too tired to use my energy for anything other than making it to my bed. When my body hit the sheets, I was asleep before I could even think about food again. I woke up to the sound of the door closing. Through squinted eyes I saw the outline of Tajel's body.

"Sorry. I wasn't trying to wake you," she whispered.

"What time is it?"

"30 minutes before we're off shift," she answered.

"Thank the gods," I sighed in relief.

I heard Tajel snort and I looked back up at her. "Sorry, just didn't expect that to come out of your mouth."

"Why?" I asked. I sat up, running my fingers through my hair.

"You don't make random comments like that normally," she answered. "It sounded silly coming from you."

"Do you find it so easy to insult me?" I wasn't angry, merely curious.

Tajel studied me a moment, taking her time to respond. Her lips pursed as she considered my question carefully. "I find it easy to be honest."

I wasn't expecting her to say that.

"Sometimes honesty is not kind or gentle, even when you want it to be," Tajel explained. "But I would like to add that you are an amazing paramedic, and I don't say that to many people."

"So, I'm supposed to feel honored by that?" I questioned dryly.

Tajel pointed at me. "You make it especially easy for me to be honest."

"Because, I don't want to kiss your ass?" I sneered.

"Actually, my ass has never requested to have your lips on it," Tajel retorted. "I'm beginning to think you're trying to find things to hate about me."

I scoffed. "Why would I do that?"

"Because you hate me for making you forget that you're straight."

"Wow. " *Fuck.* But I wasn't straight. "Hate is a strong word."

"I will do the paperwork. It's only fair since you did everything at the start of our shift."

Tajel was about to head out and my need to make things better overpowered me.

"Wait," I called out.

Tajel appeared amused. "You like to have the last word, don't you?"

"Not even," I said seriously. "Look, I've been a pain and honestly, I'm surprised you haven't requested a new partner."

Tajel laughed.

I was confused but continued anyway, "I want to make this work. I don't want you to think I'm a bitch. At least, not most of the time."

A smile began to form at the corner of my lips and Tajel narrowed her eyes at me.

"See, there's that smile," she said.

"Let's start over," I urged, confident that things could improve between us.

Tajel crossed her arms over her chest, seemingly intrigued by my proposal. She smiled, and her dimples emerged. I mentally moaned. *Fuck, why does she look so good?*

"How?"

I was too nervous to make eye contact.

"Um, let me take you out to dinner. I-I mean...not a date...just dinner." I was sure she was enjoying seeing me squirm. "I just know you were h-hungry before. I can buy you that tuna melt, is all."

This was embarrassing. I needed to stay silent before I said anything else.

Tajel chuckled and patted my arm. "Relax, I know you're straight."

"I'm not," I blurted.

Why Arianna? Why did you say that? This woman probably thinks I'm crazy.

Tajel gave me a solemn look, her casual grin gone. "I know that."

They were simple words but words that meant a lot to me nevertheless. I felt that Tajel and I finally reached a mutual understanding. Somehow, I knew she accepted why I denied being gay.

"I might want two tuna melt sandwiches." Tajel winked at me.

I opened the door to leave. "Deal."

Chapter Six
Arianna

Tajel and I ended up at some cozy diner.

"I've been coming here since I was a kid." Tajel drank some of her raspberry lemonade as the waitress brought our food. "Thanks, Melody."

"No problem, sugar." Melody lightly pinched Tajel's cheek before heading back to the kitchen.

"What?"

"Nothing." I decided to concentrate on my fish sandwich with macaroni salad. "Do you know everyone?"

Tajel ate a few of her fries. "No. I don't know everyone, but Oregon is small compared to Los Angeles."

"I've heard."

"Have you been sightseeing yet?" she asked, and I shook my head. "That's insane. You must explore. It's cold as hell right now, but there are still places to visit."

"I will."

We ate in silence for a little while, neither one of us sure of what to say. *Why did I offer her dinner? Oh, that's right, I wanted to start over*.

"Look, we don't have to hang out to be good partners." Tajel wiped her mouth with a napkin. "I can tell you're not comfortable with me."

It would be easy to agree, go our separate ways, and keep a strictly professional relationship with Tajel. It would also be cowardly. I honestly wanted to get to know her.

Though we started off shaky, I had a feeling we'd be good friends.

"Unless you don't want to, I don't see why we can't try and be friends."

Tajel finished chewing before replying, "I'm—"

A woman approached our table, and I recognized her as the same woman from the other night at the bar.

"Hey, hun," the woman purred at Tajel. "You been thinking about me?"

I found myself infuriated. This woman behaved as if I was invisible. I remembered Tajel leaving with her and thinking about what they probably did together. *Damn...I'm jealous*. This was beyond unfair.

"Hey, Gina," Tajel said coolly.

So, that's the bimbo's name. Okay, that's harsh, Arianna.

"I'm kind of busy right now," Tajel added, leaning her head toward me. "This is Arianna, my partner."

Gina barely acknowledged me. "Cute...but when you're done...call me."

She sauntered away smugly.

Tajel rolled her eyes, mumbling something obscure, then turned to me. "Sorry about that."

I had enough. "I need to get home."

I stood and Tajel did the same. "Hey, what just happened here?"

"Nothing. I'm tired."

"That's bullshit, and you know it." Tajel stepped out of the booth where we were sitting. "What did I do this time?"

"I am a fool," I remarked as I started to leave.

Tajel followed, refusing to accept my retreat. "I'm not trying to sleep with you."

"No, you achieved that, and now I'm simply one more woman you've crossed off your list." I wrapped my arms around myself tightly.

I knew I crossed the line.

"So, you think I fuck every woman I meet, and I have some slutty reputation here?" Tajel's voice climbed an octave. "Maybe a long time ago." Tajel turned to leave but twisted back around to finish yelling, "Fuck you! You know what? The night I met you at the bar, we never slept together! You were wasted, and we ended up talking for a few hours instead before you fell asleep in my bed."

Tajel walked back to the table to get her tuna melt. She folded it inside of a few napkins, and then left. She couldn't leave behind her tuna melt. But she did leave me staring after her with my mouth open. *Fuck. I should earn a trophy for 'bitch of the year.'*

I was so wrong about Tajel. In fact, thinking that I was another woman on her list wasn't what pissed me off. I was jealous and lashed out because of my petty feelings. I couldn't wait to get back home to tell Danielle how I screwed up for a third time. I'm sure she would be thrilled to hear it. *Three for three, Arianna. Great job.*

*

Tajel

Finally, it was Saturday, my favorite day of the week. I just finished a 48-hour shift with Arianna and we were able to remain professional with one another, but it was awkward. 'Awkward' was probably the most appropriate word to describe the past two days. Awkward and distressing. I could probably use more words to describe the experience but there was really no need.

"One week with Ms. Castaldi and no distress signal yet." My uncle patted my back with a mix of astonishment and pride in his voice. "Impressive."

He was exaggerating a bit about my past partners and their eagerness to get away from me, but not by much. It wasn't entirely my fault, though. I was always saddled with incompetent partners. However, my uncle couldn't ever see that.

"I came here for the barbecue chicken, not a new lecture." I sat at the table with my Aunt Laura as she made my plate. I was spoiled by her and I absolutely loved it.

"Roosevelt, don't start on my little one tonight. She's worked a long week."

My uncle shook his head at his wife. "Honey, the girl has to learn."

My aunt cleared her throat. "Last time I checked, Tajel has been a grown woman for some time now."

It was difficult not to hide my smile.

"Now you just eat up and pay your uncle no mind," my aunt said.

I took her advice and shoved a bite of chicken into my mouth as I listened to my uncle grumbling.

For most of dinner I ate quietly, thinking of my week with Arianna. The woman frustrated the shit out of me. Right when I thought we were heading in a positive direction, she goes and blows it up. Why was she always so quick to judge? And why did I care that she did? It was not my first experience with someone making assumptions about my life and I never reacted that way before. My blood began to boil the moment she assumed I slept around. And, so what? Why does it matter who I slept with? She wasn't my girlfriend. That would never happen.

Our night together was a mutual thing. We wanted to sleep with each other and then go our separate ways. And we didn't even do that. The fact that we didn't have sex should have made everything much easier. I tried telling her when she first became my partner, but she had to be insulting and say she made a mistake. *Fuck her*. Why was she on my mind on my favorite day of the week?

My aunt walked me to the door after we finished dinner and handed my jacket to me. It was our thing. It was my aunt's way of having her personal time with me and learning about anything new in my life.

"Sweetie, you were awfully quiet tonight."

She wrapped my scarf around my neck as I was working out what to say. I've never lied to my family before and I didn't want to start now. But I had to choose my words carefully.

"Yeah, well...truth is... it's been a rough week."

"Oh? How so?"

When she was done helping me into my coat and scarf she handed my beanie to me. I played with it nervously.

"Is it work or is it a woman?"

I looked up at her with a weak smile. She was great at reading me.

"Ah, both," she guessed, correctly.

"I'm not into this woman or anything. It's just, she made a wrong assumption about me and it's been bugging the shi—heck out of me." I nearly forgot for a moment that my aunt hated hearing foul language, especially from me.

"And the work part?"

"The woman is also my partner," I whispered.

If my uncle found out any of this, I'd be a dead woman. I glanced around to make sure we wouldn't be overheard.

"Relax, he's watching television." Even so, out of respect for my privacy, she lowered her voice. "I understand the difficulty of finding the right partner. That goes for finding it through work or love. Whatever is going on between you two—"

"Nothing," I replied briskly. "Either we argue, or we don't talk at all."

"You two never shared one normal conversation?" I knew I couldn't say anything now. "Honey, I know how important your work is to you. The fact that this is bugging you suggests there is something more to it."

"There's nothing going on between us," I said defensively. There wasn't.

"Maybe not physically, but it's not hard to see that you're conflicted. You've certainly had your share of annoying partners. But she's the first person who's got you so, emotional."

My brow raised at my aunt's choice of words. Emotional. *I don't get emotional.*

She knew exactly what I was thinking. "All I can tell you is to be you. If this woman can't see what an amazing partner you are, then you shouldn't spend any time thinking about her."

My aunt was right. "Thanks, Aunt Laura."

"Love you. Get home safe," she said, kissing my cheek.

"Going to Sasha's. She asked for some of your peach cobbler, by the way."

She laughed aloud. "Tell her that if she wants it so badly she can come to dinner with you next Saturday and get it herself."

I chuckled. "I'll let her know."

My uncle called out for his wife, "Laura, stop spoiling Tajel and come settle in for the night."

She breathed exasperatedly and then smiled at me. "Good night."

She kissed me on the cheek again and I was out the door. I made up my mind on the drive to Sasha's place that Monday would be a new day, and I would not let Arianna affect me any longer.

Chapter Seven
Tajel

We were 16 hours into our 24-hour shift. Felipe was on the couch with Rogan.

"Slow shift." He tossed a chip into his mouth.

I took a seat next to Felipe and snatched the bag of chips out of his hand.

"I should kick your ass," I snarled. Felipe was always eating my food.

"Where's your partner?" he asked, ignoring my threat.

"I don't know. I'm not her babysitter." I was annoyed that he brought her up.

"How does it feel to work with another woman?" Manny, our field supervisor, interrupted as he entered the room.

Ugh. I was ready to leave.

"You find out if she's like you? Or can I slide—"

"Shut up, Manny!" I snapped. "Why are you even here this early?"

"To make sure you don't screw anything up or try to horde the new pussy on the block, especially since yours is unavailable."

"Wow, Manny, you're going way too far," Rogan warned, straightening himself.

Felipe hopped off the couch and put himself in between Manny and me before I let my anger get the better of me.

"Bro, you need to leave." Felipe knew how to diffuse tense situations.

"I'm sorry. She just pisses me—"

"Nothing I or anyone ever does gives you the right to say what just came out of your mouth." I clenched my fists, still ready to punch him if he continued. "And don't you even speak, look, or breathe in the direction of my partner, or I promise you, I will get you when you least expect it."

Manny rolled his eyes and walked around acting as if he wasn't concerned about my threat. Arianna chose that moment to walk in, immediately catching Manny's attention even though he was walking in the opposite direction. I was finally going to report his ass. It's one thing when he was messing with me, but he wasn't going to do it to my partner. Enough was enough, and he needed to be fired. It was long overdue. *Idiot.*

I wanted to make sure Arianna hadn't heard anything, but dispatch came over the intercom, alerting both Felipe's rig and mine to answer a call in the same location. A gunman was holding hostages at a small clinic. There was sure to be injured people. We were in our rigs and driving away in a matter of seconds.

When we arrived on-scene, the police told us to stay a block away until the situation was under control.

"I didn't think there were going to be gunshot calls this often in Oregon," Arianna said, sincerely stunned.

"What did you think? Our state was immune to this type of violence?" I asked.

"No, I didn't mean that." She stopped herself from saying more.

"Medic 112 and 72...update?" Dispatch came through the radio static.

Across from us, Felipe was sitting inside his rig with his partner. He gave me a thumbs-up to let me know he would respond to dispatch. Silence was the only thing that passed between Arianna and me, and I was fine with that. Well, not really. I played nice and Arianna stomped all over it as usual. The police called out to us, interrupting my thoughts, and now it was time to get to work.

I cautiously drove closer to the clinic with Felipe following behind. When we parked the rigs, we hopped out and promptly followed the officers into the clinic.

"A doctor has been shot, along with another," the officer told us as I carried the stretcher and Arianna grabbed the jump bag. "The suspect has been arrested."

"We have the doctor!" Felipe yelled, rushing over to his patient.

Ass. He knew I wanted the critical patient.

I bent down to our patient who had a gunshot wound in his shoulder, and said calmly, "Hey, I'm Taj—"

"Just take me to the hospital so I can go home." He waved me off, wincing a little from his gunshot.

Okay. He was clearly the type of patient who had no respect for those who only wanted to help. This asshole acted as if we were the ones that caused his gunshot wound.

"Can I check and see if the bullet exited—"

"I need to get shot more often." The man ran his eyes along Arianna's body and she grimaced, undeniably disgusted.

Gross.

"Look buddy, let me do my job." Arianna was trying to focus on caring for the man who couldn't keep his eyes off her.

"Fuck this clinic!" someone bellowed with rage. The sound was coming from a narrow hall that was to my left. "This place doesn't help anyone!"

A man who appeared to be in his early twenties emerged from the opening in the front of the clinic where we all were, carrying a gun pointed in our direction. Instinct took over my body and I lunged forward, falling on top of Arianna to shield her from the gunfire.

The sounds of gunfire filled the air, causing my ears to ring.

"Clear!" an officer shouted after some time had passed.

I turned to Arianna, worried that I might have injured her when I jumped on her. "You okay?"

She nodded. I lifted my body off her and looked in the direction of the shooter. He was lying on his back on the ground outside in the doorway. He was completely still. I looked over to our patient. Luckily, he wasn't hit by any stray bullets.

"What the hell was that?" I yelled at the officers who seemed to have no interest in responding.

Moving swiftly to the gunman along with Arianna and one officer who quickly retrieved the gun, my heart was pounding from shock. I began checking for a pulse as soon as I reached him. I used our shears to cut through his clothes, exposing his gunshot wounds – I counted four. Arianna started pressing gauze onto each bleeding hole and then she carefully moved him to one side to check for any exit wounds. Only two bullets had gone completely through his body.

"Another bullet. It's in the left thigh," Arianna noted.

I started CPR as Arianna took out the BVM when we realized he had no pulse. She grabbed more gauze to control the bleeding. He also had a gunshot wound to the left side of his chest and Arianna applied an occlusive dressing, to stop air from being sucked into his chest.

"He has a pulse again," I stated, putting him on 15 liters of oxygen with a face mask.

"Why are you helping him when you have another patient? Just let his ass—"

"Don't even begin to question my job. This patient's a priority no matter his crime. We do our job."

The shooter's saturations dropped again, below 86%.

Arianna's hands trembled, and she was having some difficulty holding onto the tube that she would place down his throat.

"Arianna." Her eyes snapped up to me. "I won't let anything happen to you. We're safe now. Take a breath."

She shook her head vigorously and closed her eyes. She took a few deep breaths and then opened them, her determination and focus renewed. Her hands were steady, and her expression was serious. I watched as she used a jaw-thrust maneuver to open our patient's mouth and airway, sliding the tube slowly down his throat as I continued to press down against his chest. His heart stopped again.

Near the end of my thirtieth compression, I felt something snap beneath the palm of my hand. "Fuck! I broke a rib."

I finished my compressions right when Arianna began bagging him. *Damn, she is quick.*

After a few more minutes, I checked his pulse a second time. "Nothing."

I looked at our patient for only a second, but it was long enough to realize how young he was. What was a young man, practically still a kid, doing shooting a place up? A few fire paramedics hopped in the back of the ambulance with me. We made it all the way to the hospital still giving our patient CPR, airway control, and even the use of an AED from our Lifepak. He was done. 15 minutes without a pulse. It was over, but we would let the doctors make the call.

Another unit of ours approached us from behind as we were walking back to our rigs.

"Yo, Tajel! We heard what happened. You two okay?"

I waved him off as I marched toward the officer who questioned me at the scene. Without thinking, I punched him squarely in the jaw. A few other officers who were standing nearby rushed over to us to rip us apart.

"Don't you ever fucking question my methods again, especially when you fucking cops said the place was cleared and you nearly got us killed!"

Arianna was beside me in a flash, helping the officers keep me back.

"I should arrest your ass!" another officer shouted at me.

"And I should report every one of these fuckers who did not do their job thoroughly. That bullet could have easily hit me or my partner. We don't have vests like you do, but it's clear now we should wear them around you morons."

Arianna pulled on my arm again, so I turned to face her. Her eyes were gentle and understanding. Of course, she understood. She could have gotten shot.

"Let's go. They've learned their lesson and I'm sure their sergeant will deal with them."

Through her touch and the soft tone she used with me, a new calm settled over me.

I walked away from the officers with Arianna.

"I'll drive, "Arianna offered.

I was about to argue but I thought better of it. With the way I was feeling, I was in no position to drive, so we cleaned out the back of our ambulance, first rinsing all the blood out and then wiping everything down. The walls, seats, the –ceiling – blood had a way of ending up in areas you never expected to find it.

20 minutes passed before more crews came out of the hospital pushing their gurneys.

"Shit, I heard what happened." Felipe raced over to me while Rogan loaded the gurney into their rig. "How are you two?"

"I'm fine," I lied.

Arianna only looked at me but said nothing.

"Sure, yeah," Felipe said, clearly not satisfied with my answer. "I'll see you back at station."

He gave Arianna a meaningful look and walked off. We climbed into our rig and I took my place on the passenger side. As I waited for Arianna to start driving, I turned to look at her. She appeared to be undisturbed by everything that happened today, but I knew that couldn't be the case.

It was obvious she wanted to say something, but she remained silent. Arianna had a terrible habit of always saying the wrong thing, but I wanted to hear what she had to say now. Maybe it was momentary insanity. I couldn't help it.

"Just say it," I blurted, unable to stand her silence any longer.

She sighed. "Feeling scared or sad, expressing any emotion isn't weakness. Not expressing emotions or even admitting you are feeling anything, that's true weakness."

I pointed to the officer I punched. "I think I expressed an emotion."

What does this woman want from me? To cry on her shoulder?

"To show that you were tough?" Arianna looked straight at me. "You punched him because you were scared."

I refused to comment on that remark. *Bullshit. I wasn't scared. I was angry.* "Drive."

Arianna said nothing else to me, but reported to dispatch, letting them know we were clear. The dispatcher directed us to head back to the station, and I sat stewing in my anger for the entire ride. I had a right to feel angry. It wasn't easy being a female paramedic, but I worked my ass off to be treated with respect. Being questioned by that officer sent me over the edge. Why? Because he thought his opinion was worth more than mine. It was something I experienced many times when dealing with men in our line of work.

We made it back to the station in one piece.

Chapter Eight
Arianna

Chief wanted both of us in his office for a full report on what happened at the scene and the scuffle at the hospital. After we were done I was dismissed, but Tajel remained behind. I headed for our sleeping quarters, intending to immediately strip off my uniform and hop in a shower. My skin felt hot and sticky, and my uniform was clinging to my body so tightly I believed my shirt had turned into a straightjacket.

Grabbing my overnight bag, I rushed to the shower and stripped away the rest of my clothes. I didn't wait for the water to warm up before getting in. My body relaxed as the cool water fell onto me and before long, it was at the temperature I wanted.

Once I was done, I changed into a clean uniform and found Tajel waiting for me in our room. I paused in the doorway, waiting for Tajel to say whatever was on her mind. I could tell she was bothered.

Tajel was entirely rigid. Her eyes were focused on me. "I'm not weak."

Did what I said earlier really upset her that much?

I took a step closer to her so that she could see my sincerity, if nothing else. I was bad at choosing the right words. I never meant to offend Tajel and I was desperate for her to know that.

"I know that you're not. That's why it's all right for you to be honest with your feelings. I don't think you are weak." With another step, I nearly closed the gap between us. "I know what real weakness is, because I have been utterly weak for so long."

Tajel shook her head. "You're not weak."

I maintained my seriousness. "Yes I am. Don't lie for me."

"You're not weak at least, not right now."

The kindness in her words soothed me more than she probably intended. The fact that she was being nice to me at all, especially after my third time slaughtering any chance at getting along with her, surprised me. She didn't have a mean bone in her body. Not really. Whether Tajel tried to or not, she wasn't capable of holding a grudge.

"Thank you." Before she could ask why I thanked her, I explained, "You put your life at risk and kept me from harm."

"I probably should have done that for the patient instead."

I pursed my lips, considering her observation, then smiled. "But you didn't."

Absentmindedly, I reached out to her, taking her hand into mine and squeezing it.

"And thank you for earlier. I heard what Manny said to you. After my behavior at the diner…"

Tajel accepted my apology for the third time, and I was beginning to think she enjoyed our arguments simply because she liked to see me squirm when I would finally apologize. Time slipped away from us. It was probably only a few seconds, but I realized I couldn't handle the tension in our linked fingers. When I managed to pull away, I noticed her knuckles were bruised.

I took an ice pack from my medic kit that I kept in the bathroom and popped it to activate the ice. I wrapped the pack in a small towel and placed it over her hand.

"You should be more careful. We need these hands."

Our eyes locked, and my heart raced as everything around us faded. A knock on our door made me leap away from Tajel and she gave me an amused grin. *Yes, I'm pathetic.*

"Hey Tajel, can I eat the rest of your chips and dip?"

It was Felipe. *Of course.*

"That means he already ate them," Tajel told me in a low voice. She rolled her eyes.

"Play with him a little," I whispered, giggling.

"Bro, I'm kind of hungry. About to come and eat 'em now!" she shouted at the closed door.

It was quiet for a few seconds, and then Felipe's voice broke the silence, "Uh...umm...well... Give me like fifteen minutes and I'll just bring them to you! You've had a rough day!"

"He's about to run his ass off in the cold to buy a new bag of chips and dip." Tajel tried to keep her voice down, but laughter threatened to burst forth.

I laughed and quickly covered my hand with my mouth.

"Never mind, go ahead! Just eat my chips. I'd rather sleep, honestly."

"Cool," Felipe said in a high-pitched voice, happy he hadn't been discovered. "I mean...get some sleep. Thanks!"

"Mmhmm," Tajel replied loudly enough so he would hear and then said to me, "I should make his ass get me a new bag. He owes me like 50 bucks worth of chips now."

"Does he eat everyone's food?" I asked, hoping he would not go for mine. I liked what I normally brought to work and would be annoyed if he touched my food.

"No, just mine. We have an understanding. He knows what he can't have of my food."

"Like what?"

"Anything my aunt makes me." She walked over to the bed with the ice pack still covering her hand. "We should get some sleep."

I nodded in agreement and when I finally fell onto my bed my eyes were closed in a matter of seconds.

*

Tajel

Here I was again, playing nice with Arianna, and this time she hadn't fucked up for an entire week. I was relieved that we could have a normal, civil conversation. It wasn't without any difficulties, though. She was like an inspector marking down everything I said and did, waiting to pounce over any perceived slight.

"Hey...I'm going to recertify as a flight medic. I thought...maybe you'd want to join me and get yours."

Arianna's eyes lit up. I smiled at her and parked the rig in the station. It was Friday evening and we still had an hour left to kill before the end of our shift.

"No point in waiting to get it later, so yes, that would be a blast." Arianna's cheerfulness was refreshing. "Thanks for inviting me with you."

"No problem."

As we walked into the station Chief approached us with a stern expression on his face. "Tajel. Ms. Castaldi. "

"Chief. " I stuck my hands in my pocket.

"Chief," Arianna greeted him.

"How was your shift?"

Why were his eyes on me when he asked that? I wasn't as bad as he kept making me seem.

Arianna seemed not to notice our Chief narrowing his eyes at me. "It was great. Tajel's an amazing partner. Never a dull moment."

The natural pink of my cheeks flared into a deep crimson. *Calm down, Tajel*. Lately, talking to myself had become second nature. Chief smiled and turned his attention back to me for a moment. I knew my nervousness was perceptible to him. *I am acting guilty. Stop.*

"I would like to invite you to dinner this Saturday, Arianna. My wife is making chicken enchiladas."

"She's a pescatarian," I said without thinking.

Arianna gave me a curious expression, then turned to Chief with a wide grin to accept his invitation. "I'll eat whatever your wife makes. I can make an exception."

Chief smiled. "My wife can make a delicious vegetarian enchilada." He looked at me. "We'll save the meat for the rest of us."

"Thank you, Chief."

Chief left and we continued to our sleeping quarters.

"Are you coming to dinner tomorrow?"

She caught Chief's implication. "Well...umm...I don't go around shouting it from the rooftops, but... Chief is also my uncle."

"No way." When I didn't laugh, she asked, "You're serious?"

"I eat there every Saturday. My aunt can really cook. I would not be at his house if she wasn't married to him."

Arianna frowned. "I'm sure he loves you tremendously if he puts up with you at work."

"Wait, I'm not difficult."

"All I'm saying is, you should be proud that he's your uncle. He's highly accomplished and seems like an amazing man."

Why did she have to chastise me? The stubbornness rising in me diminished when Arianna spoke again.

"My father was like your –uncle – smart, ambitious, hardworking, and a great man beyond all expectations. Then, he stopped being who I grew up loving. Who I admired. I still love him though and understand why he changed."

I could only stare at Arianna. Maybe she wasn't trying to, but she let me into her life just a little, and I would not dismiss that.

"I'm sorry. You're right."

Arianna realized she shared more than she intended. She had a habit of doing –that – she regularly spoke before she thought but it was normally a bitchy remark. This admission of hers was refreshing.

We were alone in our sleeping quarters, so I reached my hand out to brush her arm to comfort her. "Hey, I will never use your words against you. Don't think what you told me was a mistake."

Arianna smiled timidly, her cheeks flushed. "I'm sure there are moments you will want me to keep quiet."

I laughed. "Yes, but now is not that time."

After talking for a while longer, we both packed our overnight bags and headed out the door.

I was about to get into my car when I spotted Arianna standing by the front entrance. "Are you waiting for someone?"

Arianna checked her wristwatch. "Danielle. I don't have a car yet and I usually take hers, but she needed it today, so she said she'd pick me up. She was supposed to be here by now."

I found myself unable to leave her there alone. "I can drop you off if you want?"

"Umm…" Arianna looked around as if praying that her friend would show up so she wouldn't have to be alone with me.

"Look, I'm not contagious and I thought we moved past—"

"No. I'm sorry."

"No," I repeated, feeling the word on my tongue as it slipped past my lips.

"No... I mean – yes." Arianna sighed, her body relaxing as she did. "I mean...I wasn't thinking anything bad regarding you and your intentions."

"Then what? Is there something you're afraid you'll say or do?" Part of me was intrigued but also hopeful to hear her answer.

"I think I've already said every rude or stupid thing I could say to you," she said with faint embarrassment.

"Hey, I'm not judging you for your past mistakes." I smiled awkwardly. "Are you afraid of what you'll do?"

Her skin, usually a shade darker than mine, was pale now, as if all the blood drained out of her. Her brown eyes scanned the ground, and a few lose strands of her hair fell across her face.

"Of course not."

Arianna was incredibly cute, but I could not afford to be thinking of Arianna as attractive. For one, she was my partner. Secondly, she could go right back to bitch mode.

"Have you always been this shy?"

"What? I'm nowhere near—"

"Let me clarify." I held my hand up so I would not be interrupted. "When on duty you are very brave, confident, and focused. Off duty...on personal time...your awkwardness is kind of cute." I quickly added, "Not that I'm trying to imply—"

"I got you."

"Look, we can stand here and talk about this all night, or..." I motioned to my car.

Arianna took one last look around. "A ride would be nice."

Well, that was surprising.

We found ourselves walking to my car in silence and I opened the door for her. *If only Sasha could see me now.* I never opened the door for women. I never dated a woman long enough to care about opening the door for them. I'm certainly not Arianna's girlfriend, nor do I intend to date her, but I couldn't help myself around her. Arianna brought out the romancer in me.

Don't overthink this. Arianna was a woman who could piss me off lightning fast, then instantly make me forget she did anything wrong. As I made my way to the driver side of my car, I thought to myself, *don't fall for this woman.*

Chapter Nine
Tajel

I pulled up to Arianna's apartment and put my car in park.

Arianna sat motionless for a time, staring out of the window. When she faced me she wore a nervous smile, and I wasn't certain why.

"I'm sure whatever it is—"

"Would you like to come up? Last time I was supposed to take you out to eat, I screwed things up. I can make you that tuna melt."

I grinned. "If you recall I took my tuna melt home with me."

Arianna lowered her head. "Right."

"But, I'd love to see if your tuna melt is better."

This seemed to bring back that bright smile I adored. It was the one that came naturally and without thought. Was it wrong to want to see Arianna smile like that? The way the left side of her mouth curled up when she smiled was adorable.

"I can make a really great tuna melt. I've mastered making anything with fish."

I was convinced. I shut off my engine and followed behind Arianna to her apartment. I suppose I'd never taken the time to really appreciate her beauty since the night I first met her, but now I felt free to observe. The beauty she possessed was different from any woman I'd ever known. Cliché to say, but it was true.

Arianna's beauty wasn't flashy or glamorous. Her hair was thick and crow black, falling to her elbows. I walked up beside her to get a glimpse of those large chestnut eyes bordered by thick eyelashes. If I didn't know any better, I would think she was wearing mascara. Her eyebrows had an exotic, inward slant. Unlike me, she was still in her uniform. Her shirt was untucked and unbuttoned, a white undershirt was visible and hugged her breasts. I also took time to admire her thin lips and narrow nose, which was especially narrow when she smiled. Under the left side of her chin was a small scar.

"Something wrong?" Arianna's teeth were white and perfectly straight. "Tajel?"

When her hand brushed my shoulder, I stifled a groan, snapping out of my trance. *Fuck. I need to go home.*

"It's been a long day." *Yes...I'll blame it on a long day.*

"Hey." Arianna had my attention. She ran the palm of her hand over my jaw. "What's going on in that mind of yours?"

Her smile magnified the fluttering in my stomach, twisting it in knots of pleasure.

I blinked a few times, trying to restrain the words that were threatening to spill out of my mouth. I barely noticed we were still standing right outside her front door. I knew I was going to do or say something stupid. *Hands in your pockets and don't touch her.* I did just that, offering her a shaky smile instead of words. The front door opened suddenly, and Danielle and Sasha nearly collided with us.

"Shit!" Danielle shouted as she leaped back. She gave Arianna a sheepish grin. "I swear I was on my way to pick you up."

"It's the truth. That's why we didn't finish—"

"Cooking! We didn't finish cooking," Danielle interrupted.

I let out a breath, relieved I could focus on them rather than my confusing thoughts. Was it possible that I was attracted to Arianna? *No.* She was annoying, rude, and was always questioning me. *Fuck, but she is sexy. Yes, so sexy.* I couldn't let go of her rudeness, though. Well, rude was putting it lightly. So why did I find myself attracted to her? If anything, I was attracted to her unpredictable nature. *This might affect my chances of joining my uncle's SWAT team.* It didn't make sense to be attracted to her. The last time I experienced anything like this was four or five years ago. And those feelings were one-sided. *Don't forget that, Tajel.*

Sasha spoke to me, "Hey hun, you all right? You're looking weird."

I did my best to fake a smile. Arianna gave me a curious look.

"I'm great. Fine." I didn't sound confident.

"So..." Danielle's attempt to ease the tension was not going well at all. "You gave my *chica* a ride home?"

"It was no big deal," I said nonchalantly. *Hell of an acting job, Tajel.*

Arianna studied me. She turned back to Danielle. "Can I get into the apartment or did you two destroy it?"

"No destruction." Danielle scratched the back of her head.

She opened the door and we all entered together.

"I need to change," Arianna announced, heading to her room with Danielle following behind.

Sasha and I were left alone in the living room.

Arianna stuck her head out from her doorway before disappearing into her room. "Make yourself at home."

I nodded, my hands still in my pockets. I paced around her living room as if there was no place to –sit – she had two couches and an ottoman. I was nervous as shit.

"What's up with you?" Sasha asked, scrutinizing my anxious body language. "Why are you acting so...nervous?"

"I'm not." My tone was a bit defensive.

"You're so full of shit." Sasha smirked. I said nothing, and she paused as if she had figured out what I was thinking. "Did something happen between you—"

"Shush!" I covered her mouth with my hand. "No. Absolutely not."

My eyes darted to Arianna's bedroom door. I felt a grin form on Sasha's face underneath my palm.

"Don't give me that look." I removed my hand from her mouth, whining to myself.

"Oh, my God," she exclaimed as quietly as possible. "You want something to happen between you and Miss Snappy Doodles!"

"Hey!"

"You were the one that gave her that nickname." Sasha rolled her eyes. "The fact that you're getting defensive with me over this is proving my point, by the way."

"You're annoying," I said, trying to ignore her.

"But I'm right." Sasha tried to pinch my cheek. "You have a crush on Miss..."

My burning glare earned her silence, but only for a minute.

" I get it. I can tell she's a great woman. Danielle wouldn't be friends with anyone who wasn't as amazing as her. And, she's beautiful."

"So, you and Danielle are dating now?"

Without hesitation Sasha answered, "Yes."

"Right."

Arianna picked that moment to walk out wearing a tank top that complimented her so well that it made me almost forget she was my partner. My work partner. I couldn't believe I had to remind myself. She was also wearing a pair of fitted jeans and her hair was drawn into a ponytail. I forgot again. *Partner. Partner. Partner.* I had to keep telling myself that. *I should go right now.*

"Hey, you know I just got a call from my aunt. She needs my help with some plumbing." That lie came too easily.

Arianna smiled, but it wasn't hard to tell that she was disappointed. I wished I could erase the lie, but it was too late. *Stupid mouth.*

"All right. I guess I'll see you tomorrow night."

The door was in sight and relief was sweeping over me because I was almost out of the apartment. Unfortunately, Arianna followed me.

"You don't have to trouble yourself."

"Who said walking you to the door would cause me any trouble?"

Damn. She had me there.

"Thanks again for bringing me home."

How did her voice sound cuddly? "No problem."

As soon as I realized my attraction for this woman, I couldn't get the thought of her out of my head.

"Being a good Samaritan?" she asked.

"I wouldn't drop just anyone off." *I meant that.*

Arianna opened the door for me. Sasha, who had also accompanied us, pretended to accidentally bump into Arianna, sending her falling into my arms. My hands gripped her waist, steadily holding her until she could regain her balance. Our eyes locked as she straightened herself and I stifled my second groan of the night. *Masturbating, here I come.*

"Thank you." She laughed with ease, extracting a smile from me. "I'm either always apologizing to you or thanking you."

"No one's perfect," I teased and the blush on her cheeks deepened. Arianna looked away, only for a moment.

"Oh, sorry." Sasha smiled mischievously. "I'm heading out with you."

"Super," I said without any effort to fake excitement.

"Oh, shush."

Sasha turned back to Danielle, giving her such a passionate kiss that I couldn't help but look at Arianna. She turned to me, probably feeling as awkward as I was in the face of such enthusiastic kissing. I decided to break the uncomfortable scene by being silly. I made kissy faces, teasing our friends until they were done, and then Sasha was dragging me out of the apartment.

"See you!" I called out to Arianna as Sasha walked with me to my car.

*

Arianna

"What's going on with—"

"Nothing," I interrupted. I walked into the kitchen and removed a container of ice cream from the freezer. "Don't start."

"Okay, I won't." Danielle grabbed herself a spoon, waiting for me to open the ice cream. "But I will say, Tajel was looking at you with—"

"Stop," I barked. "You want me to be with anyone at this point. You're seeing what you want to see."

"I wouldn't go that far." She dipped her spoon into the ice cream first. "But it would be nice to see you with a woman who looks at you the way she—"

"You don't quit." I shook my head. "She finished hating me only earlier this week. Yes, she's attractive and I believe she feels the same way about me. She wouldn't have tried to sleep with me that first night if not. But that doesn't mean that us getting together would be a good idea."

"You're right. It couldn't possibly be a good idea for two attractive women to be together and to be happy."

Danielle walked off with the ice cream. I followed her, not finished with our conversation or my snack.

"I'm not going to fall for that."

"Don't be blind."

I glared at her, unwilling to accept her suggestion.

"I only want you to accept—"

"I work with her and I think you're wrong."

The conversation was over. We both knew it. Danielle kissed my cheek, her lips cold from eating ice cream.

"I'm glad you moved here."

"It was what I needed," I agreed, getting a big spoonful of the ice cream.

Danielle gave me a pleading look.

"Go ahead and say it so I can say *no*."

"You can't say *no* to your best friend," I laughed, and she continued, "There's this woman I know… I think you two would hit it off."

"First you try to push me toward Tajel and now you're trying to get me to go out with some new woman?"

"Hey! I honestly think you and Tajel would be great together. But you don't see it, so go out with someone else."

I rolled my eyes. "No."

"You can't say *no*. Just...gosh, Arianna! The whole point of you moving here was to start living the way you wanted to. You like women. Date them."

She was right. I'd limited myself back in Los Angeles because I never wanted my family to find out that I am gay. Here I was, free and able to start dating without looking over my shoulder. What was one date? Closing my eyes, I rested my head on the couch, and Danielle knew she had sold me.

"Great! Her name's Iris. She's cute as hell, with a lot of personality." Danielle went on for a few minutes about Iris as if her description would make me more excited. "How about tomorrow night?"

"What? That soon?"

Danielle smiled. "What are you waiting for?"

"I have dinner plans tomorrow night."

"Then after," Danielle persisted. "What about nine? It's a Saturday night."

"All right." It was clear I wasn't going to get out of this date.

"She says nine is perfect, and she'll let me know where," Danielle informed me while looking at her phone.

"Great."

I was no longer interested in eating ice cream. I felt like I was the one being eaten. *One date. It's harmless. One date.*

Chapter Ten
Arianna

I stood at the front entrance of Chief's home, my nerves rapidly taking over. Shaking, I rang the doorbell. An older woman who looked to be in her 50s answered the door.

She welcomed me with a gracious smile. "You must be Arianna. Please, come in."

I returned her smile as she motioned for me to come inside. She wasted no time in offering to take my coat and then I followed her down a small hallway that led to the living room. The dining room was to my left. The table was already set and Tajel and Sasha were already sitting, drinks in hand. I was glad to see her. I don't think I could have handled being here alone.

"Hey, you made it!" Tajel exclaimed. "I was sure you'd get lost."

I smiled. "I'm quite capable."

Chief came over to me and offered me his hand. "Ms. Castaldi."

"Chief." I took his hand and shook it.

"Oh, let's leave all that formality stuff outside of this house," the older woman who introduced herself as Laura, chastised.

"Very well. If you're comfortable with that?" Chief asked me.

I nodded.

" You could call him Uncle Rosy."

"Tajel." Chief frowned at her playfulness.

Tajel conceded, "Or you can just call him Roosevelt."

I chuckled nervously. "Roosevelt sounds better than Uncle Rosy."

"I second that," Roosevelt chimed in.

He followed his wife into the kitchen leaving Tajel, Sasha, and me alone together.

"How are you?"

I shrugged. "The same. Kind of disappointed you didn't let me make you that tuna melt."

Why did I care about that? I'm sure Tajel wasn't starving. Especially since she had an aunt who could cook.

"There's always next time."

Tajel certainly had a way of making me feel more at ease. She has been great at that since the beginning of our partnership, even though I was such a bitch to her.

I knew I needed to apologize to her. "I was just telling Danielle last night that I'm glad you don't hate me anymore. God, I was terrible to you."

Tajel reached out her hand brushed against my arm and soft, kind words followed, "I never hated you. You were merely a kidney stone, now resolved."

"Kidney stone? Those things hurt like hell and could cause some serious damage."

"Bad example, but you get what I'm saying."

I knew she was right, but I was ready to move forward. "Then let's put it behind us."

"What's behind you?" Chief, er, Roosevelt asked curiously.

"Uncle," Tajel almost growled, bothered by her uncle's nosiness.

"Roosevelt, don't bother my baby." Tajel's aunt returned from the kitchen to embrace Tajel protectively.

Tajel leaned into her aunt's arms, a broad grin spread across her face as she looked at her uncle.

"What about me?" Sasha pouted.

Laura smiled and gave Sasha a loving hug.

"Cute, real cute. Stealing my hugs from my aunt." Tajel shook her head playfully.

"You can share." Sasha giggled quietly. She looked at me and added, "Well, not everything."

That remarked earned a withering stare from Tajel that went unnoticed by her family. Tajel motioned for me to sit beside her. I took my seat as Laura and Roosevelt came out with the food, placing everything in the center of the table. I wasn't sure if anyone here prayed over their meal, but I received my answer when everyone began eating as soon as their food was plated.

After a few bites, Laura asked, "Have you gone exploring yet, Arianna?"

"Not yet. I will soon though," I replied between mouthfuls.

"I've already given her this lecture," Tajel said.

"Don't tell her what she's missing, honey. Show her." Tajel's aunt gave her a knowing smile.

Tajel turned to me. "I can show you around, if you want. Unless Danielle has that set up with you, of course."

"She's been rather occupied." My eyes shot over to Sasha. "Plus, she's a bad guide. Back in Los Angeles she worked at the LA Zoo and I spent a day with her at work. She got us lost."

Everyone laughed.

"That's terrible," Laura said, choking back a laugh. "Well, Tajel's an amazing guide."

I knew what Tajel's aunt was trying to do – she wanted to ensure her niece's romantic happiness. Laura continued, giving her compliment after compliment because she knew that Tajel was too modest to talk about her accomplishments.

"Has Portland caused you to experience any culture shock?" Roosevelt was endeavoring to steer the conversation to a more neutral topic.

I didn't even have to think about my answer. "So many people in Los Angeles are only concerned with themselves. They would run you over without bothering to look. And, I've never had any of my bosses invite me to dinner with his or her family before now. People are very welcoming here."

"Glad you approve," he said after taking a sip of water from an oversized glass.

"What about your family? Were they upset by the move?" Laura questioned.

I should have expected someone to ask me that, but I was completely caught off-guard. *Oh God, I couldn't think. Say something.*

"How does any family handle one of their own leaving?" Tajel piped up, hoping to spare me from any further interrogation.

"You have a great point," Laura observed, putting another enchilada on Sasha's plate.

After that, the focus of conversation wasn't on me and I was relieved.

I felt someone's hand squeeze mine underneath the table. I looked over to Tajel and she gave me a comforting smile.

"Breathe," she whispered.

I lowered my voice as well and asked, "Does it look like I've stopped?"

She nodded, and I smiled.

"Thanks," I said, taking a deep breath.

Dinner ended after a couple of hours of conversation, laughter, and some of the best enchiladas I've ever eaten.

Sasha approached me at the front door. Her arms were crossed, and her hands were tucked underneath them. She bit her lip apprehensively.

"Please tell me if you have an issue with me dating your best friend. I mean, you work with mine, and if Danielle and I—"

"I do not dictate who Danielle dates, no matter the circumstances. If you two are meant to be together, then no one should get in the way."

Sasha let her arms drop to her sides, seemingly reassured.

I continued, "You seem really cool and Danielle likes you. That tells me enough."

"Cool. All right. Well, I got to get back in there and get my peach cobbler."

"Okay. Sounds yummy." I smiled.

Tajel came over to me, holding my coat. She offered to help me put it on, so I slid my arms into the jacket and then turned to thank her. She smiled at me – a sweet smile that made me forget for a moment that there were ever any problems between us.

"Thanks... I'm glad you were here. I would have been far more nervous if you weren't."

"Glad to be of service."

I zipped up my jacket. "You're a piece of work."

Tajel nodded in agreement, sticking her hands in her pocket. Something was on her mind. The way her eyebrows furrowed and her lips shifted to one side told me so.

"You going to tell me what's on your mind?"

She barely raised her head to look at me. "Nothing."

I didn't believe her, but I didn't press her.

"All right. I should go. I think I've thanked your aunt and uncle too many times already, but can you tell them again for me?"

Tajel was noticeably still distracted. Laura came around the corner with a container of what I presumed was leftover veggie enchiladas.

"Here you go, dear. Don't worry about returning that anytime soon."

I was already looking forward to eating the leftovers.

"Thanks again. And your kitchen looks amazing. I love cooking and I would consider myself so lucky to have a kitchen like yours."

"You are too sweet."

"Good thing you have a great handy woman to help with your plumbing."

"I know! Thank God for my baby. She fixed my kitchen sink last week and it's working better than ever."

With that, my eyes darted to Tajel. She helped her aunt last week, not last night. She lied. I don't know why, but the fact that she had lied to me with such ease really bothered me. I felt the anger in the pit of my stomach. It was hard like a rock, and it gave me the urge to scream. Did she hate being around me that much?

My lips formed a tight smile as I waved to the group and turned sharply, heading for the door.

Tajel sensed my anger and the reason for it.

"Wait." Tajel did her best to cut off my path. "Let me explain."

I shrugged. "What's to explain Tajel? If you didn't want to be around me anymore all you had to do was say so."

"It wasn't like that," she whispered, trying to keep the others from overhearing.

She opened the door and motioned for me to come with her outside.

Once we were out of earshot and outside, she continued, "I wanted to spend more time with you. You're sweet and cool."

"You know what? I have no patience for liars."

"Arianna, don't jump to conclusions. Please. I fucked up the moment I lied, and I knew it. I don't like liars either, and I'm still angry with myself for lying to you. Can we go somewhere and talk?"

I considered going with her, but I was still too upset. I wanted to leave. "I can't."

"Arianna, come on."

"I can't because I have a date tonight."

"A date?" She sounded surprised. Or maybe she didn't believe me.

"Am I not good enough to be with a woman now?"

"No – yes...you're more than deserving." Tajel took on an apologetic demeanor, stepping toward me with pleading eyes. "I'm sorry."

"You confuse the hell out of me, you know that?" I ran my fingers through my hair. "I got to go."

Tajel didn't say anything else, and I walked over to my car as quickly as I could, eager to get away from her.

*

Tajel

"What happened?" Sasha came out with her peach cobbler in a Tupperware container.

"I messed up."

We walked to my car and Sasha spoke first in an effort to figure out how my conversation with Arianna ended.

"She found out that you lied to her?" Sasha sucked air in through her teeth.

I didn't respond to her question. I didn't have to. We both knew I made a mistake.

"She's going on a date tonight."

"So, why do you care?" Sasha knew I was attracted to Arianna, she only wanted to force me to say it aloud.

"I think I like her, okay? Now be quiet."

"But—"

"Not a damn word," I warned.

Sasha put her fingers to her lips and moved them to the side, as if to show that she was zipping her mouth closed. That didn't help, because it seemed she was still too curious. She raised her hand like an enthusiastic young student, bursting to ask her teacher a question. I got in my car and started the engine while she climbed into the passenger side. There was no way I would let her speak until I said what I needed to say to her.

"She's my partner," I said while driving. "If we started dating and things went sideways, it would affect our partnership. Besides, we've already had enough difficulties because of her lousy attitude."

"Don't be a hypocrite." Sasha realized too late that her comment was harsh.

"Wow."

"You just told Arianna over an hour ago to let the past be the past. I heard you. And now you're using your past with her as an excuse as to why you shouldn't be into her. How is that fair?"

It wasn't. She was right.

"She told me I confused her."

"Well, of course! You're charming, beautiful, and an amazing paramedic. And when you're around her, you are sweet and affectionate, a side of you rarely seen by anyone. But you two go back and forth – one day you're upset with each other and the next day you have trouble keeping your eyes away from one another."

"Okay...I see your point." *Damn, Sasha can go on.*

A car behind mine honked. I guess the light must've been green for a while. I pressed the gas, waiting for Sasha to speak since I knew she wasn't ready to let this go yet.

"I've seen you with other women and I've never seen you act this way before." Sasha fidgeted with the clasp on her shirt. "If she starts dating some other woman, I think it will drive you insane."

"I know. And, you're right." I pulled up to Sasha's apartment. "But I still don't think it's a good idea."

"I'll support you no matter what you decide." She leaned across the middle console to plant a kiss on my cheek. "I would invite you in to have a slice of my peach cobbler, but I don't want to share. Besides, Danielle is coming over."

I scoffed as I unlocked the door for her. "Get out and call me later."

I watched Sasha walk up to her apartment, making sure she got to her door. As soon as she was inside, I drove away thinking about our conversation. I was attracted to Arianna. I knew that the night I met her. Before tonight, I thought it was simply a little crush and nothing more, but I realized Sasha was on to something.

Arianna was different from other women I'd liked or dated. She was the best partner I was ever assigned since becoming a paramedic two years ago. I already trusted her in the field, but the thing was, I couldn't trust her outside of work. Arianna told me she was straight, even though she wasn't. She was also quick to judge, as if she was always searching for something to prove that I was a terrible person. But underneath all of that, she was endearingly vulnerable.

I should not be thinking about her. The thought of her out on a date was irritating me more than it should. *A date? When did this happen?*

After 20 minutes, I arrived home and wasted no time heading to my bedroom. I didn't even want to go out. For the first time in years I hated my Saturday.

Chapter Eleven
Tajel

"You want to drive?"

Arianna and I were in the middle a 48-hour shift finishing up a call, and even the mild conversations between us was not enough to ease the tension.

"Sure." Arianna took the keys and climbed into the rig. "Com 2, Medic 112 is clear and available."

"Medic 112, copy."

It was too quiet while we waited to be directed to a new location. I wanted to say something to break the silence, but I wasn't sure what to talk about.

"How was your date Saturday?" I needed to know. I should have kept my mouth shut, but I couldn't.

Arianna drummed her fingernails on the steering wheel absentmindedly. "It was fine. She's actually picking me up after my shift for our second date."

"Wow...That's fast." My surprise didn't go unnoticed. *Great job, Tajel.*

"Medic 112, call coming out of Cleveland High School. Possible assault."

Arianna responded to dispatch, and then we rushed off toward the school with the sound of our sirens ringing in my ear. I was familiar with the area in which the school was located, so I acted as our navigator. It was not long before we were on-scene, and we jumped out of the rig, our minds entirely devoted to our cause. We took everything we needed and raced to the front entrance of the school where an officer escorted us to the principal's office.

I was expecting a young teen, a boy or girl, waiting to be taken to the hospital with tears pouring from their eyes. What we got was a woman in her late 30s, sitting in a chair which was turned to the side. Her face was obscured by her hair, and she was wrapped in a coat as tightly as a caterpillar in its cocoon.

"I'm Tajel." I pointed to Arianna when she walked in behind me, "This is my partner. Her name's Arianna." I looked over to the officer who was standing nearby. "Can you give us a moment?"

"I need—"

"Please, leave. We know what to do." Arianna left no room for argument, so the officer vacated the room swiftly.

"I'm the principal here," a woman about the same age as our patient informed us. "I'm also her closest friend."

I nodded my understanding. She wanted to stay, and if our patient was fine with that, so were we.

"Can you tell us your name?"

"Her name's—"

"Ma'am, it's important we hear it from her," Arianna advised the principal as respectfully as possible.

I asked our patient again for her name and this time, she answered. In a few minutes, I could get all the answers I needed about her condition except for one. The worst part was coming. I knew it. I crouched near our patient, but not too close, to give her the comfort of space.

"Are you in any pain?"

She shook her head and I moved on to the next question.

"Do you feel there's anything we should know about?"

Again, she shook her head.

I took a deep breath as quietly as I could, knowing my next words could possibly bring on a deeper emotional reaction. "Were you...sexually assaulted?"

She gazed at me and the pain in her eyes was clear. I knew the answer. Her tears continued to flow between gasps and screams.

"Have you washed any part of your body?"

"No." Her voice was shaky and unsettled.

After a few more uncomfortable questions I told her what to expect at the hospital and I assured her that we would get her there safely. She didn't say anything else, but I could see the relief in her eyes. She would not have spoken at all if Arianna and I weren't both women.

"I would like to come." The principal's words sounded more like a demand than a request.

"You can ride up front with me," Arianna told her.

The principal left her vice principal in charge and followed us as we sped toward the rig. The ride was a blur, but I concentrated on keeping our patient as calm as was possible for someone who had recently endured what she had. When we made it to the hospital our patient cried on and off, looking as if she wanted to scream. It was difficult to watch her being taken away, even if it was by doctors. Her pain was disquieting and palpable. Victims of sexual assault always tore my heart apart.

We were done with our call, and time rolled by as we continued about our day. I began to wonder what Arianna was thinking about. Was her heart broken at the sight of that woman's pain too? Did she feel what I was feeling right now? There were times my job simply asked too much of me. Being in a career that immersed you in suffering sometimes made you feel as if you were drowning in tragedy. It could seriously mess with someone's mind and body. The end of our shift couldn't come quickly enough, and I was grateful when it did.

"You still mad at me?"

I needed for Arianna to move past my lie. After what we saw today, our problems seemed too trivial to continue worrying over.

"I'm not sure." Arianna wasn't even looking at me. "Are you going to tell me why you lied?"

"Damn it, Arianna! You're not being fair."

Arianna tried avoiding my eyeline as she walked past me and headed to our sleeping quarters, but I managed to block her exit.

"Will you be still long enough to let me explain?"

"Explain why you lied?"

"It's not that simple."

"Move, Tajel." The look in her eyes told me she was serious, and I knew I shouldn't press the issue for a while.

I stepped aside, watching her leave and following a safe distance behind. As she exited the front entrance, a woman who was leaning against her car walked over and embraced Arianna. I would be lying if I said that seeing her wrapped in the arms of another woman did not bother me. And I was officially done lying.

*

Arianna

"You are good at pool," I complimented as Iris knocked another stripe into one of the holes.

"I do play regularly, and I've entered a few competitions."

"So, shooting pool is a sport now?" I was a bit clueless about the game.

Iris appeared at my side and let me know it was my turn. I hadn't noticed she missed her last shot.

"Prepare to fear me," I said in a playful manner.

"I already do," Iris replied jokingly, but I caught her eyeing my body as I moved around the pool table.

A familiar laugh from the entrance of the bar made me glance up from the table and over Iris's shoulder. Danielle was at the front arm-in-arm with Sasha. I wasn't expecting to run into them, but it wasn't a shock for any of them to come here – it was our favorite bar. I knew they would see us eventually, so I was about to return my attention to the game when I noticed Tajel trailing in behind them and looking bored. Being a third wheel was utterly awkward.

"There's Danielle." Iris waved and when Danielle noticed us, she didn't seem too surprised to see me. "I invited her and Sasha on a double date tonight. Last minute decision. Danielle said she thought you'd like that."

Well, that explains the lack of surprise on Danielle's face. As for Tajel, that was a different story. She stopped midstride and turned to say something to Sasha before heading to the bar. I watched as she ordered herself a shot and knocked it back hastily.

"Hey gorgeous," Danielle whispered. "We had to bring her."

I knew she was talking about Tajel. I kissed Danielle's cheek and lowered my voice to reply, "Had to? That better be the truth."

"Honest," Danielle murmured.

"So, you two want to join the game?" Iris asked.

Danielle and Sasha nodded and for a while, I was having a lot of fun. That is, I was having fun until my gaze drifted over to Tajel. Seeing her alone tempted me to approach her. I couldn't, though. I couldn't abandon my date. I felt Iris's hands slide around my waist, pulling me toward her. Iris asked me if I was having a good time, and I smiled in response. I was. Iris was great.

30 minutes passed and my concern for Tajel only increased. I was still angry with her, so there was no reason for me to want to be next to her, but I couldn't stop this swell of worry rising inside of me. I watched as Tajel knocked back another shot. *How many shots has she drank?* When Gina appeared next to her, everything began to move in slow motion. She was a leech looking at Tajel as if she were her next meal. It wasn't anger, it was fury that funneled through my body now. I knew my attention was more on Tajel than on Iris, but at that moment I didn't care.

"Your turn," Danielle said, missing her shot.

I was ripped from my trance and back to the game, my friends, and Iris. The fury seemed to have fled, at least momentarily. I counted the remaining balls. Three. I leaned over the table, finding my angle, and lining up my shot. From the corner of my eye, I noticed Gina pull Tajel off the bar stool and then walk with her toward the exit, their arms around one another.

"Hold up." It was Sasha's voice, and it stopped me from hitting my target. "She's not leaving with that viper."

For whatever reason, the words were out of my mouth before I could stop myself. "I'll go."

All three women turned to me with stunned looks on their faces. I was surely not the right choice for the task of wresting Tajel away from Gina. It should be Sasha. She was best friends with Tajel and I... *What am I?* Our friendship wasn't in a good place now. I was also on a date.

Fuck me. "Look...I'm sorry. I should help her. She's my partner at work and we had a really rough shift."

Iris's smile was understanding. I wasn't sure if it was genuine – she couldn't possibly be thrilled about me ditching her on our date, but I would find out one way or another later, probably through Danielle.

"You sure?" Sasha asked.

I nodded, waved to Iris, and hugged Danielle before heading out. In the parking lot, I found them leaning against Tajel's car, Gina kissing Tajel's neck.

"Get away from her," I ordered.

Gina was about to argue when Tajel's eyes snapped open. She looked completely disoriented.

"I'm not...I'm not in-interested."

Tajel's speech was slurred but it was clear enough for Gina to take a step back.

Gina glared at me. "Bitch. You just want her for yourself."

I ignored her and marched over to Tajel to take her keys from her. "You're crazy if you think you're driving tonight."

"I-I wasn't going..."

I unlocked the car and helped Tajel into the passenger side, buckling her seatbelt for her as she laid her head back against the seat. I jogged around the car after closing her door and climbed into the driver side, immediately starting the car. After repeatedly asking Tajel for her address she was able to tell me where she lived through her slurring. It took me about 15 minutes to get to her house, which I vaguely remembered leaving after I thought we'd slept together the night we met. Once we were inside I searched her fridge and found a bottle of Gatorade. I opened the bottle and handed it to her.

Tajel drank the entire bottle in a few, long gulps while standing lazily in her kitchen. She lifted her head and there were still traces of Gatorade on her lips.

"What are you doing here?"

"I drove you home."

Tajel pushed herself away from the counter, but she looked as wobbly on her legs as a newborn colt. I rushed to her and managed to steady her.

Tajel shoved me somewhat forcefully. "You can get back to your date now."

Her temper was confusing. I was only trying to help.

"Why am I even here? This was stupid." I shook my head, pressing the palm of my hand to my temple. "You look fine now. Sleep it off, and you'll have a nice hangover in the morning."

"Go back to your date with your new girlfriend." Tajel put her hands on the counter to keep herself stable.

"Damn it, Tajel! Enough!" I snapped.

"Enough of what?"

"Tajel, don't push me right now. There's no excuse for your behavior." I shut my eyes. *Why did I feel like crying?* "You seem to be fine. I'm going to leave now. Goodnight."

I was almost to the door when Tajel called out to me, moving around the kitchen counter, using her hands to help her walk.

"I'm sorry, all right? I fucked up." The gray in her eyes made me stop. "Just, stay."

"I have to go."

"Please, don't go back to her."

"What's your deal? I left my date to help you out, though I'm not sure why now. You're obviously fine."

"Well, I'm not."

I crossed my arms, refusing to believe her. There were no words to describe how conflicted I felt. Tajel kept confusing me. She would want me around one day and then push me away the next. I did the same to her. We simply weren't compatible.

"Please. Come here," Tajel pleaded. She held her hand out.

I should have left then, but I didn't. I walked over to her.

"What do you want?"

Tajel held no humor nor anger in her expression. Need was in her eyes. I stopped myself a few feet away from her.

"Come closer."

I moved another foot closer and Tajel reached for my hand. I let her take it. Tajel moved away from the counter, straightening herself as my body stiffened. My heart was pounding so loudly I could hear it in my ears. Without another word, Tajel tilted toward me, but I was frozen entirely. Then her lips brushed against mine. I still couldn't move. I was unable to process what was happening.

Tajel's lips hovered close to mine after she ended our kiss, her hand cupping one side of my face as she whispered, "Please..."

That was it for me. When Tajel's lips found mine again, my lips moved along with hers. She took control of my body, wrapping her arms around the small of my back. I opened my mouth wider, giving her more access and she wasted no time in kissing me deeply. Tajel slipped her hand underneath my shirt, and I moaned as her thumb made circles on the flesh of my back. Slowly, I slid my fingers along her shoulders and then up to the nape of her neck as I continued to familiarize myself with her lips. *What am I doing?* Tajel's kiss caused me to momentarily forget our partnership and how complicated things have been between us since we first met. This couldn't happen. It could jeopardize everything. I pulled my head back, shuddering from the sensation of our kiss.

"We can't do this." I removed myself from her arms and stepped away from her. "Tajel, you're drunk."

Tajel's gaze returned to my lips briefly, and then up to my eyes again. We stared at each other for a few minutes. I wasn't certain of the time, but I knew the seconds that passed while we looked at one another was more than I could bear.

"Yes, I am. But you're not and you kissed me back." Tajel reached for me again, and once more I retreated. "Just because I'm drunk it doesn't mean that I don't really want you."

"We can't," I said firmly, moving toward her door.

I practically ran out of Tajel's home, fearing all the while that she would call me to come back to her. If she had, I might have done just that. She was so fucking right. I dove headfirst into that kiss. I let her consume me. I took out my phone and dialed Danielle's number. I was thankful she answered. She agreed to come pick me up, and 20 minutes later, she and Sasha were parked in front of Tajel's apartment. Sasha climbed out of the car and I replaced her in the passenger seat.

"How is she?" Sasha asked. "I'm going to stay the night with her."

"She's fine." I didn't want to say more.

I turned my face toward middle console, hoping to avoid Sasha's stare.

"Oh, okay." She kissed Danielle and went inside to be with Tajel.

"Not tonight, Danielle. I just...can't."

Usually when something was troubling either of us, Danielle and I would sit with a bowl of ice cream and talk things through. Tonight, my emotions were chaotic and confusing. Tonight, I needed to be alone.

Chapter Twelve
Tajel

I woke up groggy, fighting the sleep that threatened to overtake me. A throbbing headache swept across my forehead, adding to my misery. The smell of fresh coffee and something cooking lured me out my room, but I knew that if I ate anything there was a good chance I wouldn't be able to keep it down. I walked weakly to the kitchen.

"Good morning, sleepy head." Sasha put a mug of coffee and a bagel in front of me. "Sit."

"Shit." *Well, I guess I'm eating.*

I took a sip of my coffee and I closed my eyes, letting the bitter flavor wash over my tongue. My head was still throbbing, and I felt slightly nauseated, but I tried to breathe through it.

"What was I doing last night?"

"Trying to drink away your misery."

"Did I succeed?"

Sasha's face said it all. "Quite the opposite. You've made things worse for yourself."

I wasn't sure if I wanted her to continue or not, but Sasha would go on no matter what I wanted.

"You got drunk. Arianna took you home. You—"

"Wait, wasn't she on a date?"

"Mmhmm." Sasha rolled her eyes after seeing me grin. "She brought you home and tried to sober you up."

She left her date for me. Somehow, it seemed like a piece of the story was missing.

"What happened?"

"I don't know, but Arianna sat outside in the cold until Danielle and I got here. I thought she was either going to cry or scream."

The blood drained from my face thinking of the possibilities. *Shit.* All I remember of last night was feeling angry at seeing Arianna with that woman.

"I need to see her." No way I could let this linger.

"I don't know about that." Sasha knew something. I stared at her intensely for a moment and she sighed. "I talked to Danielle earlier this morning and she said Arianna has been locked up in her room since last night."

"Fuck," I groaned.

What did I do? I tried to take some meditational breaths to ease the stress circulating inside of me. Jealousy. Whatever I did had to be because of my jealousy over her date with another woman. Lying and jealousy were officially crossed off my list of things never to do again.

"Give her time."

I scoffed. "We have a shift tomorrow night. Maybe I should switch partners, give her additional space."

"If you end your partnership with her, your uncle—"

"Not completely end our partnership. That will be up to her." I took another sip of my coffee to relax my nerves and then I settled on a decision. "I can tell my uncle I have a doctor's appointment I can't reschedule and to exchange my shift for another. Or I could call one of my coworkers and get them to switch with me."

"You sure you want to do that?"

"Look, I'm not enduring a repeat of our last shift. I do not want this kind of tension in our partnership."

"If you're sure."

Why does Sasha keep saying that? "I'm sure."

*

Arianna

"Hey, *chica*. You practically lived in your room all day yesterday and today, and now you're leaving for work. You going to talk to me before you go?"

For more than a day, Danielle had been knocking on my door to check on me. She told me she was making sure I was still alive. There were no words to say. I mean, there were, but none that I knew how to express properly. We walked out of our apartment together, heading to Danielle's car in silence. But on the way to the station, she refused to allow the silence to continue.

"We've known each other since we were little. You've had enough time in that room to yourself, and now it's time to tell your best friend what happened."

I sighed. *Just say it.* "Tajel...she, uh...she kissed me."

Danielle was quiet for a while. I looked over to her to make sure she heard me correctly. "And...what's so wrong with that?"

I frowned. "She's my partner. And she was drunk!"

"And?"

"And, I kissed her back." Danielle opened her mouth to speak but I cut her off, "I shouldn't have done that. She's my partner and she was drunk! Plus, we can't even get along for more than a week before we have an argument."

"Well to be fair, the first few times were your fault."

I narrowed my eyes at Danielle. I hated that she was right.

We were parked in front of my station and Danielle turned to me with a serious look on her face. "You need to talk to her."

"I can't."

"Arianna Castaldi, talk to her! And for once, give her a chance to explain herself."

Danielle left me with a lot to think about. She was unquestionably right – I owed Tajel a chance to explain her side of things. But what was there really to explain? She kissed me. *Why did she kiss me?* Maybe that's what needed explanation.

"Hey partner!" Felipe was clearly in a chipper mood.

"Partner?"

Was Tajel sick? Maybe she drank more than I thought.

"Yeah, we're together for today. Tajel needed to switch." He smiled.

"Oh," I said without feigning excitement. "Sure."

I climbed out of Danielle's car, giving her an irritated look. Here I was, about to take her advice and Tajel wasn't even here. I headed to our sleeping quarters and found her belongings spread out on her bed. I didn't understand. *She switched partners without telling me. Now who's the coward?* Well, this would make my day easier. I wouldn't have to talk to her. I shut my eyes, taking a moment to calm myself. I could get through the day. Putting my mind on the right track, I readied myself for the next 24 hours.

*

Surprisingly, Felipe wasn't a bad partner. He was easygoing and knew when to be quiet. After the shift, we walked into the station and right away, I saw Tajel heading to our sleeping quarters. I wasn't sure if she saw me or not.

It was nearly dawn and she would be leaving shortly to go home. *Ignore her, Arianna.* The thought of confronting her crossed my mind, but I couldn't. If she wanted to talk, she could come to me.

God, I did want to confront her, though. My thoughts kept returning to our kiss and how badly I wanted to kiss her again. But something about it terrified me. Tajel emerged from our quarters and walked on, completely ignoring me. She wouldn't even look in my direction. *Oh, no.* My eyes began to water as the pain rushed upward and then out.

I raced to my quarters and hid there until my face was no longer puffy from crying. I needed to get a grip on this. Ten minutes passed before dispatch called out to my unit over the intercom. I wiped my eyes, making sure I left no evidence of crying on my face. I left the room ready to finish my shift.

*

Tajel

"Honey, you are better than that," My aunt said to me after I told my her the latest scoop on Arianna's and my feuding relationship, and my role in making it worse. I thought she would be on my side.

"You remember kissing her, probably confusing the dear woman even more, and then you ignored her. You also never told her you would be switching partners."

"I thought giving her space would be better."

"Perhaps. But you still should have let her know."

I sat on the couch in my family's living room. My aunt was holding my hand, squeezing it lightly as she talked.

"You care for this woman and she deserved more than you gave her."

I fell back against the couch feeling worse than I did when I arrived. "You're supposed to kiss my cheek and tell me that everything will be all right."

"Oh, no. You are not a child anymore. You've mishandled the situation. You need to fix it."

She was right, of course, but it didn't make it easier to hear. I only nodded in response.

"Good. Now, will you be staying for dinner?"

I shook my head. "I lied about why I needed to switch partners today, so I don't want to talk to Chief."

She kissed my cheek. "Everything will work out, honey. Give it time."

I left a few minutes later, not wanting to push my luck and risk my uncle finding me here when I was supposed to be in a doctor's office right now. I spent the rest of the day thinking over the entire course of my partnership with Arianna, as well as the events of last night and everything my aunt had to say about it. I knew what I had to do. I made my decision.

The next morning, I went for a run and ended up at Arianna's apartment building. *I can do this*. I texted Sasha while I waited outside of the building, allowing my breathing to return to normal. It was a short wait – two minutes after I sent her the text, she responded, telling me that Danielle was fine with me dropping by. I made it to the door of their apartment and I thought I was going to vomit. My palms were sweaty, and my heart raced. I knocked softly, almost hoping that no one would answer. That was wishful thinking. Sasha opened the door to me.

I raised an eyebrow. "No wonder you had an answer for me so quickly."

Sasha rolled her eyes. "Don't get all cute with me. Not today, Tajel. You need to talk to Arianna and make this right."

I threw my arms up in surrender. "I know. I already got this lecture from my aunt."

Danielle hissed, "I certainly didn't like what I saw when I picked her up at the station last night. She looked worse than when I dropped her off at work and that's saying a lot."

"I have no excuse."

"Damn right, you don't!"

I understood Danielle's anger. I hurt her best friend.

"I'm so sorry. I haven't given you one reason to like me, but I'm here now to try to fix things."

Danielle didn't say anything else. She only pointed to Arianna's room. Sasha gave me a weak and sympathetic smile. I took a deep breath, hoping that I could be strong enough to repair the damage I'd done. I knocked on her door and waited for her to answer. *What if she didn't open the door or respond?* But I had to try. Sasha and Danielle headed to the couch and turned on the television as I knocked again.

"Arianna? It's me, Tajel."

Nothing. *Figures.* I sighed, knocking again. Nothing.

"Is she in here?" I asked.

Danielle nodded. "Keep trying."

"Arianna, please open the door." I pressed my ear to the door to listen for any indication of movement but there was nothing. "Fine. Then I will say what I need to say from where I'm standing. I don't care who is listening."

Still no movement.

"I should have called and talked to you about—"

Arianna opened the door before I could say more. "Leave, Tajel. I don't need this today."

I ignored her and continued, "I know I was drunk but—"

"Damn it, Tajel!" Arianna looked over my shoulder to the couch where both our friends sat together. "Come in."

She stepped to the side to allow me to enter. As soon as I walked through the door she closed it forcefully. *This isn't going to be easy.*

"What do you want?"

"For starters, I want to tell you how sorry I am for not saying anything about switching partners. I should have let you know."

"Did you really have a doctor's appointment?" Arianna was waiting for a lie.

Oh, I am so done with lying. "No."

Arianna was quiet for a few seconds, probably surprised I finally told the truth. "Is that the only thing you are sorry about?"

"No." I thought I was shrinking under the power of her glare. "I'm also very sorry that I kissed you when I was drunk."

Arianna remained unmoved. *Fuck.* I knew then I had to be painfully honest.

"And I'm sorry that I was such a coward that I didn't kiss you when I was sober."

If what I said shocked Arianna, there were no signs of it on her face or in her demeanor.

"I accept your apology. You can go now."

I wasn't going to leave. I needed us to move forward and I honestly couldn't take any more of this back and forth. Either we worked through our issues or we ended our partnership.

"See, this truthful thing works both ways. I deserve the truth from you too."

"I need time to figure out—"

"What do you need to figure out, Arianna? From what I can tell, you've had more time alone in here than you really needed." I pointed to the stack of dirty dishes on her nightstand.

For the first time since she opened the door, I noticed what she was wearing – a tank top and pajama pants with a wolf print pattern.

"Stop looking at me," Arianna growled.

"I can't help it," I replied. "You want me stop lying to you, right? So, fine. I want you. You're incredible, beautiful, and totally unpredictable. And, I was extremely jealous seeing you with another woman."

I took a step closer to Arianna, but she moved away from me.

"I've been through something like this before. I fell for someone I shouldn't have, then I found out she didn't feel the same way."

"Tajel...I..."

"I want you to admit your feelings." I needed to know I wasn't alone in this. "Tell me the truth. And if you feel nothing, maybe I can stop feeling so lost."

For an agonizing amount of time – who really knows how long – Arianna's eyes wandered around the room as if she was trying to come up with some excuse not to respond. I could give her a moment or a few hours, however long she needed. Our next shift didn't start until tomorrow evening anyway. We had time. I needed to learn patience.

Arianna's eyes slowly returned to me, and then her gaze shifted to my lips. I smiled widely and sincerely, feeling at last that there was raw truth between us. This time it wasn't me that closed the distance. Arianna glided over to me and cupped my jaw with her hand. We let the magnetic force of our attraction pull us together.

"You weren't a part of my plans," Arianna whispered to me.

I respected her honesty. I took in a slow, deep breath. "I believe you."

It was almost as if our bodies refused to separate from one another. I could feel the heat emanating from her mouth and stifled a groan in anticipation of the possibilities.

"I may disappoint you. I haven't been a great friend to you," Arianna admitted.

My hands rested at her waist as I pulled her even closer to me. "That's only because we've been going about this all wrong."

Arianna was breathing heavily, her arousal evident in every breath she drew. She whispered, "Are you sure you want—"

"I'm sure." My mouth fell onto hers and our lips synchronized in their movements.

Arianna moaned, wrapping one of her arms around the nape of my neck. Her tongue slid into my mouth with easy precision and I welcomed it eagerly. Passion and desire swelled in my body, and the sensation of our kiss was becoming too intense for me to stand up straight. My legs began to weaken, so I twisted Arianna around and pushed her to the bed. We fell on top the covers, our bodies entangled.

Our mouths disconnected, and we used that time to admire each other. Even though we wanted this moment to go on, we knew it couldn't. Sasha and Danielle were in the living room. I straddled Arianna's right thigh and propped myself up on my left elbow as I ran my hand up Arianna's outer thigh and then to her stomach. I kept going from there, my fingers gradually finding a home underneath her shirt. She moaned while her body shuddered under my touch.

I lowered myself to press a soft kiss onto her bare stomach. Arianna's body was trembling, the skin of her stomach transforming into gooseflesh each time my lips made contact. I took time to bask in the melody of her moans. Slowly, I lifted her shirt up as my lips moved along her ribs. Working my way up and around her breasts, I made sure my hands stayed in rhythm with my kisses. The palm of my hand discovered her breast and squeezed. Arianna arched her back, letting me know her breasts were incredibly sensitive.

I focused only on touching Arianna, enjoying the softness of her skin and hearing her heightened breaths. Somehow, I could feel Arianna's eyes on me. I looked up at her, my fingers never stopping. Offering her a smile, I returned to the task of kissing her while her hands made their way to my face. I nipped on her top lip before gazing back at her.

"So, that night we met, and I thought we had a one-night stand?"

"Mmhmm?"

"What did we talk about?"

I smiled. That night, she was drunk and revealed her deepest thoughts and feelings so freely. I thought she might feel uncomfortable around me if I ever told her what really happened that night. I knew things she probably never wanted me to find out. I only hoped that now she would tell me things while she was fully cognizant and because she wanted to.

"You spoke of how much you wanted to live a life of your choosing and have your family accept you as you are, and of how much you wanted to feel another woman's love. Feel the weight of her body over you. Kiss you with a fiery passion and make love to you. And you hoped you would not fear any of it once that woman was within your grasp."

Arianna looked away. She bit her bottom lip, and I wondered now if she regretted that night.

"I said all of that?"

I used my right hand to direct her face back to where I could see into her eyes. "That, and you hoped that woman would be me."

Arianna's mouth fell open and I did my best to hold in my laughter.

After a few seconds, Arianna shoved me playfully. "You're so full of it."

I giggled. I liked the way I felt when I was with Arianna like this. It was entirely new and thankfully, without tension.

"Let's just promise that we try and do better from now on. For some reason that night, I wished for it to be me you learned to love." I shook my head, knowing how silly I must have sounded. "Who knew you'd turn out to be my partner?"

"I surely didn't."

I snorted. "I know. Our first few shifts demonstrated how much you loved being near me."

"Hey, I was stupid for not seeing how important you were then. I just...I've never opened to someone or had anyone affect me as you have. "

"I affect you?" I was intrigued.

Arianna chose not to answer, and it didn't bother me at the moment. I kissed her softly and sighed with contentment. I would move at her pace. That was probably for the best, since I wanted her to like me and to remain my partner. But, this was still a risk, and Arianna's mood swings had to be taken into consideration. Maybe if we kept work separate from our personal lives, we would be heading down the right path. I also knew that it was important that I not say anything to my uncle about whatever it was that Arianna and I were doing together. *What are we doing?*

We kissed for several minutes until we were ready to face our two nosy friends.

Chapter Thirteen
Arianna

What am I doing? Letting myself feel this way and exposing myself in every manner that I wasn't used to. We spent the day under the watchful, scrutinizing eyes of Danielle and Sasha. I was nervous and uncomfortable, so Tajel and I maintained our distance. It was difficult for me to be present with them in the moment because I couldn't pull myself out of my own head.

I tried to be positive – it was a new day. I hadn't kissed Tajel since yesterday morning in my room and honestly, I was afraid of working the next shift with her. I wondered what she was thinking.

"Hey, partner!" Felipe approached me with a warm smile.

"I'm happy with Tajel as my partner, but I appreciate the compliment."

Felipe laughed. "Well, you're the first. But, I'm glad she has someone who likes her."

If only you knew how much I like her. If I had my way, however, no one would ever know. Tajel was probably over me by now and ready to move on to a new woman. I needed to stop thinking as if she saw me as more than a momentary affair. *Why did she say all that last night? Did she truly mean everything she told me?* She was sweet to me even though we have had some issues in our partnership. That night we were supposed to hookup, she listened to me for hours. I'm sure I complained and gave myself new resolutions.

"Hey..."

I looked up to see Tajel standing next to me, a worried expression on her face. How long was I in my head? I hoped not too long. I had already confused her on so many levels. I have pushed her away, pulled her in, and then pushed her away again. I'm sure I could qualify for a free therapist appointment, if there was such a thing.

"How was your day?" I asked casually as we walked toward our sleeping quarters together.

"It's been slow."

"Slow..." I repeated as I opened the door for her.

Tajel closed the door and before she said whatever was on her mind, a call came in from dispatch over the phone in our room.

"We have to go. Hostage situation at Hog's Brewery. Two possible stabbings."

I dropped my stuff on the bed and raced out of the station with her, scrambling into our rig and driving away in less than a minute. Tajel alerted dispatch that we were en route and after that, the entire drive was a blur of colored lights, nondescript buildings, and pedestrians. I felt the sudden burst of adrenaline and I tried to slow my breathing, knowing that I would need to be calm and focused.

"Ever done this before?" I asked Tajel.

"Once."

I lived in Los Angeles and I'd never been put a situation like this. I have experienced calls where officers resolve a situation like this before I walk in, but not a hostage situation where I was standing by. If I'd known this could happen in Portland I would have moved here earlier. Penniless or –not – with or without Danielle.

"I've never done this before," I admitted.

This is what we lived for. The action and adrenaline rushes. I was far from being a cowgirl rushing into danger, but I surely liked being near it.

"It can make you feel every emotion in seconds."

Tajel parked the rig across from the bar on the street corner.

"Follow my lead," she instructed.

In this situation, I wasn't going to be a prideful woman. Tajel had the experience and rank, so I would proceed under her direction.

"Com 2, Medic 112 on-scene."

"Copy Medic 112, be advised sheriffs will be talking with you about a possible hostage approach."

"Copy that."

Tajel peered into the driver side mirror. She was watching as several law enforcement cars arrived on-scene. Two fire trucks parked on the opposite end of the street, which was taped off for emergency vehicles. We were facing toward the bar, so when it was time we could drive up easily. The night sky was decorated with red and blue emergency lights.

"Sheriffs are approaching now. Medic 112 will be available by handhelds," Tajel updated dispatch.

"Medic 112, copy. Be safe, ladies."

Tajel left the rig running as the sheriffs jogged over to us. We stood outside waiting for instructions.

"Evening, ladies." It was one of the sheriffs who greeted us. "Not how I expected my night to start, but you know how it goes sometimes."

We both nodded.

"Well, we have a situation, obviously. An older man was asked to leave the brewery and refused. He then stabbed two customers who were trying to get him out of the building. I believe it all started because he was harassing some girl in there. Always some fucking girl making a man crazy."

I fought the urge to educate him – we should be referred to as medics, not ladies, and his remark about the woman inside the bar was infuriating. Maybe he didn't know any better. But right now was not the appropriate time for an argument.

"We asked if he would let medics come in and get at least one hostage out, and he said he only wanted women to go inside." The sheriff laughed, and his partner gave us an apologetic look. "So, you two girls are going to go in since he doesn't consider you two threatening."

"You should supply us with bulletproof vests, Henry," Tajel ordered.

The sheriff who'd been talking to us changed his expression immediately. His smile disappeared. He snapped his fingers at his partner.

"Always a smartass, Tajel," he said displeased.

"Always the same overweight prick I've known for years." Tajel smirked. "When are you retiring?"

He walked off, leaving his partner to grab our vests.

"He's nice," I observed sarcastically.

I looked across the street to where the bar was located. Several officers and other paramedics circled the building.

"He's very prejudiced and sexist."

"I caught onto the sexist part," I replied.

Tajel scowled. At that moment, Sheriff Henry's partner returned with our vests.

"The suspect only wants you to bring in a stretcher and one jump bag. He's also requesting pain meds for himself."

"Let me guess, Fentanyl...Morphine?" Tajel had clearly done this before.

He nodded.

"You ready?" Tajel asked.

"Yes."

I took a deep breath and cleared my mind. I was nervous and excited all at the same time. If my parents saw me on the news they'd flip out. Realizing how dangerous this was, I took another deep breath.

"Well girls," Henry began, "you two go in. Keep your hands visible all times. Limit your conversation with him. Please don't try to defuse him. You're not capable of that. Just get out with the patient in one piece."

"Are we cleared to go in? I can explain the rest to my partner without you."

Sheriff Henry waved us off.

"If he approaches us with the knife in his hand, ask him politely to give us the space we need to get the patient out. Don't let him think you're a threat, so no matter what he says or does, don't react. Be like a zombie."

I nodded occasionally as she continued to explain the protocols and to give advice.

"If you don't want to do this, we don't have to," Tajel offered, her expression was serious.

"I can do it as long as we're together." I put on a second pair of gloves and Tajel adjusted my bulletproof vest. "Is this what you want to do? SWAT medic?"

"Yeah." She continued fixing my vest. "Is that okay?"

Last thing I wanted was to hinder her. "Yes. I'd support you in anything you wanted to do."

I could see my words meant a lot to her. Tajel grinned. "Good."

She looked around. The sheriff motioned for us to move in.

"We got this," she encouraged.

We approached the bar calmly. I carried the stretcher and she was toting the jump bag.

"Why isn't SWAT or any type of incident commander here?" I was used to the procedures in place in Los Angeles.

"We usually do, but this situation happened suddenly, and nothing is nearby. We're outside of Portland and by the time the SWAT or any professional IC officer or negotiator arrived, the hostages could be dead. The condition of the two hostages are unknown right now. My uncle is building a SWAT, or what is now being called SERT team. Special Emergency Response Team. That's the team I will be joining whether my uncle likes it or not."

Tajel noticed my nervousness and smiled at me.

"We will be fine. Do you trust me?"

"I trust you." I remembered how she protected me when we responded to a call that involved an active shooter.

"Glad to hear you say that."

Standing in the street inside the circle of law enforcement cars as shields, we faced the bar. There was a small patio with a black gate made of metal as additional barrier to cross. The front door was made of glass that was blacked out. A few posters obscured our view of the inside of the brewery. There were a few large windows to the left side of the building that were also tinted like the entrance.

We both took a few deep breaths, and then Tajel knocked on the front door of the bar.

"That better be the fucking paramedics!" someone shouted from inside. It was probably the suspect.

"Sir, my name is Tajel. I'm with my partner, Arianna." Tajel's voice was loud and her pronunciation precise. "We are the paramedics. Can we come in?"

Tajel grabbed the stethoscope from the jump bag quickly and put it around my neck. We heard movement and a few voices that we believed belonged to hostages. It wasn't clear what they were saying, but the fear in their muffled voices was palpable.

"Pay attention to –everything – how many hostages there are, if anyone else is injured, any other weapons around…everything."

Tajel's instructions were helpful and a distraction from the nightmarish situation we were in together. She opened the door slowly after the suspect yelled his approval allowing us to enter.

"I only want to see the two of you. No fucking tricks."

"Only two female paramedics, like you requested," Tajel hollered to him, trying not to let her voice be engulfed by the cries and whispers of the hostages.

I counted nine hostages. Of those nine, two were injured. *They must be our patients*.

"No tricks or I swear...I'll stab someone else," the suspect threatened.

The lights were dim, so it was hard to see everything clearly, but I spotted the suspect with relative ease. His body was rigid, and he was gesticulating erratically. There was a woman who sat in a chair in front of the elongated bar counter, too close to the suspect for her to run without him being able to reach her. He stood at the far-right end of the brewery where the path to the restrooms led. His hair was thinning, not much at the top, and almost pasty as it clung to his sweaty head. He had an ivory complexion that was in stark contrast to the dark, dense stubble on his jaw.

The hostages were divided in two groups – a group on each side of the bar. The first of our patients was a man who was sitting on the floor leaning his body against the bar counter, holding his side. I could tell by the way his chin rested on his chest and the amount of blood pooling out of his side, that he was either gone or close to it. There was no indication of breathing, but I did as Tajel instructed and kept my expression blank. There was another man amongst the group who was crying in agony, writhing around the floor on his side. A young woman was cradling his head in her lap.

"Sir?" Tajel called to the suspect.

"Don't call me that. None of that formal shit. I'm Jason." He waved the knife around angrily.

"Jason. I would like my partner to go check on the man by the bar counter. And I would like to check on the man with the group by the pool tables. Is that all right?"

Jason scratched the corner of his head while still holding the knife, then nodded exaggeratedly. "Go."

His manic state made me nervous, but I kept my expression neutral. Tajel pointed to the bar, directing me over to the man who was near death as she calmly walked over to the man who was crying in the lap of the young woman. I checked the patient for a pulse, finding nothing. Then, I checked his pupils for a reaction. Nothing. I saw no movement in his chest. As far as I could see, the man was dead. I stood and walked over to where Tajel was assisting her patient and shook my head. She nodded. We knew we could not let this man know he had killed someone. He might lash out if he knew. But if he asked directly, I wouldn't lie.

"Sir, we're the paramedics. Let us help you," Tajel pleaded with the injured man who was screaming at her to leave him alone. "If you want to leave this place, let us check you out."

The man relented, wincing when he spread his arms to allow us to see the two stab wounds in his abdomen. One wound was in the upper-right quadrant of his stomach and the second on his lower-left. In one swift motion, I opened our jump bag and pulled out the shears needed to cut off the man's shirt.

"You brought a weapon!" the suspect shrieked, yanking a woman off the floor.

She screamed in panic as he dragged her toward us. The knife was to the woman's throat.

"Toss the shears over to him," Tajel ordered.

I chastised myself for taking the shears out of the bag. I slid them across the floor to the suspect, hoping he wouldn't believe that we were threatening. Unfortunately, I was wrong.

"Hey, hey." Tajel stood and put herself between the suspect and me, sensing danger.

I realized he was close enough to harm Tajel. I held my breath as fear gripped my body. My eyes began to water at the thought of Tajel being harmed by this man.

Tajel, however, remained calm. "We're here to help. Them and you."

"You're here to help me, huh?" Jason asked in a mocking tone. He used his knife to point to the bag we brought. "I'm going to check that bag before you touch another damn thing."

We both moved away from the bag, our hands in the air. He ordered the woman he'd been dragging to pull the bag away from us and search it. When she was done after finding nothing he believed to be menacing, he pushed it back to us and then pointed at the dead man by the bar counter.

"Why...why aren't you helping him?"

Fuck. I was hoping he wouldn't come close enough to notice the other patient. Now we were facing the possibility of this man unleashing his anger on everyone, including Tajel and me. I sucked in air through gritted teeth, not sure of what to say to him. I knew we would have to tell him the truth, though.

I stood slowly, and Tajel sighed before saying, "He's dead."

At this moment, I wasn't sure if we'd make it out of this place alive.

Chapter Fourteen
Tajel

"What did you say?"

The suspect paced frantically after receiving news of his victim's death. He began to hyperventilate, breathing raggedly. Tears flooded his eyes. He tightened his grip on the woman's arm.

"I... I didn't mean – how did this happen?" He wailed as if in agony. "Oh, fuck. I-I can't go to prison."

"Jason," I said his name softly, trying to keep him placid. " I'm not judging you. Talk to me."

Our original plan would be destroyed unless I could find a way to make him believe I cared about his well-being too.

He was distraught, waving his knife around his face which was soaked with tears, snot, and saliva. "I...it all happened so fast. I was drunk!"

"Mistakes happen. Sometimes they're small, and sometimes they're big. I know all about that."

"Have any of your mistakes ever killed someone?" he questioned me, clearly doubting I could relate to him.

I sighed. I didn't like discussing my past with anyone, but if I was going to share it would be to save someone else's life.

"Yes."

Arianna was stupefied, but she said nothing.

"My mistake cost me my parents' life."

He looked at me in disbelief and then his demeanor softened. It was too difficult to talk about losing my parents without a few tears escaping the barriers of my eyelids. I wiped them away using the back of my forearm while trying to keep my focus on Jason. I never forgot the fact that Arianna was watching me.

Sensing my discomfort, Arianna moved to distract him. "Jason, would you like something to take the edge off?"

He looked at Arianna and nodded.

Arianna smiled. "It's in my bag, okay?"

"Get it, please," he pleaded as if whatever she gave him would make all he'd done go away.

Slowly and carefully, keeping her hands raised, I watched as Arianna went over to the jump bag and dug out our medicine case. She unlocked and opened it, taking out a few drugs.

"Is alcohol the only thing you've had today?"

"That's all. I'm not allergic to anything. Please, just give me the shot."

Arianna cautiously approached him. "You have to lower that knife."

He complied. Arianna put an I.V. in his right arm. He sat on a stool, the other arm still wrapped around the woman's neck. She injected medication into his I.V., used a saline lock, and taped the extension to the I.V. in his arm. She stepped back. Jason maintained his grip on the woman and pulled her beside him around the bar counter to grab a glass. He told her to fill it with water while he held the knife against her back. Once she was finished she stepped away from him.

"What did you give him?" I whispered.

"Versed."

"Good call." I made sure Jason was still preoccupied, and then looked behind us to the injured man. "I think it's safe to check on our patient now."

Arianna agreed and went over to the patient. He was having difficulty breathing.

"I... can't...take...a..."

"Stop speaking," Arianna ordered gently but firmly. "I need you down here, Tajel. Air is flooding his lungs."

I placed my gloved hand over his stomach where he was stabbed. I wanted to seal it and stop the bleeding. I listened to his lungs again. One side was completely diminished.

"He appears to be experiencing a tension pneumothorax."

Tajel handed me an occlusive dressing. We placed the adhesive part down over his stab wound.

"Oh, God, is he going to die? Please! This can't be happening!" The woman sobbed and continued to hold the man's head.

"Ma'am, we need you to relax and back away," I advised in a hushed tone. "Jason, can I help our patient now?"

Jason leaned against the counter lazily. The drugs were already working. He waved his hand.

"Goooo...on," he slurred.

I moved quickly, grabbing the jump bag to retrieve a needle decompression, the blood pressure cuff, and another stethoscope.

I checked his vitals. "He has distended veins in his neck and trachea deviation."

Arianna seized the decompression needle from my hand and hovered over the patient. She pressed her fingers over the left side of his chest, counting to his second intercostal muscle at his midclavicular line and pushed the needle through his skin, muscle, and bone. In a matter of seconds, he could breathe, and I heard an audible release of air. I tried to control his bleeding while Arianna put him on 15 liters of oxygen.

The woman whom Jason had kept with him sprinted over to us. "He passed out!"

Arianna and I transferred our patient to the stretcher and then we lifted him together. We didn't waste any time heading to the exit.

"Everyone, stay seated and put your hands in the air when law enforcement comes inside," I instructed the remaining hostages.

We exited the brewery, our gurney waiting for us right next to the front entrance. As we put the patient on it, the sheriffs rushed past us and into the building.

We started rolling our patient to the rig which was a block away as Sheriff Henry approached us with a dubious expression on his face. "What the hell happened in there?"

"No time to talk. Figure it out." We got the patient inside the rig. Arianna remained in the back and I climbed in the driver side and called dispatch. "Com 2, Medic 112 en route to Providence Portland Hospital."

When we arrived at the hospital, we brought the patient inside and gave the doctor and RNs our report of his condition. Arianna and I moved the man into a vacant room where the hospital staff took over. I bumped into my uncle on the way out. He looked like a man who had just found the child he lost in a store.

"Son of a bitch dispatchers told me what happened after you were sent out on the hostage call!"

My uncle hugged me without warning and I didn't resist.

"Chief. I'm—"

"Drop the formality, Tajel." He kept me in an embrace. "You could have been hurt. God, everyone knows the sheriffs here need more training."

I shrugged. "Most of them were fine. Just one in particular who needs some additional training...or at least some help to submit his resignation."

My uncle finally let me go. "I'm glad you're safe. Your aunt is so worried about you, but I told her not to come. You'd really have to pry her off you if she did."

"Thanks," I said, relieved that Aunt Laura wasn't with him. I loved my aunt, but she could certainly get overly emotional. "I'll call her after work."

"It would be better if you visit instead. Tomorrow? She won't feel good until you do. She wanted me to send you home."

I laughed. "I'm fine."

"That's what I told her." He looked around. "Where's your partner?"

"Right here," Arianna said, walking over to us.

She had clearly been keeping her distance by hiding next to the rig. I watched her approach and took note of her anxious behavior. My uncle talked to her for a moment and then told us to head back to the station.

"Ready to get back to work?" I asked.

Arianna nodded, and we headed out together.

16 hours later and we finally made it back to station in one piece. It seemed as though people everywhere in Portland were falling ill or getting hurt – from a pneumonia call to a hypoglycemic patient. No more traumas. The morning was turning into late afternoon when Arianna and I decided to head into our sleeping quarters. We were both

thoroughly exhausted, and I just wanted to curl up in my bed and sleep.

I removed my boots and my uniform and slipped underneath my covers, but for some reason, sleep eluded me. I was very aware of Arianna's breathing as she slept across from me in her bed. I stifled my stirring desires and shut my eyes. I laid still and quiet for a while, sneaking a peek at Arianna occasionally. I needed to get a grip. She had a moment of weakness the other day. That was all that kiss was. I shouldn't start imagining a life together with her.

I twisted around, rolling onto my back to stare at the ceiling. I decided to stop thinking about Arianna. If I didn't, I'd never fall asleep. It took maybe 15 minutes of counting the flaws in the ceiling's design for sleep to finally welcome me. I have no idea how long my slumber lasted, but I knew it wasn't long enough when I was awakened by a soft whisper in my ear and I had an unbelievably difficult time opening my eyes.

Still groggy, I awoke to find Arianna kneeling beside me on the floor. I turned my body to face her, giving her my full attention.

"Um...I just, uh...wanted to say, I'm sorry for nearly getting us killed. You know? With the shears?"

I was too tired to conjure up any sort of emotion, but I managed to say sleepily, "Nothing is your fault. You were doing your job. And you saved everyone's ass when you gave him Versed. It put him right to sleep."

She nodded, and I wondered if that was the real reason she woke me.

"I'm sorry about your parents."

I froze, unsure how to respond. I was certainly awake now. "It happened a long time ago. Don't worry about it."

Arianna spoke softly, "But it's plainly still an open wound in your heart."

I smiled, but it was a smile only meant to reassure her. "Yeah well...my wound and my heart are both my problems to deal with. Get some sleep."

I did not want to talk about my past or my parents anymore.

"All right."

Why did she wake me up for that? Now I would never be able to get back to sleep. 20 minutes of tossing underneath my sheets and it felt as if my skin was on fire. I was upset, and Arianna was the cause. I groaned in frustration and decided to get out of bed. There was no sense in staying in bed if I couldn't sleep. Maybe food would help. I put on my uniform bottoms and before I could get my boots on, I stopped myself.

No, I can't let this go. I walked over to Arianna's bed and shook her lightly. She rolled onto her back and looked up at me.

"Is that why you woke me up? If so...why would you do that to me? You think I wanted to relive my past with you after the night we had? You couldn't wait for a more appropriate moment?"

Arianna sat up and rubbed her eyes vigorously. She only studied me, blinking rapidly.

"You can't—"

I should have seen it coming but I didn't. Arianna kissed me, snatching all my words and breath away.

When our lips parted, I exhaled, not realizing I had been holding my breath. "If that's what you wanted all you had to do was say it. Don't torture me."

"I'm sorry."

"Don't apologize, just communicate better. The one time I had you drunk you were completely honest. Do that sober. Okay?"

She agreed.

My heart raced, a rhythm fast but precise, and with a pulse I felt beating in my head. My stomach twisted in knots as my clit throbbed. I leaned in slowly, taking a shuddering breath, and kissed Arianna affectionately. Arianna moaned as both of her hands made their way to the back of my neck, pulling me in. I bit her playfully on her bottom lip while my left arm curled around her back, slipping under her shirt. The touch of her skin against my fingertips felt intoxicating, making me continue. Arianna whimpered at my touch.

Our lips parted, but only long enough for us to catch our breath.

"You make me feel insane. A good kind of insane," I told her.

"You sure about that?" She giggled and tossed her hair backward over her shoulder.

"Only when you give into me." I kissed her again, this time more urgently.

My lips brushed over her jawline and then down to her neck. Arianna offered herself to me, extending her neck further so that I had more skin available to kiss. She slipped backward onto her mattress. I followed, straddling her. I removed the cover that blocked her from me, then slid my pants down and positioned myself on top of her. Her legs spread for me to move in between them, and I did so happily, grinding against her center. Both of us gasped for air as we climbed to the height of our pleasure.

"I want you badly right now." Arianna was imploring me to keep going.

I kissed alongside her neck, whispering in her ear, "I want the same."

I pulled her shirt up and over her head and then got to work on her sports bra, desperate to reach her breasts. I guided her bra over her head with Arianna assisting me so I could get my mouth over one of her taut nipples. She whimpered even louder when I sucked on it gently and let my tongue skim over it.

"I'm going to cum."

I chuckled and brought my lips back to hers. "I haven't done anything yet."

"You certainly have." She sank her head into the pillow, sexually frustrated.

Someone knocked on the door and I flew out of Arianna's bed, panicked. Part of me felt like the door would magically pop open at any second. Arianna was still as stone. I was on the floor trying to slow my heart rate.

"Yes?"

"Can I have your chips?"

I snarled at Felipe, "Bro, you seriously going to wake us up over some chips and dip?"

I heard muttering. "You're right. Sorry. Go back to sleep."

"Felipe, eat my damn chips!"

"Thanks." Felipe sounded relieved. That meant he already ate my chips. "Go back to sleep."

I rolled my eyes.

Arianna looked to me. "The door is locked, right?"

I nodded. "We're safe."

"He didn't hear us?"

I shook my head.

Arianna leaned back in her bed and absentmindedly scratched her arm.

I crouched next to her. "Have you already changed your mind about us?"

"Who said I changed my mind the first time?"

I looked at her as if to say, 'I'm not a fool.'

"I was nervous. I never changed my mind."

Good. "How about we get some sleep and I'll take you home once we're off? We can talk more then."

"Deal."

Before she could turn away I couldn't help stealing a kiss. Arianna laughed and called me a thief. I chuckled at that and fell asleep with no problem at all.

Chapter Fifteen
Arianna

I was in need of Tajel's attention, but for the rest of the week we were strictly professional. Maybe too professional. I wondered if Tajel was still interested, but I knew I was being silly. Of course, she was still interested. The things she said to me the night of the hostage take down – those words were full of undiluted honesty. I believed in her, and I believed in our possibilities.

It was late afternoon on a Saturday, and I had just finished napping after a 24-hour shift.

"Knock, knock."

It was Danielle opening my door before I could even answer.

"I brought you..." She stepped aside to reveal Tajel standing next to her.

Tajel appeared to be irritated with Danielle. I'm sure my best friend was asking her a million invasive questions about our blossoming relationship. I hadn't told Danielle much because there wasn't a lot to tell.

"She didn't tell me you were still sleeping."

"What else would she be doing in her room alone?" Danielle asked sarcastically.

"It's fine," I replied and shifted in my bed, preparing to sit up. "Thanks, Danielle, for your assistance. You can go."

Danielle blew me a kiss and left Tajel alone with me in my room. Once the door was closed, Tajel looked around, taking note of the setup. I had a lot of burgundy decorations in my room so I'm sure she must be thinking that I really like that color. I was about to stand when I remembered I wasn't wearing bottoms, only panties and a tank top. It shouldn't have mattered so much, it wasn't as if Tajel hadn't seen me unclothed before, and in more intimate circumstances. Nevertheless, I decided to stay under the covers in my bed.

"I don't get a hug, or at least, some kind of greeting?"

Shit. Bad manners.

"Sorry. How are you?" I struggled to sound nonchalant. Tajel chuckled.

"Some greeting." She pointed to my bed. "Can I—"

I motioned for her to sit before she said anything else. *She's within touching distance now. I can handle this.* Tajel's charming smile distracted me from thinking about my lack of clothes. I blushed and hoped she didn't notice. She scooted closer to me and I thought my heart was going to leap out of my chest it was beating so rapidly. The hair on the back of my neck stood straight up and I felt my blood pulsing under every inch of my skin.

Tajel moved closer to me again, and I understood then that she was seeking to cause me to react to her nearness. My mouth slowly opened, and a heavy breath escaped from in between my lips. If Tajel heard, she made no indication of it. I laid back against my pillows. She sat beside me, her arm stretching across my stomach. Her face was only a few inches away from mine.

"What are you doing?" After I asked, I realized I should have kept my mouth shut.

"What does it feel like I'm doing?" Her mouth drew closer. I nearly stopped breathing. "I've missed you."

"I thought you changed your mind or something."
Idiot. Why can't I ever say the right thing?

Tajel's brows furrowed. "Why would you think that?"

"Forget it. It was stupid of me to say that."

"You weren't stupid. Foolish, probably."

That didn't make me feel any better.

"When will you stop doubting my intentions?"

My damn mouth. I need to fix this. "I'm sorry. I keep screwing up. It was just...the rest of the week, especially after that day."

"Look at me, please." Tajel's seriousness was unmistakable.

I wasn't aware that I had been looking away. I locked eyes with her, working hard not to turn away again.

"We hadn't talked much about what happened and you behaved as if we weren't even friends. Just coworkers."

Tajel was about to argue but instead she laid her head against mine.

"I'm sorry. It was certainly not my intention to make you feel that way. I was...scared. My uncle can read me so easily, and I was worried he would see the change in our relationship."

I perked up, understanding instantly. I carried that same fear with my family. The difference was, Tajel was out to hers. Being that we were partners, it made it hard for her to come out to him or anyone about what was happening between us. I still didn't know what was happening between us.

"I didn't believe you could get scared. I never thought of you feeling that way."

"Ha, ha." Tajel's laughter echoed in my room. "I never said I was impervious, particularly when it involves my uncle."

"No, you did not."

Leaning against me, Tajel groaned loudly. "Don't think I don't know that you're hardly clothed underneath this blanket."

I was about to ask how she knew when I caught sight of my uniform bottoms lying in a clump on the floor.

"You wouldn't take advantage of me, would you?" I asked with a hint of hopefulness.

"Depends." Tajel shrugged. "You want me to?"

I couldn't form the words, so I simply nodded and in seconds, Tajel's lips met mine. I trembled, tasting the lingering flavor of a raspberry candy.

I breathed in her scent. "I want more of this." Our lips brushed, my hands hesitant to touch her face. "I'm nervous."

"Why?"

"Because...I actually like you," I admitted.

Tajel smirked. "You better."

I chuckled, but I was serious. "I've never taken a risk like this before."

"With someone you work with?" Tajel asked.

"That...and with someone I really like. My family has never been supportive of my sexuality."

"Religious?"

"Conservative." It was hard talking about my family without feeling the urge to plunge my face into freezing water first. "I lived in a bubble all of my life, even after I moved out of my parents' house. That's one of the reasons I came here. I thought that if I was far away from them, I would finally be able to be myself."

God, I'm talking too much.

"I usually don't talk so much about myself. Sorry." I covered my face in embarrassment.

Tajel removed my hands from my face. " You are sharing parts of yourself with me...being honest and open without being drunk... this is what I want."

"You sure about that?" I asked in a playful manner.

"Positive." Tajel kissed me again and smiled affectionately. "I would like to take you on a date."

My heart sped up too fast for my body to process anything properly, and then my skin flushed.

"Is that a yes?" Tajel pointed to my cheeks. "You're blushing."

I cringed. *Did she have to point that out?*

"What?" Tajel laughed. "It's adorable."

"Stop," I whined.

I'm sure my face was entirely red at this point. I wanted to hide under the covers, but she'd just chase me underneath them. Tajel snorted and I glared at her, trying my best to appear angry and not amused.

"Did you just snort?"

Tajel tried to stand but I seized her arm, preventing her from retreating. *Look who's embarrassed now.*

"That was very cute." I maintained my grip on Tajel's arm and she narrowed her eyes at me. "I'm serious."

I caught hold of her blue, plaid shirt and pulled her toward me to plant a kiss on her lips. "I think everything about you is cute."

I started unbuttoning her shirt.

"Arianna, you are very tempting."

"Good." I kissed her again and my hands wrapped around her neck.

Tajel broke our kiss. "I want to."

"Then why are you stopping this?"

Her breathing was ragged, and it indicated to me that Tajel wanted me as much as I wanted her. "I want to do this right. You're not like other women. And sex...as good as it is...I don't want to start off that way with you."

I wanted to argue her choice to not give into our physical desires. I didn't know a lot about her past relationships, but I certainly knew about mine. In the end, rationality won, and I conceded the point. If we were going to have a good start to our relationship, we couldn't rush things. I understood that.

However, it wouldn't stop me from kissing her. I gave her a quick peck and then asked, "So, this date... when will it be happening?"

Tajel's smile produced dimples, and my legs trembled beneath the covers. "Tonight? Seven?"

I glanced at the clock on my nightstand. That was four hours away. "That works for me."

Tajel was buttoning her shirt back up. "Can't have Danielle thinking I took advantage of you. I'll pick you up." She kissed me quickly and stood. "Dress warm but delicious."

"Delicious." I shook my head. "Get out so I can start my day and get ready."

Tajel lingered in my room for another minute before leaving. I wrapped the covers around me and smiled.

Danielle appeared in my doorway with a wide grin plastered on her face. "Seems things between you and Tajel are spicing up?"

I shifted under the covers. "They are."

"I knew you two would work out."

Of course, you did. Danielle was clearly happy that I was finally giving myself a chance at happiness.

"Don't look at me like that," Danielle pouted. "I'm your best friend. I know what's best for you. Don't dismiss this."

"Danielle, I am not dismissing anything. In fact, we have a date tonight."

"You do?" She was so surprised she almost lost her footing. She had to reposition herself against my bedroom door.

"We do," I beamed.

Danielle shrieked and then leaped onto my bed to embrace me tightly.

"Thank God! She is hot, and I know you wanted her."

"Okay, okay." I ripped Danielle off me. "Get off. I need to get up."

"All right." Danielle left my bed and practically danced out of the room. "I can't wait to help you get ready!"

I said nothing in response. Arianna was my best friend after all. The last time she helped me to get ready for a date we were nineteen. That was eight years ago. Plus, I wasn't going to deny her the pleasure of helping me pick out an outfit because she really loved that part.

For the first time in my life, I would be preparing for a date without feeling dread at the thought of my family scrutinizing what I was wearing or who I would be going out with. I never actually told them I was gay or flaunted my women in front of them. I never said I wasn't gay either. It was just never discussed. A few of my relatives would try to hook my up with their guy friends and I'd just dismiss it every time. No more of that pressure of trying to please my parents all while being gay. I was free, without limitations. And if Tajel wanted me to look good tonight, so be it. I would do more than that. I called to Danielle from my room and then I took a moment to look at myself in my dresser mirror as Danielle reentered my room.

"Danielle...let's make me look delicious tonight."

Chapter Sixteen
Arianna

"I don't know. Should I be doing this?"

I was becoming so unsure of getting involved with Tajel. It could destroy our partnership and I wasn't willing to let that happen.

"Seriously, Arianna? What happened to the confidence you had only a little while ago?"

She was right, as usual. "Is this too much?"

I turned away from the mirror after scrutinizing myself for nearly 30 minutes.

Danielle admired me excitedly. "If I didn't know you...I would totally dump Sasha to talk to you."

I rolled my eyes and turned to face the mirror once more. "No, you wouldn't."

"You're right." Danielle giggled and then used her hand to smooth a few wrinkles on my bedclothes. "I would try to have you as my side piece."

I searched my dresser for something to toss at her. "You're an ass."

"I'm a fine ass." Danielle smirked and then crossed her legs. "At least, that's what Sasha tells me."

"She was lying." The sarcasm in my tone was unmistakable.

"Only haters say that."

Danielle and I couldn't stop ourselves from laughing. The doorbell rang suddenly, and I stiffened.

"Breathe," Danielle advised. "I'll distract your date for a few more minutes. Come out with confidence and leave all of that bullshit you're worried about in here."

Danielle closed the door, leaving me alone to try to calm down. I decided to give myself one last look in the mirror before leaving my room to greet Tajel. I wore a cream-colored, long sleeve dress that fell to my mid-thighs. It was a body-hugging dress with a scoop neck – I didn't want my outfit to be too revealing for our first date. Chic, black stockings and suede boots paired with chunky accessories completed my look.

"Okay. You can do this," I reassured myself.

I left the room, grabbing my clutch purse on the way out. When I saw Tajel in the living room, I bit my bottom lip, happily anticipating our time alone together. She wore an acrylic pullover that exposed enough of her breasts to make me feel as if I was beginning to overheat. She also wore fitted jeans and black ankle boots. *Damn, with those gray eyes and dimples, I could stop breathing altogether.* Tajel smiled at me approvingly.

"You two make me feel so fucking flustered. Where are you taking her?" Danielle was behaving like an overprotective parent.

"She'll find out once we get there." Tajel winked at me.

"Whatever." Danielle waved us off, plainly irritated with Tajel's secretiveness. "Get out."

Tajel offered me her hand. "Ready?"

Our fingers interlaced, and the sensation gave me goosebumps.

"Look at you two!" Danielle squealed.

God.

"Danielle, leave us be."

141

She appeared unbothered by my request as Tajel and I left together.

"She always finds a way to embarrass me," I told Tajel while we were walking to her car.

I noticed her looking at me and smiling.

"What's the look for?"

"Eres una mujer hermosa."

I couldn't stop myself from smiling as well. She was so adorable. "You speak Spanish?"

"I never cared to learn. You give me a reason to." Tajel squeezed my hand. "It's a part of you, *sí?*"

"Sí."

We kissed and Tajel growled teasingly. "We better get going before I turn you around and drag you back into that bedroom of yours."

We laughed and then Tajel opened the door for me. If I had any doubts left in me, they disappeared after that kiss.

*

Tajel

Jimmy Mac's was a restaurant that featured live jazz. It was the perfect place for our first date – jazz could be sensual, and it would be nice to enjoy that with Arianna. We walked inside, and I instantly spotted the black, leather seats and the elegant, hardwood tables. There was a stage centered on the back wall of the restaurant where a band was already playing. Dim lighting helped create an intimate atmosphere. There was a candle at every table. Waiters were dressed in black and red. It was a pricy place people enjoyed paying for.

My sister approached us. "Hey, Tajel. Your table is ready."

"Thanks, Brooklyn."

"Mmhmm." She was studying Arianna who was looking me, curious as to how I knew the hostess so well.

"Arianna, this is my sister, Brooklyn. Brooklyn...this is Arianna."

"Nice to meet you." Arianna respectfully offered her hand and Brooklyn took it happily.

"Is it *my* table?"

"Of course." Brooklyn gestured for us to go, her gaze returning to the stack of papers on the host stand.

When we found the table, I said to Arianna with a silly grin, "Here you go madam."

She rolled her eyes.

Once Arianna was seated she asked, "You have your own table?"

"Yo, Tajel!" a voice from somewhere in the restaurant called to me.

"Hey, Theo," I greeted as soon as I realized who the voice belonged to.

I introduced him to Arianna. He was wearing his neat, gray suit. Even in his sixties he still had women accompanying him gladly.

"Lovely lady," he complimented. "I hope you let her hear your amazing voice."

"It's a possibility."

Theo smiled and then walked over to the side stage to wait for the artist who was performing to finish his set.

"You sing?"

"I fool around a little."

Arianna looked at me in disbelief. "You're full of shit."

"Why is that?" I was but I wanted to know how she knew.

"You never half-ass anything you do."

I shifted in my chair to face her. The corner of my lips raised into a smirk. "You know me already, huh?"

Arianna's expression was serious. "No. Just a few things. A few important things. But I'm looking forward to knowing more."

"What can I get you ladies?" Brooklyn appeared at the table with two menus.

"I would like a strawberry lemonade," I answered. I turned to Arianna, who couldn't maintain her serious demeanor. "What?"

"Nothing." She then addressed my sister, "I would like the same, please."

Brooklyn then asked for our appetizer order and afterwards she headed to the kitchen. I wasted no time turning my attention back to Arianna. *Damn, she looks so sexy.* I needed to make sure this date went well.

"I'm glad you said yes to this date."

Arianna smoothed out her dress. "I didn't think I would agree to it at first."

"Why?"

One of the musicians began playing a solo on the base guitar, garnering the attention of everyone in the restaurant. We postponed our discussion. There was no way we could continue anyway, the sounds of the music and crowd combined prevented us from hearing one another. I didn't mind too much. Music was always a way for me to escape from my emotions, specifically from my past. After the volume of the music softened, I decided Arianna and me should continue our discussion.

"Are we being smart?" Arianna's serious demeanor had returned.

"Do you think we're worth exploring?"

Arianna was quiet for a minute, then replied, "Yes."

The relief I felt was immediate, and I brushed my jaw with my fingertips absentmindedly as I watched Arianna finish her strawberry lemonade.

"Stop looking at me like that," Arianna said, her straw still positioned between her teeth. She kept her eyes on the band.

"You don't want me to look at you?"

"I do." Arianna tried to keep her composure while a smile threatened to emerge. "You make it hard for me to focus."

"Focus," I repeated, almost tasting the word on my tongue.

Arianna's gaze dropped to my breasts and then quickly returned to my eyes. Clearly, she was enjoying the view. I stopped myself from teasing her about it, instead choosing to use this time to learn more about her. Arianna was utterly intriguing. She tested more than half of the nerves in my body, and yet I was still drawn to her. But our partnership was precious to me and I did not want to risk that, period. However, despite the possible consequences, I wanted to be with her.

Two hours into the performances and after delightful meal, we were ready to go.

"Thanks," Arianna said.

"For?"

She sighed. "Asking me out. Bringing me here."

We were by my car, shielding our faces from the harsh wind with our hands. "Weather forecast is never correct."

Arianna shivered, and I offered her my coat.

"I'm fine."

"Hey, no arguing." I put my coat around her shoulders and waited for her to slip her arms into the sleeves.

She finally relented, shaking her head. "I'm not used to the weather."

"I do have one more place to take you." I held out my hand, which she took without hesitation.

"Then...we had better get to it, right?" Arianna smiled.

We started walking down the block toward our next destination. My stomach fluttered as I enjoyed the sensation of her hand in mine.

"Where are we going?" Arianna's voice interrupted the sounds of our shoes on the sidewalk.

I pointed to a place across the street before we crossed. "There."

"Melt 'N Mouth." Arianna snorted, "Sounds like a porn shop."

I laughed, opening the door for her to walk through. Vibrant hues of blue and pink greeted us as we strode through the place.

"Honey, you came!" My aunt walked over and hugged me tightly. She noticed Arianna who appeared to be nervous. "Oh, relax, sweetie. My husband doesn't know anything. It is not my place to tell him about you two."

"I tell my aunt everything."

"Well, thanks for keeping this a secret," Arianna said, clearly relieved.

"Of course. I know the risk you two are taking."

"We're going to sit. Can you start us off with a hot fudge brownie with vanilla ice cream on top?"

My aunt nodded, and I escorted Arianna to an open booth nearby.

"What kind of ice cream shop is this?"

"It's more like an ice cream lounge," I corrected. "Some of the sweets are normal...some have a little cannabis in it."

Arianna laughed until she saw that I was serious. "Are you kidding me? There's weed inside of the desserts? Your aunt works at an illegal—"

"Firstly, my aunt doesn't work here, she owns the place," I explained. "Secondly, marijuana is legal in Oregon."

"Wow, really?" She was genuinely surprised.

"If you're 18 or older and not pregnant, you can have a brownie with a certain amount of weed."

"Well," Arianna examined the other patrons eating their desserts, "California is definitely not like Oregon."

"I'm so glad you moved here."

"I needed to leave." Arianna sat across from me in the booth. I felt the distance between our bodies and it was driving me nuts.

I got up and pointed to the empty space next to her. "May I?"

"Sure."

Arianna slid a little to the left to allow me to sit next to her. She wasn't looking at me, though. Her fingers made circles on the skin below her ear.

"God, you make me nervous."

"I'm not doing anything."

Arianna laughed, her fingers continuing their movements above her jawline. "There you go again, sounding so smooth."

I let my head rest in the palm of my hand and faced her. "What are you talking about?"

"Your charm. Those dimples." Arianna covered her eyes with her sleeves. "I can't believe how much you affect me."

I gently brought her arms down away from her face. "Look at me. I can't help it when I'm around you.

Especially, when you look as beautiful as you do right now."

Arianna played with the curls of my hair. *Damn.* It was as if she instinctively knew exactly what I liked. I was a sucker for my hair being played with.

"Here's your brownie and ice cream." My aunt served the dessert and then left without another word, giving us privacy.

"Can we take that to go?" Arianna looked at me suggestively, and the insinuation wasn't lost on me.

"Yes."

When my aunt next passed by our booth, I asked for a container for the dessert. Once it was boxed, we quickly exited the restaurant, heading straight for the car and thinking excitedly about the possibilities the night presented.

"Your place," Arianna demanded.

"Are you—"

"Are you really trying to convince me to change my mind?"

"No. I only want you to be sure." I leaned closer to Arianna. "We don't have to do anything."

Just outside of the car, Arianna pressed her body against mine, our lips touching softly. Keeping myself steady proved nearly impossible since Arianna's touch was causing my thighs to shake uncontrollably. We couldn't continue here, I was aware of that. People in the restaurant, including my aunt, could easily see us.

"We should go."

"You'd like that now, huh?" Arianna teased seductively.

I bit my lip. "I liked it before. I was only trying to be a gentlewoman."

I opened the car door for Arianna. "After you."

Arianna climbed into the passenger side and I caught a whiff of her scent. It was delicate, like flower petals, and I started counting the minutes until we could be alone together. I couldn't help but be thankful for Arianna entering my life. She was all I have ever wanted in a woman, and if kissing her made my body feel wild and sensuous, I could only imagine how it would feel to have sex with her. But, I wouldn't know until it happened. Until then, I needed to get us safely to my place. I could do that, hopefully.

Chapter Seventeen
Tajel

15 minutes to my house. I could get there without driving us off the road, suffering from a sexual haze. Right? Fuck, she's making my body overheat again. I concentrated on controlling my breathing.

"You are making this very hard," I told her, pressing lightly on the brakes at a stop sign. Several more stop signs to go. *Freaking great.*

"Is it supposed to be easy?" Arianna asked, placing her hand gently on my knee.

I shrugged. Her scent filled the air in the car and my nipples began to harden.

"Depends on the circumstances." *You got this, Tajel. You're in control.*

I turned a corner hoping that somehow we'd teleport there.

I caught Arianna staring at me. "What?"

"How are you so calm while driving and yet, I can see that your body is in strong need of attention?"

"You want me to announce to everyone in Portland that we're about to have sex?"

"I'm not usually as forward as I have been with you." Arianna smiled shyly. "I just wouldn't be able to maintain composure like you."

"Please don't stop being forward. Don't stop being the woman who isn't afraid to get what she wants. That's who

150

you are, whether you realize it or not. Own your confidence." I reached across the middle console, squeezing her thigh. "And trust me…I'm working really hard to not go crazy. I want you."

I could tell that Arianna wanted to kiss me again. The corner of her lip twitched, and it was easy to see that she was thinking about her next move. I wouldn't move first. This had to be her choice. Her eyes bored into mine and my blood pumped through my body down to my center. *Fuck, my clit was throbbing.* I couldn't wait any longer. We were nearly to my place.

When we arrived, I led Arianna up the stairs. Holding her hand made me feel special. I could not forget, however, that being with Arianna could compromise my chances at joining my uncle's SWAT team. Before Arianna, my career always came first. Women came and went, but they never lasted long. I never gave any woman the opportunity to affect me in that way.

My mind wasn't only focused on the intimate experience we were about to share, I also wondered about what would happen afterwards. Tomorrow. I wanted more of her already and I had yet to fully understand what Arianna meant to me. I simply knew she was special.

I found my door unlocked. I questioned whether I remembered to lock it before leaving, but I felt certain that I had. Frowning and bracing myself for whatever might await inside, I opened the door and pushed it forward gently.

"Is something wrong?"

From the inside of my apartment I heard a voice, forcing me to take a step back. "I think someone broke…"

I listened to the voice again, and immediately recognized who it belonged to. *Why now?* I sighed in frustration, looking back at Arianna. I couldn't send her away. I had to deal with this before I could take her home.

"We should leave and call the—"

"I know who it is." No sense in procrastinating.

"Oh...dude." My brother didn't pause when he saw me, but instead continued the conversation he was having with someone over the phone. "Make that two boxes of pizza."

I snatched the phone out his hand and spoke into the receiver, "Sorry about this. Can you cancel those orders?"

I waited for a response and then hung up the phone. Arianna lingered close to the front door, running her fingers over the stitching of her clutch purse.

"Ah, come on, little sis. I haven't eaten in days."

I was unmoved. "Tyler, give me back my money."

Tyler stared at me for a minute or two, completely dumbfounded. He smiled, but it wasn't a sincere smile, it was a nervous smile. It was obvious that he was trying to figure out what to say to me, but when he saw Arianna, he no longer needed any more time to think.

I returned to Arianna and grabbed her hand. I whispered to her, "I'm sorry about this. I had no idea he was coming."

"There is no reason for you to apologize. I can call a taxi..."

I didn't want her to leave. "No. I can get rid of him."

"And we can get back to what we were about to do, just like that?" She snapped her fingers and shook her head.

I sighed. She had a point – there was no way we could restore the mood after this.

"No." I didn't want to be alone, though. "At least let me take you home?"

"You always knew how to get the ladies."

My brother's words made me grimace, especially since Arianna was standing beside me. Arianna was expressionless, however, but I knew she couldn't be happy right now.

Tyler put his arm around my shoulders, his musty smell made me embarrassed to claim him as my brother. "She stole my girlfriend once. Bitch wasn't that special, though. Or was she?"

"Tyler." I wiggled my way out from under his arm and glared at him. "Stop."

"That look. I know that look." Tyler smirked, his lips dry and cracked. He shook his index finger at me. "You should be careful around her...if my sister doesn't get you killed like our parents she'll only break—"

"Tyler!"

My entire body was shaking. Tears stung my eyes. Only Tyler could ever rile me up to the point of tears.

"Just shut up."

"All right. I'm backing off." He held his hands up as if surrendering. "Can I order that pizza now? I'm starving."

"Give me the money you took out of my drawer." I couldn't stop the trembling in my muscles, but my feet remained planted firmly on the floor.

He looked at Arianna, then at me again. "Is she going to punch me?"

"Don't talk to her!" I screeched. I held my hand out, still waiting for my money.

"You sure you want it?"

I said nothing, and he dug his hands inside the pockets of his torn, dirty jeans. He smiled cheekily as I watched him rummage for my money. Everything was a joke to him. When he found my money, he held it out to me. He then put his finger up, signaling for me to wait. He shoved my money into his boxers, rubbing it against himself, around in circles. I was overwhelmed by his insulting behavior.

"You still want it?"

My own brother. We were close once and now this was our relationship.

"We're twins, by the way," Tyler continued trying to talk to Arianna.

"Do whatever you want with it."

Disgusted, I grabbed Arianna's hand and led her out of my apartment and to my car. I was silent. I opened the door for Arianna, still managing to remember my manners. I was literally shaking. She didn't get in right away, instead reaching out to squeeze my hand which was resting on top of the passenger side door. That helped me take a breath and she climbed inside. On the drive to her house, I never said a word. I honestly couldn't recall the drive – all I was able to think of was how furious I was with my brother. We did manage to make it to her place, but I wasn't sure if I committed any traffic infractions along the way. I turned off the car and remained quiet and unmoving. There was so much pressure in my chest I was sure it would burst open at any moment.

"I'm sorry. Please know that I'm not the girl he described. That's my past and I really—"

Arianna placed her index finger over my lips. I blinked several times, surprised by her gesture.

"At first, his words scared me. This is the first time I've opened myself up this much." Her fingers linked with mine. "But, then he went on...and those things he said to you...He was cruel, and I saw your spark vanish. I don't want to see anyone take that spark from you again. Not me, not anyone, not ever."

I smiled weakly as a tear slid down my cheek. Before I could wipe it away, Arianna stroked my cheek with her thumb, smearing the tear across my cheekbone.

"I'm not going to run."

"Are you sure you—"

Her lips were on mine before I could finish. When she put her hand on my thigh, I inhaled sharply and shivered. Arianna buried her fingers into my hair as our kiss deepened. Shaking, I squeezed my thighs together. I was so amazed by how much I responded to her touch and warmth. She had my heart already.

"Come up." Her words were nurturing. "I want to take care of you."

I nodded and was about to climb out of my car when I reminded myself that my brother and his friends were still at my house.

"Shit." I sighed and slammed the palm of my fist against my forehead. "If I don't deal with Tyler tonight, I have no idea the state my apartment will be in tomorrow."

"I understand. You're right." Arianna's fingers were still curling around strands of my hair.

"I can't believe my brother would just show up after almost two years. And of course, he had to show up tonight. I'm so sorry."

"I'm not upset. He hurt you, not me."

We talked a bit more and then I walked Arianna up to her apartment.

She turned to face me. "I really enjoyed our night."

"Even the end?" I was worried that she would reconsider our relationship, even though she said she wasn't upset.

"Well, it would have been better not to see that, but because of it I feel like I know you a little better."

I gave Arianna another kiss and wrapped my arms around her waist.

The sound of the front door opening interrupted our kiss. Danielle and Sasha almost knocked us over, clearly not expecting to run into Arianna and me right outside the door.

"Oh..." Sasha grinned. "I can see your date was excellent."

Arianna and I both rolled our eyes.

"Good night. Please call me once you are finished." Arianna kissed me again and then disappeared into her apartment.

"I will," I said. "Can I pick you up tomorrow?"

Arianna reappeared in the doorway smiling. "Call me once you're on your way."

"Will do." I couldn't wait until tomorrow.

I left with Sasha following close behind, talking to her about my brother showing up at my house.

"I'm coming with you. You are not going back there alone."

I didn't waste time resisting. I knew Sasha would follow no matter what I said.

"And you're calling your uncle before we get there."

I was about to argue and decided against it. "All right. Let's do this. "

Chapter Eighteen
Tajel

There was no way to avoid this disaster. This was my house, so it was my problem. Sasha had a solid grip on my forearm, not allowing me to get out of my car. I slapped her hand, trying to free myself, but it was no use. Sasha was determined to keep me from going inside my apartment.

Sasha grunted in frustration. "Don't go in there until your uncle arrives."

"I called him, but I don't need to wait for him."

I finally freed myself and scrambled out of the car, slamming my car door shut. The music coming from my apartment could have been heard over a block away. It was so loud that it felt like it was causing vibrations in the pavement.

"I don't understand what makes him think that what he's doing is cool?" Sasha chased me up the stairs, probably planning another attempt to stop me from going inside.

A vehicle pulled up and parked along the curb of my street. By the low rumbling sound the engine made, I could tell it was my uncle's truck. He jumped out, shutting the door with such force I thought for sure the glass of the window would break.

His order was directed at me, "You wait down here."

I was in no mood to be told what to do. "This is my place. I'm going inside."

My uncle skipped a few steps trying to catch up to us. He took the lead, putting himself in front of Sasha and me at the front of my apartment building. The door to my apartment was already ajar, and the stench of weed floated outside, causing the fury I'd been quelling to resurface. My brother and two others I did not know were sitting on my couch leaning toward my coffee table. They were slicing up their drugs and giggling like giddy children.

"Tyler!" My uncle opened the door fully.

Generally a calm person, my uncle's composure was lost when it came to my brother. He stomped toward where they were seated – they were completely oblivious to our presence. He swiped an open soda bottle from the table, then proceeded to pour its contents all over my brother and his friends.

One of my brother's friends pulled out a knife from his pocket, slashing it in the air to try to cut my uncle's chest. Spotting the knife as it emerged from the man's pocket, my uncle stepped backward to wait for an opening before landing a blow on the guy's jaw.

"Yo!" Tyler shouted. "Bro, that's just my crazy uncle!"

Tyler walked up to his friend who was still wielding a knife and hunched over in pain from the punch.

Tyler turned to our uncle and said with a chuckle, "Unc', he was just messing with you."

"What part of that was supposed to be a joke?" I fumed.

Tyler raised his arms defensively. "It's no biggie, Tajel. Besides, you know how to save his life."

My brother wasn't bothered by the fact that a fight almost occurred that could have ended badly for either our uncle, or his friend, or both. He didn't care about anyone's safety, not even his own. At least, he didn't care enough.

"You son of a bitch!"

I was ready to lunge at him when Sasha took hold of my waist. I struggled against her arms, but she only tightened her hold.

"Fuck you, Tyler!" I screamed.

"Damn, bro. You weren't lying. Bitch is a firecracker." His knife-wielding friend decided to put his weapon back in his pocket and took a moment to scrutinize me. "What's your name?"

"She's not interested," Sasha hissed in disgust.

"Bro," Tyler said, "Remember? She eats pussy."

Tyler then noticed that Arianna wasn't with us. I could tell that was who he was searching for.

"Where's that hot, Latina babe you had with you?"

I knew I had to change the subject before he went too far. Looking around my house I discovered beer and vodka containers strewn about the floor. I'd only been gone for an hour and yet it seemed that I had walked into the aftermath of a house party that raged for half a night. The other friend of my brother's who hadn't said anything since we burst through the door, tried to relight his joint, but I marched over to him and snatched it out of his hand.

"What the fuck?" the man whined. He didn't bother standing.

"Get out of this house. All of you." My uncle pointed to the door. "And if you think I don't have the police commissioner's number on speed dial, try me."

The guys looked at each other and then at Tyler as if seeking his direction.

"Don't look to him. He's leaving too." I was able to keep my voice steady.

Tyler laughed. He always laughed at awkward or scary situations. I suppose he honestly believed he could camp out at my house.

He sniffed and wiped his nose multiple times, then snorted. "Fine. Bad time to come. Ruined your date."

"Get out," my uncle repeated. He didn't want them in my house for one second longer. Neither did I.

"Bro...is that you?" One of the guys grimaced as they sniffed the air. "Dude, is that shit on your shoe?"

Tyler lifted his foot to examine his shoe. "Yeah, I guess so. I don't even know when I stepped into it."

Great, there is shit tracked all through my house. I believed that I did not smell it before because of the overwhelming stench of weed in my apartment. Instead of cleaning his shoe with one of the napkins lying on the table next to the half-empty boxes of pizza, Tyler raised his foot and scraped the bottom of his shoe on my coffee table. I watched as he put his foot down, revealing a glob of animal waste on the edge of the table. My eyes watered, a mixture of anger and hurt.

That was my brother. I blinked rapidly, trying not to give him the satisfaction of seeing me cry. They left my house not bothering to take their trash with them. I didn't care. I just wanted them gone. When the door closed behind them, I stared at the door for a while, making sure they were not coming back. I heard shuffling and turned to see that my uncle was already cleaning up the empty soda bottles. I felt violated. Sasha slowly wrapped her arms around me, telling me it was all right to feel what I was feeling. I made up an excuse to go in my room, leaving Sasha and my uncle to clean my brother's mess.

*

I Belong with Her

Arianna

Danielle and I were sitting in her car parked in front of Tajel's apartment. She turned off the ignition and then looked at me. "You sure you want to go up alone?"

I spied Sasha's car in a parking spot across from us. "Sasha's here. Maybe it's best that you come up with me."

I tried calling Tajel's phone and when she didn't answer, I became worried. I needed to know how she was doing and hoped that I did not cross a line in coming to her apartment unannounced. Danielle and I climbed out of her car and headed over to Tajel's apartment.

A few seconds after I knocked on her front door, Sasha appeared. "Hey, we forgot you were coming!"

She opened the door wider, allowing me to see that Chief was in Tajel's living room.

Shit.

She spoke again, this time in an exaggerated tone, and she seemed to be addressing Chief as well, "I know we were supposed to go for drinks, but I believe we will have to reschedule!"

Chief overheard the three of us talking and noticed me in the doorway as soon as he looked up from his task. "Ms. Castaldi..."

Damn it. I should have waited and given Tajel a chance to call me before barging over here.

"Chief." My voice was perceptibly shaky. "I'm... uh..."

As if on cue, Tajel emerged from her bedroom, her eyes red and puffy. It was difficult to resist the urge to run over and hold her. I couldn't help myself. I cared so much for Tajel. My feet remained planted firmly in place, knowing that I would have to wait for Chief to leave to be affectionate with her. *I hope he leaves soon.*

Almost as if he were actively trying to avoid my inner wishes, he continued working, tossing the last of the empty beer cans into the trash in the kitchen. As he washed his hands I snuck a quick glance at Tajel. Thankfully, there was no sign of anger on her face because of my presence. She appeared to be relieved, and I thought my heart was going to leap out of my chest. I smiled weakly at her, hoping that I hadn't drawn attention to myself.

Chief walked over to us, wiping his damp hands on his pants. "Whatever plans you ladies had you mind having it another night? Tajel will be coming back home—"

"No, I'm staying here."

Tajel seemed set in her decision, even though Chief persisted for some time in his attempts to try and reason with her. I could tell that in scary moments like this Chief was picturing Tajel as a young child in need of him to shield her from the world. He responded the same way after the hostage call at the brewery.

"She won't be alone tonight, uncle," Sasha said, reassuring him.

While Chief was studying Tajel, Sasha winked at me.

"All right," he relented, taking one last look around the apartment to search for any lingering hazards or threats. "I prefer you here than my niece being alone tonight."

Tajel put her hand on his arm. "Uncle, please. I will be fine."

He put his hand over Tajel's and nodded. "I'm glad you two are getting along. You call me if he returns. Your aunt is going to get mad at me for not bringing you home."

He planted a kiss on Tajel's forehead.

After talking for a few more minutes, Chief left the apartment, making sure the door was locked on his way out. Sasha went over to Danielle, who had made herself scarce while Chief was there, and the two of them headed to the couch to give Tajel and me some privacy.

"I should have waited—"

I was interrupted by Tajel's embrace. Her arms snaked around my mid-back, squeezing me firmly. "It's been a long night."

Tajel shivered and I could tell that she was scared. I decided to not voice my concern until later because I didn't want to make her uncomfortable or upset.

Tajel ran the tips of her fingers up and down my arms. "Can you stay the night?"

"What about Sasha? I thought she wanted to keep you company?"

Tajel whispered, "Sasha can't take care of me the way you can."

There was no need for Tajel to clarify. I was already feeling aroused. I hadn't ever been touched the way I instinctively knew Tajel would touch me. My sexual experience with women was limited, and during each of those encounters I was unable to fully enjoy myself since I was still denying who I was. Thinking of having sex with Tajel both excited and scared me. I liked her more than I wanted to admit. Accepting my feelings for her meant something. And most importantly, I wanted to be the only one taking care of her.

"We don't have to do anything, but—"

"I'll stay."

I watched as her eyes lit up, grateful that I said *yes*. I knew she'd be happy with me only holding her tonight and that meant a lot.

"Hey, I'd love to sit and chat but it's getting late," Danielle said, calling our attention away from each other.

Sasha snickered and pulled Danielle up from the couch. "Not even a glass of wine before we go?"

Sasha was teasing, but Danielle shook her head.

"All right. We're already out the door."

Not even a minute after Sasha and Danielle left, Tajel came over to me, interlocking our fingers as she faced me.

"Are you all right?" I asked.

"I'm fine."

I smiled, massaging her knuckles with my thumb. "You going to tell me what happened?"

Tajel kissed my cheek. In a soft, hushed tone she said, "Not tonight."

Tajel freed her fingers from mine and unfastened the belt of my coat. My heart drummed, and my clit did the same. Her hands explored the skin underneath my clothes, traveling from my hips up to the side of my abdomen. I closed my eyes, enjoying the circular motion of Tajel's thumb right below my breast.

I asked, "Are you sure?" I was already breathless. "I don't want you to do something out of—"

Tajel's lips met mine for a brief kiss. She pulled away before I could properly process what had happened.

"I only want to focus on us." She slid her hand under the collar of my coat. "No more questions unless you really need answers right now. I just need you to help remind me of why I fight so hard to be happy."

I nodded. I could do that. Tajel kissed me again, this time more sensually. I moaned into her mouth, tasting her desire for me. My arms dropped to her waist. Heat permeated my body as our lips melted together, and all I wanted was to feel her on top of me. Tajel began unbuttoning her pants, but I swatted her hand away before she could complete the task. I wanted to do it for her, and so I did.

Tajel slid my coat off my shoulders and it fell to the floor. "*Qué guapa eres.*"

I grinned as we kissed. I loved to hear her speaking Spanish. "You know how hot you sound?"

"It turns you on," she said.

I deepened our kiss, tangling my fingers into her hair. "*Siempre.*"

Swiftly and urgently, I tore most of her clothes off before we even made it to the bedroom. I was so wet, and I couldn't wait for more. I knew it would be a night to remember.

Chapter Nineteen
Tajel

"Are you sure?" I lingered by the door.

Arianna answered me by closing the door. Slowly, she stepped backward toward my bed, undoing the bun that kept her hair in place. Her thick hair fell in waves around her face, enhancing her beauty. Every motion of her body was mesmerizing. I exhaled shallowly. I couldn't control my heart rate and my hands were sweating. *Grow some balls*. Ridiculous of course, I only had lady parts. My clit throbbed, and my nipples stiffened at the intoxicating sight of her. She now stood in front of me in a matching pair of bra and panties and they looked as silky as the wetness between my thighs.

"Are you coming?" Arianna's tone was lustful.

The hesitant, unsure part of Arianna that drove me mad, was no longer present. Arianna expelled so much confidence and sexuality. The modest way she kept her emotions at bay before was now engulfed by boldness and desire.

Arianna had already removed most of my clothes, leaving on only a bra and matching blue briefs. She waited for me on the edge of my bed, her thighs rubbing against the fabric of my comforter. *Fuck, she is taunting me*. I slinked toward her and wove my fingers through her hair. Arianna closed her eyes, her head following the movements of my fingers.

She drifted closer to me. I leaned in to plant a kiss on her neck. I used my fingers to trace circular designs onto the skin of her shoulders, gradually descending to her forearms and wrists. Arianna shuddered and bit her lip. I inhaled her scent, a mild lavender that emanated from her pores.

Placing my hands gently at the curves of her hips, I spoke softly into her ear, "How badly do you want me?"

Arianna's smile warmed my heart. *"Te quiero mal."*

Instantaneously, goosebumps emerged all over my body. I went in for a kiss, but Arianna decided to be playful, swerving her head back a few inches to avoid my lips. I grinned and tried again, and again, I missed. A chuckle escaped Arianna's mouth. Our eyes locked, and the heat between us flared, burning away any remaining doubts.

On the third attempt I caught her lips, and she put her hands on either side of my face, stroking the skin at my jawline. Electricity zipped through my veins when our bodies met. She used my neck to drag me closer to her, deepening our kiss. When our lips parted, I pressed my forehead against hers. We listened to our breathing for a few minutes, enjoying the momentary pause. I was wet, and I knew Arianna had to be as well. There was no reason to rush this moment. *Patience.* I twisted her around and laid her on my bed. I separated myself from her long enough to reach into my nightstand and grab my stethoscope.

"Qué estás haciendo?"

Her use of Spanish shouldn't have surprised me, but it did in that moment, and I couldn't help but giggle. *"Qué?"*

"What are you doing, silly?"

"I want to listen to your heart." I stuck the earbuds of the stethoscope in my ears and steadied myself on the bed.

"Now?"

I ignored the goofy look she gave me. I pressed the stethoscope against the skin on her chest. Right away, I heard a solid, rhythmic beat. Maybe I was being a little cocky, but I wanted to quicken the pace of her heart.

"You are very sexy." Arianna's cheeks flushed at my words, and her heartbeat accelerated. I dragged my lips against the outside of her ear. "I really want to taste you."

Arianna closed her eyes and smiled. She pulled the stethoscope off me and tossed it to the floor. "You got what you wanted, now give me what I want."

My lips inched down the high curve of her neck and Arianna gasped when I reached her collarbone. She extended her neck, giving me more space to give her exactly what she wanted. The salt of her skin mixed well with the lingering lavender scent.

Wrapping my hands around Arianna's thighs I lifted her upward and moved her further back on the bed. I crawled on top of her, exploring her thighs and then her pelvis with my lips.

Arianna squirmed, exhaling softly. "God, you're too much."

Her words goaded me on, and my hands traveled up her abdomen, only stopping at her breasts. My fingertips brushed her nipple, causing Arianna to moan loudly. Her thighs tightened, so I had to use my knee to keep her legs from closing.

"Don't you dare," I warned her playfully.

"Fuck...but I need to cum right now."

"No, you don't." I kissed her cheek. "Your body is just overwhelmed from never having such a great lover before now."

I straddled her. Arianna slapped my arm playfully. I laughed and returned my attention to Arianna's neck, tickling her skin with my tongue. She giggled and tried to get out from under me. Our teasing soon ended, both of us breathless from our laughter.

Arianna fingers smoothed away a stray strand of hair from my face. "I can't believe I'm with you...like this."

I couldn't wait any longer. I leaned in, capturing her lips in a passionate kiss. Arianna fumbled with the clasp of my bra, successfully unhooking it after a few failed attempts. I couldn't blame her; our kiss was worth concentrating on. Feeling a bit assertive, I tossed the covers off the bed and pried her legs apart again and then my hand slithered up her inner thigh.

I wanted to make our time together last, so I moved my hand back up to her left breast, squeezing it and sliding my tongue over its rigid nipple. From the corner of my eye, I noticed Arianna's hands clenching my sheets. Deciding her other breast was lonely, I shifted, capturing her right nipple with my lips. Arianna groaned, lightly tugging at my hair to bring our mouths together for another kiss.

Her lips swelled with the intensity of our kiss and I could feel the rush of adrenaline coursing through my body. I wanted her. I wanted her right now. Gradually, I made my way to her center, leaving a trail of kisses in my wake. My tongue grazed the hem of her clit and Arianna hips shot up. A deep, throaty groan was all I heard outside of the pounding in my ears.

Arianna's hips rotated with the twirling movements of my tongue. I gripped her thighs, sucking her clit into my mouth. The taste of her pink flesh sent my own into a spiral of heated desire. Wetness flowed out of her in ways I'd never seen from another woman. The thought of me making her this wet made my own thighs clamp together in pleasure.

"Oh...I'm almost there."

I knew what to do next. I slid my middle finger in and out of her, taking full control of her clit with my mouth and flicking my tongue upward repetitively. She cried out, her body twisting in ecstasy. Arianna came quickly and forcefully, her juices squirting into my mouth before I had the chance to move. Not that I wanted to move. I continued to penetrate her with my finger as she trembled from the urgency to orgasm again. She tightened against me. Fluid flooded around my fingers as she came again. I slowed my pace and moved myself to her side. I kissed her lips to let her taste herself, trying to regain control of my breathing. We did not speak right away.

Arianna was breathing heavily. "Gosh. Maybe we should put a towel underneath me next time."

I laughed. The sheets were truly soaked. "So, there will be a next time?"

"You are not funny," she grumbled.

"Yes I am." I kissed her cheek and wrapped my arm around her waist. "I'm definitely available for a next time."

I laid my head on her chest as she played with the curls of my hair. "Don't go falling asleep on me. I still owe you an orgasm or two."

I lifted my head to look at her. " Tonight was about you."

Arianna gave me a serious look. "Tonight is about us."

"Yeah," I agreed quietly. "Can I just be held for now?"

Arianna smiled, and I placed my head back on her chest.

Of all the women I'd ever slept with, none ever wanted to please me like I pleased them. I had many orgasms in my life, but half of them were caused by masturbation. The rest occurred when I heard the orgasms of the women I was fucking at the time. Clearly, Arianna was a giver.

"Next time, it will be you first." Arianna kissed the top of my head. "I would like to treat your body the same way you just treated mine."

I smiled, but I still felt a little uncomfortable. Shutting my eyes, I thought of the intimacy we just shared. I truly liked Arianna and did not want to fuck this up over fear and a closed mind. Listening to her heartbeat I slipped into a relaxing sleep. I decided to focus on right now. Right now, I liked the way I felt.

If I kept my head screwed on right I would be able to keep her. Just one issue. Well, maybe two issues: either I might mess this up or my uncle could stand in the way. Tomorrow I needed to overcome self-doubt and my fears. After that, I would need to win my uncle's support. How would that happen? Not a clue, but it was a something to reach for.

Chapter Twenty
Arianna

Two months had passed, and things between Tajel and me had yet to die down. We dated in secret, not wanting to expose our relationship, especially to Chief. I was comfortable with our discretion and saw no reason to shake things up.

"I can't believe Tajel hasn't chewed you out for eating her chips and dip." Felipe dug into the open bag on the table. "She would beat my ass if I did."

I rolled my eyes as he took a bite of a chip. "Tajel already knows you eat her chips and that you replace them."

Felipe started coughing. He covered his mouth with his hand until the coughing subsided. "She does?"

I laughed at his reaction, and then drew his attention to the chip crumbs on his moustache. He began wiping them away, and a look of embarrassment overtook his features. We were sitting on the couch in the break room watching the television on mute. Felipe scanned the room as a few of our coworkers passed us heading to their sleeping quarters. His body language suddenly changed, and he seemed uncomfortable. I scrutinized this shift in his demeanor, which did not go unnoticed by him. It only made him appear more uneasy.

"I... I was wondering…" Felipe scratched the back of his head trying to seem nonchalant.

"What is it?"

"I'm getting to it." He smiled awkwardly and then I realized what was coming. "I thought...since you're new here… I mean... we are all friends here… "

He closed his eyes and gulped.

"You want to go out sometime?"

Damn. I did not see this coming. I should have, though. Tajel warned me this would happen. It was painful. I heard someone clear their throat behind us, and I turned to see Tajel with her arms crossed over her chest. Her icy gaze was directed at Felipe, but it softened when she saw me. I hoped she wouldn't react harshly. Felipe didn't know about our relationship.

I lowered my head. I knew I should have listened to Tajel, but I had been too focused on keeping our relationship secret. She, however, was always more focused on us. She looked at me and then at her bag of chips on the table. Tajel walked around the couch to snatch a few chips from the bag. Her curly hair was swept up into a huge bun, and I could tell she was upset even though she was trying to pretend she wasn't.

"Am I interrupting you two?"

Felipe slid to the opposite end of the couch, rubbing his hands against his thighs. "Nah."

He wore a quizzical expression as he studied Tajel and me. Tajel was content, tossing chips into her mouth with her eyes glued to the television. But there was tension in the corner of her eyes and I bit my lip worrying that she might let her anger erupt at any moment. I smiled weakly at Felipe and we all sat on the couch in uncomfortable silence until Tajel unexpectedly stood a few minutes later.

"I'm still tired." She walked toward our sleeping quarters and the impulse to chase after her was strong.

"Wait." I jumped up, forgetting that we were at the station.

"Castaldi." Chief's booming voice sounded as though it had emerged from thin air.

Shit.

If Tajel was curious about why Chief was calling my name, she did not stick around to find out. She continued to our quarters. I struggled to swallow the saliva pooling in my mouth. *Don't freak out. He didn't see anything.* I smiled as best I could as he approached me.

"Chief."

"You have a moment?"

I nodded and followed him to his office.

"Take a seat." He gestured to the empty chair in front of his desk.

As he made his way around his desk to his oversized chair, my feet tapped the ground nervously. "Is everything all right, sir – uh, Chief?"

He smiled, never taking his eyes off me. "I'm fine. Are you?"

"Yes, Chief. Of course."

I could tell he did not believe me.

"I called you in here because I just wanted to see how you were adjusting." He casually flipped through a few papers on his desk.

I cleared my throat. "I'm still learning, but I'm quite comfortable finding my way around Portland."

"Well, everyone seems to love you, including Tajel. That's rare."

I needed to be careful going forward from here. There was no rule against coworkers dating, but I still thought it was smarter not to expose my relationship with Tajel.

I Belong with Her

"Well...to be honest... We did not start off too great." *Why did I say that? Now he will think Tajel has done something wrong.* "I can be critical and she's easygoing like you."

"But you two are fine now?" he asked.

"Yes. She's an amazing partner and a great friend."

He stopped thumbing through the paperwork on his desk. "My wife enjoyed your company the last time you came over. It would make her happy if you came again for dinner."

"Sure thing." I spoke with a smile, but I was sure I was going to faint. I couldn't say *no*. That would be too suspicious.

"All right, you are dismissed. I'm glad things between you and Tajel are working out."

As I left Chief's office and walked back through the break room trying to control the urge to vomit, Felipe approached me.

"So, was that a *no* on going out with me because I'm not your type, or because you and Tajel are together?"

"Are you being serious right now?" I held my chest, still feeling nauseated, and sped away from him not wanting to have this conversation at work.

He followed me to the kitchen, where there was no one else in sight.

I sucked in a breath. "I don't know where you came up with that idea, but I don't—"

"Hey, hey! Why are you being so defensive? Relax. Tajel's my friend and I'm happy—"

"We're not together," I growled, immediately regretting my words.

I closed my eyes and sighed. I couldn't keep it a secret from Felipe any longer. And I hated lying.

175

"Tajel and I... are seeing each other."

Felipe rubbed the back of his neck. "Damn. She heard me asking you out. If I would have known..."

"It's not your fault. It's my fault."

"But you—"

"She told me you liked me. I didn't listen. I could have avoided this."

"Then you should go to talk to her."

Thank goodness he was so cool about this. "Thanks. I really appreciate this."

He nodded. "Don't worry. We never had this conversation."

I smiled and went to find Tajel.

*

Tajel

I paced around the room telling myself not to take this so seriously. It's not like I had to worry about anything. With a bisexual woman that could be a different story. While I continued to pace, the door opened, and Arianna came into view.

"Hey," she said.

"Hi," I responded coolly.

"Felipe knows." Arianna shut the door behind her and leaned against it. "I freaked out."

Hearing her say that upset me. "Why?"

"Why?" She sighed and stared at the ceiling. "Because...that could expose us. I don't want the entire world knowing about us."

"It wouldn't be the entire world. Only the people that matter."

Shaking her head, she said, "I'm not ready for that."

"Then when?" My voice was raw and scratchy. "Do you not see this as a serious relationship?"

"Of course, I do!" She ran her hands through her hair, stopping at the back of her head. "I thought you didn't want to tell anyone, especially your uncle."

"What if I did?" Arianna looked away, and I regretted my question. "Never mind."

"Please don't shut me out." Arianna came over to me, a pleading look in her eyes. "I'm sorry I didn't listen to you. This is all new to me."

I nodded.

Arianna kissed me, almost making me forget what we were talking about. "Can you give me time? Let's seriously discuss what this could mean for the both of us."

I could be patient. I listened as Arianna told me what happened with Felipe. I smiled. "I'll talk to him."

Before our lips could reconnect we got a page from dispatch. Our romance would have to wait until later. Right now, we had a life to save.

Chapter Twenty-One
Tajel

"Com 2, Medic 112 is on-scene."

Arianna and I hopped out of the rig, meeting at the back doors. She pulled the gurney out as I unstrapped the stretcher. We were in front of Voodoo Doughnuts, a popular place even I went to on occasion.

"Tajel!" One of the employees named Toni came rushing out in a panic. "It's Madeline."

Automatically, I took the lead. "What happened?"

"She came in and she just fainted."

Arianna ordered for everyone to give us space to work and then she bent down over her, checking for a pulse. "She has a pulse."

I nodded and moved to the other side of the patient. I addressed Toni, "Did she fall?"

"No."

I repositioned her head to check her airway. "She eat anything?"

"No!" Toni cried. "Damn it, Tajel! She walked in, barely standing up straight, and then she passed out."

"How did she seem?" Arianna asked. She was now doing a full assessment. "Tajel..."

I looked over to see Arianna holding the extended arm of the patient. There were what looked like several years' worth of needle marks all over her arms. Although, to my recollection our patient had been using for less than a year.

"She was with..." Toni decided not to continue.

"What?" I growled, looking up at her for a second.

"I saw her climb out of Tyler's car."

My body stiffened upon hearing my brother's name. "Okay."

"Whoa!" Arianna exclaimed. "Turn her or she will aspirate."

We maneuvered our patient onto her left side as she began vomiting.

"Her breathing is shallow."

Once she finished vomiting, we returned her to her back. "I'm going to intubate through her nose."

I measured my nasal adjunct to help with her airway, placing it from the tip of her nose to her earlobe to measure it properly. Right away, I placed the hose inside her nasal cavity, twisting against her resistance.

"I'm going to give her succinylcholine to temporarily paralyze her if we're intubating."

Arianna handed the BVM to me. I began assisting our patient with her breathing. The nasal hose was not giving her enough oxygen.

"Let's go to our original –plan – we should intubate," Arianna suggested, pulling out the intubation kit.

"Will she be all right?" someone asked.

I set up an intraosseous infusion, drilling the IO needle through the tibia of her calf bone. Setting up the line, I added Narcan to the list of drugs to use. A few minutes later, the fire crew was positioning our gurney closer.

I watched as her saturation rose, holding my hand out. "Wait on intubating. She's improving."

People gathered around us, their camera phones capturing our work. The impulse to slap their phones from their hands was ballooning inside of me, but I held it in as best as I could. *What is wrong with people?* They were violating our patient's right to privacy. When she could breathe adequately on her own I placed a non-rebreather over her face, giving her oxygen.

"You ready?" I asked Arianna.

"Yeah."

The fire crew helped us place the patient on the gurney and into the rig.

Arianna finished taking her vitals. "She is hypotensive… weak pulse. But saturations are improving."

I administered a second dose as Arianna packed our jump bag. "We need to go."

I hopped out of the back of the rig and sprinted to the driver side to alert dispatch we were leaving the scene. I turned on the sirens. The hospital was five minutes away.

"She's waking up!" Arianna yelled.

"You need one of us?" the fire captain asked.

Arianna nodded. "In case she wakes up and is combative."

The fire captain agreed, telling one of his paramedics to hop in.

"See you there." He closed the door for us.

My adrenaline was pumping, and I was sure our patient's adrenaline was pumping too from the drug we gave her. As soon as I parked in front of the emergency room, I opened the back door to find our patient struggling with Arianna and the fire paramedic.

"Hey, hey, Madeline. It's me."

"Tajel…shit." She began crying, grabbing onto me as if I was her lifeline. "I fucked up!"

" You don't need to apologize to me." I squeezed her hand. "Don't talk. Just relax."

She had pulled the nasal hose from her nose. That's what happened most of the time after we gave our patients Narcan. Arianna and I pulled the gurney out of the back of the rig. We wheeled her inside of the hospital where a doctor and a few nurses met us. I gave the doctor my report, and by the time I was through I looked around but found no sign of Arianna. I decided to check for her outside, and she was there, cleaning the gurney.

"I can do that," I offered.

She shrugged. "I figured you'd want to stay and make sure she was okay."

I was appreciative that she respected that I might have wanted to stay behind. I climbed into the back of the rig, sitting beside her. I closed the door for some privacy. Arianna continued to clean the rig and I decided to help by placing the I.V. lines in the needle bins. Once we were done we both took off our gloves and sat down.

"Thank you for trusting me."

Arianna only nodded. Something was wrong. She never spoke with only gestures.

"Did I do something?" Shaking her head, Arianna started to stand until I grabbed her hand, stopping her. "What is it?"

Arianna looked at me with concern. "That was very intense."

"It was." I combed my fingers through her hair. "Talk to me."

"I lost a brother to a heroin overdose. He choked on his own vomit."

My heart ached alongside Arianna's. Every day I feared I would get the call or be the one trying to save my brother's life because of his addictions. Arianna never talked much about her family and never about a brother.

"I'm sorry."

That always seemed to be the only thing a person could say after hearing something like that. I wanted to give her more than *sorry*.

"We can only do so much as medics and sisters. The rest is in their own hands."

I watched a tear fall from her eye, and I wiped it with my thumb before she had the chance to do it herself. Arianna searched my eyes. I would not give her pity. She saw the way my brother looked that night. The path he was taking. Instead of saying anything, Arianna leaned the side of her head against my shoulder as I reached for her hand to link our fingers.

We sat quietly until Arianna felt better. "Let's clear out of here."

Walking up to the front of our rig, Felipe and Rogan approached Arianna and me.

"How was the call?" Rogan asked.

We just looked at them blankly, and so they both made a move to leave.

"Yo, Felipe." Felipe turned to me nervously. He told Rogan he'd meet him at their rig. "I'm not upset about anything. I thought you should know."

"Oh...oh. Cool." Felipe smiled.

"Keep what you know to yourself," I added.

"Please," Arianna pleaded.

He nodded. "Sure thing."

Felipe walked off and we went back to our rig. Dispatch told us to head back to the station. On the drive back we sat quietly, hardly making any sounds at all. We headed back to our sleeping quarters together. There was a little over an hour left in our shift, so I thought it might be a good idea to get some rest. I closed the door and turned to discover Arianna's lips smashing into mine.

I wrapped my arms around her. My fingers trembled trying to undo the buttons to her shirt. My body and mind craved her as if I'd been starving for the last 24 hours and she was a steaming entrée. Yanking off her shirt after all her buttons were undone, I kissed along her neck.

"Wait...Arianna." Her fingers were already at my pants. "We have to slow down."

We never had sex at work before. It was a line we agreed never to cross. I told Arianna that we'd have to be quiet, and she agreed.

"Babe, you don't have to be silent." She narrowed her eyes at me and I continued, "Not that I'm complaining."

"I'm not that loud."

"I beg to differ," I smirked.

I straddled her when we made it to the bed, pinning her down. "You should know the game by now. Whoever is the strongest wins."

"Yeah...well..." Arianna continued to struggle underneath me. "That mindset will make you lose eventually."

"I'll be waiting for eventually to arrive." I kissed her quickly and then tried to lift myself off her only to be yanked back down. "You still want to play?"

She shook her head and then I leaned down, capturing her lips as my body eclipsed hers. The kiss was deep and passionate, making my clit throb. A knock at the door prevented us from going further. I turned my head toward the sound and was thankful I remembered to lock the door. I climbed off Arianna quickly, telling her to get under the covers and pretend to be asleep. I put on my pants and took a deep breath before opening the door.

It was my uncle.

"I would have called your room phone but seems it's not on the hook."

"Sorry about that," I apologized.

"I would like to talk to the both of you."

"Sure thing." I closed the door after my uncle left and turned to Arianna who was sitting upright in the bed.

"You think he heard us?"

"No, Arianna." I tried not to sound upset. "I'm sure he wants to review our last call."

Arianna sighed. "Sorry."

"For?"

"I know you hate it when I do that." Arianna stood up and grabbed the shirt she had thrown on the floor. "Our relationship does matter to me."

I caught the end of the phone that was dangling from its cord and put it back on the receiver. "Maybe it's time to talk about where we're both at and what we want."

"Sounds good to me." Arianna gave me a quick peck on the lips and I smiled. "I forgot to tell you, your uncle invited me to dinner tonight. I couldn't say *no*."

I was not thrilled. "It's my uncle's birthday."

"What's wrong with that?"

"You'll see."

We both laughed and exited the room, making our way to my uncle's office where he would either lecture us for the choices we made dealing with our patient, or approve of our methods. We would have to wait to find out.

Chapter Twenty-Two
Arianna

I can at least admit to myself I was a bit nervous. The first time I went to Chief's house for dinner the circumstances were different. I wasn't sleeping with Tajel then, and now we were keeping our relationship secret. It honestly never crossed my mind I would be coming to a second dinner or that I would be dating his niece.

I kept trying to remind myself not to be obvious in my affection for Tajel in front of Chief. I knew that sometimes I could get carried away, but I certainly couldn't allow that to happen at dinner. *Damn it, he is going to find out.* There was no way out of this. My train of thought was interrupted when someone knocked on my car window. Luckily, I did not have to get Danielle to drop me off since I finally bought a car last month.

Tajel was standing outside of my car. I opened my door and she helped me climb out.

"Why are you standing out here?" I asked.

"Waiting for you." She stepped closer to me, noticing my nervousness. "You need to relax. Would it be such a terrible thing if he found out?"

"You really want to test that theory?"

Tajel's demeanor dampened. "Just a foolish thought."

I immediately regretted my words. I knew she wasn't enthusiastic about keeping our relationship secret. "It's not foolish. I'm glad you want to tell him and everyone else that we're together. But like you said, maybe we should first discuss it ourselves."

"You're probably right." Tajel looked at the house. "We should go inside, or my uncle will start to get suspicious."

When we entered the house Tajel's aunt was the first to greet me.

"Arianna." Laura hugged me tightly, and then whispered into my ear, "I'm sorry. My husband thought it was a brilliant idea to invite you."

I frowned, remembering that Chief said it was Laura who wished to invite me to dinner. *Shit. I don't like this.*

"I can take your coat," Tajel offered.

I shimmied out of my coat and handed it to Tajel to hang on the rack.

"Welcome again," Chief greeted me.

"Chief, thanks for the invitation."

"I'm Roosevelt outside of work. Wife's orders. Come and sit." Roosevelt motioned to the dining table. "Tajel, get her a glass of wine."

Tajel did as she was told, going into the kitchen to get the wine. We went to the dining room as she returned with a bottle of Merlot and poured some into my glass. Tajel's eyes connected with mine for only a few seconds and I smiled inwardly.

Roosevelt sat beside his wife. "You've been here for about four months now, Arianna. How are things coming along?"

Tajel took a seat across from me. It was too difficult to avoid looking at her. *Damn, she looked so sexy.* Her attire was casual – a designer shirt, jeans, and boots. Her bare arms were exposed, and I wanted to reach out and touch her skin. I pushed thoughts of Tajel's skin out of my mind.

"I've adjusted well. Learning the area has been pretty fun." I took a sip of my wine. "I've made some friends."

"I've noticed." Roosevelt chuckled, not a sound I heard often. "No offense, but my niece doesn't make friends that easily. Especially on the first try."

"Neither do I," I interjected. "I guess we just fit."

"Seems you do." His tone was different this time. It felt ominous.

He was looking at Tajel. I was growing more nervous as time passed. I didn't think on it for too long, because there was a knock at the door and then the sound of someone shouting. The voice belonged to a man.

"Let me in!" More banging at the door. "Come on, unc'!"

Tajel's face blanched. "What is he doing here?"

"Relax, Tajel." He stood up. "Excuse me."

Tajel ran her hands through her hair and as soon as her uncle turned through the small hallway that led to the front door, she whispered to me, "My brother will remember you."

"Don't think so negatively, you two." Laura joined her husband at the front door.

"I should never have come. I should have lied to get out of this." I knew coming here was risky, but I couldn't refuse the invitation.

"Hey," Tajel's voice captured my attention, "this was never meant to stay a secret. Either you want to be with me or you don't. But if you want, we can deny it if you don't want to say anything."

Tajel was giving me an opportunity to pull out of our relationship. Denying our relationship was denying her. I now realized how vulnerable she was when it came to us. I never realized before this moment how much power I truly had when it came to her. Being so wrapped up in my own fears, I had completely forgotten about Tajel's. She feared losing me, feared rejection from her uncle, and feared his disappointment.

Tajel's aunt and uncle returned from the hallway with Tyler stringing along behind them. I noticed Tajel's body tense up, and I was worried that the success of the dinner was in my hands. She closed her eyes and lowered her head.

Tyler wore a huge grin on his face. "*Hey, chico.*"

"*Chico* means boy," Tajel snarled. "She's a woman."

"I bet you know how womanly—"

"Tyler! Don't make me throw you out," Laura threatened him with a withering glare.

Roosevelt took his seat and his wife did the same.

"Tyler, sit beside your sister, please," Tajel's uncle directed.

"You don't want me to sit beside you?" His question was aimed at me.

"Leave her alone." Tajel's voice was becoming as gravely as sandpaper.

"I want to hear her ask me to sit somewhere else." Tyler winked at me. "You mind if I sit by you?"

I was acutely uncomfortable. Before I could answer him, Tajel slammed her hands on the table, using them to pivot herself upward. "Get the fuck away from her."

Judging by the look on Roosevelt's face, I wasn't sure if I should stay much longer. Dinner hadn't even been served yet, and I was beginning to think it wouldn't happen at all.

"Tajel, sit down," Roosevelt ordered.

"Why is he here?" Tajel ignored his request, her eyes on her uncle. I couldn't tell who she was more upset with.

"It's about time you both reconnected."

"So, you're choosing to do this now?" Tajel asked, doubtful of her uncle's intentions.

Tyler grinned dazedly. "I'll sit next to you, sis...so we can bond."

They did look so much alike. My brother and I looked completely different from one another, but Tajel and her brother shared the same thick, curly hair and gray eyes. As far as their relationship went, it reminded me of my brother's and mine. *This is too much.*

"I should go." I hadn't realized I said it aloud until all eyes were looking at me.

Tyler attempted to hug Tajel, but she shoved him away. "Nah... I'm still curious as to how my—"

"I'm not in the mood to stay here either." Tajel readied herself to leave. "I'll walk you to your car."

Tyler started laughing and the next words from his mouth destroyed any hopes I had left of a pleasant evening. "I ruined y'all's romantic night again?"

My body went rigid.

"Tyler, I think it—"

Roosevelt interrupted his wife, saying, "That is Tajel's partner."

"Partner...as in work?" Tyler asked, a bit surprised.

"Uncle, this is not the night," Tajel pleaded with Chief.

"You don't say," Tyler mocked without any sense of self-awareness.

Roosevelt stood.

"Honey, let these ladies go home. Clearly tonight was not a good night." Laura was trying to help, but it didn't seem that anything said now would make anything better.

"Why would you assume that these two are romantically involved?" Roosevelt pried, refusing to let go of the subject.

"Because," Tyler pointed at me, uncaring of our situation, "she's the hot Latina I saw with Tajel the night I was at her house. Before you came. They were dressed up and probably on their way to undressing if I wasn't already there."

Tajel went over to where Tyler was sitting and kicked his chair out from underneath him. "Just get the fuck out!"

"Tajel!" her aunt called her name in shock.

He managed to get on his knees before she punched him in the face.

"Fucking bitch," Tyler scowled.

"I hate you."

Everyone became silent.

I felt certain I was missing something about their relationship that Tajel hadn't yet told me. While tears began to form in her eyes, Tyler stopped smiling and sat on the floor for a minute in disbelief. Even he seemed shocked.

"You don't have to be so dramatic." Tyler rubbed his face where the blow from Tajel's fist landed and then he stood.

"I won't let you come into my life and ruin things for me again," Tajel swore. "You're no longer my brother. I'm not coming to your rescue anymore."

"Tajel, he's not well—"

"Aunt, don't enable him." Tajel finally calmed down long enough to remember that I was still in the room. "I'm sorry."

She was apologizing to me. Her pain was palpable, and my heart ached to see it.

"So, it's true. You two are sleeping together?" Roosevelt questioned in a dangerous tone.

Tajel closed her eyes, waiting. She was waiting for to me to decide our future. I understood why. I knew how she felt about us, now she needed to know how I felt. It was difficult to say anything, especially with the intense look Roosevelt was giving both of us. I was made mute and wishing I wasn't in this situation. *If only I could go back.* It was impossible, I knew. I had to make a choice. I realized then that I'd never be prepared to answer his question, but the words found me and spilled out.

"I love your niece."

Tajel's eyes overflowed with tears. My chest tightened, and I was thoroughly nauseated. Had I really said that? It wasn't the fact that I said it to him, or aloud, it was that I couldn't believe that I had said it at all. I meant it, though. I knew that much at least. Minutes passed, and I was growing anxious waiting for a response.

Laura appeared at my side, hugging me before I could resist. "Oh, I'm so happy for you two."

Tajel's expression softened. "I love you, too."

Tajel offered her hand to me and I took it, walking out beside her and proud to be in love for the first time in my life.

Chapter Twenty-Three
Tajel

I followed Arianna out of my uncle's home, unsure of what to say.

"How about you follow me home?" Arianna asked. "Just in case your brother tries to show up at your place again."

Arianna was nervous. She also wanted to talk. So did I.

"I'll meet you at your place."

On the drive to Arianna's place I thought of what I should say. I had flipped out in front of her and displayed a side of myself I never wanted anyone to see. Usually, I kept my temper in check, but my brother was great at finding my triggers. He still affected me. When we were kids we were so close, and now we were practically strangers. Time and time again, I tried to reach out to my brother to bring him back, but it never worked. It always seemed to make things worse. Before the night he appeared at my apartment with two of his friends, it had been a couple of years since I had seen him. The time before that night I thought would be the last. And now he shows up to destroy everything once again.

I pulled into the parking lot of Arianna's apartment and I parked the car. She was waiting for me at the top of the staircase that led to her door.

I jogged up the steps. "You couldn't wait for me?"

Arianna smiled. "I knew you'd get here, eventually."

Soon, her smile vanished and was replaced by a look of concern. Arianna unlocked her door and stepped inside first. I followed her, and as I entered the apartment I noticed the inside of my throat felt like rubber.

"Is Danielle here?" I asked, scanning the apartment.

"I think if she was here you would know by now."

"I guess you're right." I wanted to be honest with Arianna. I didn't do well with relationships in the past, so I didn't know how to deal with my feelings. "I'm sorry for my behavior."

"Don't apologize." Her hands gripped my arms. "I can see how much pain and grief your brother has caused you."

"Did I scare you?" I wanted to know the truth, but I was terrified of her answer.

"I was scared of you shutting down on me afterwards. I know what it feels like to be at the mercy of my emotions."

It was tough to swallow. No one liked a light shined on their faults, but I was more concerned about something else. "Did you mean what you said? That you, oh... that you..."

"That I love you?" Arianna finished what I was struggling to say. She cupped the sides of my face with her hands. "Tajel Lorraine Pierce, I'm in love with you. I meant that. Did you mean it?"

Do I love Arianna? Everything between us happened so suddenly, but somewhere in the middle of it all Arianna had become the one person I knew I couldn't live without. "Yes, I meant it. I'm in love with you."

Arianna sighed in relief. I kissed her. I was overheating, and I needed to feel her fingers inside of me. I could see in her eyes when our lips parted that she wanted the same thing. My hands explored the perfect curves of her hips. Desire flooded my body. I was wet and throbbing, and Arianna had yet to touch me where I needed it most.

When our lips grazed one another's, I shuddered. "God, I want you."

"Make love to me," Arianna begged.

My hands played with the buttons on her shirt. I smiled. "I can't stop thinking about how you said that you love me."

Though I hadn't touched Arianna's flesh, her breath hitched as if my fingers were stroking her clit. I touched my lips to hers once again, and goosebumps covered every inch of my skin. Arianna gasped into my mouth, and I couldn't wait another moment. I returned to the task of unbuttoning her shirt to bare her stomach.

"Stay the night." Arianna's voice was soft but demanding.

"I'm not going anywhere."

I finished opening her shirt to reveal her breasts. I was about to lower my mouth to take a nipple, but Arianna shook her head. Instead, she grabbed at my belt buckle, twisting and yanking me by the belt to follow her. I obliged.

When we were inside of her room, I slammed the door shut with my foot. My hands were all over her breasts in a matter of seconds. It was nearly impossible to slow myself down, but I knew I needed to. There was no reason to rush this moment. We slept together many times before but never quite like this. Tonight, we were open and honest.

Arianna unbuckled my jeans as I kicked off my boots. My jeans slid down my waist and she grinned. "I love seeing you in briefs. And that shirt."

"You want me to keep them on?"

She yanked my shirt up and over my head in response, and then removed the band that held up my hair. "I love it when your hair is down."

I Belong with Her

Reaching behind her, I unhooked her bra and tossed it to the floor. Arianna then pulled my sports bra over my head. The only thing left on her was her pants, which she was already removing hurriedly. I pressed my skin against hers when we were finally naked and kissed her again. Time slipped away from us as Arianna took my hand and led me to her bed. I climbed on top of her, straddling her legs while kissing the skin on her neck. She moaned loudly. I wasn't going to hold back.

Arianna squirmed and gasped as I flicked my tongue against her earlobe. "Fuck. Feel how wet I am."

I did just that. I slid my middle finger over her clit and felt her body begin to tremble.

"Oh..." Arianna whimpered. "Fuck."

Giving her what I knew she wanted, my finger grazed her pink flesh again and her hips buckled under the pleasure. "You feel so fucking amazing."

I couldn't move my fingers away from her clit. It felt so good and it sounded as if she were really enjoying it, so how could I? My lips continued their torture of Arianna as I sucked on her earlobe. That only made her wetter. My finger slipped inside her. Arianna tightened around my finger, moaning while my thumb circulated around her mound. I began at a slow pace but switched it up every several strokes. I could feel my own wetness slide down my thighs and onto hers.

"Oh...God." Arianna hips rose and twisted, but I maintained momentum. "Oh...I'm going to cum."

Arianna's orgasm spilled its fluids around my fingers. She cried out my name and my thighs squeezed together, feeling the pleasure of my own orgasm. We both lay quietly together afterward.

"What the fuck was that?" Arianna asked breathlessly.

I chuckled. "That was nothing compared to what I'm about to do next."

We both shifted our heads to look at one another.

"You have more for me, huh?"

I smiled. "You know I aim to please."

And please her I did.

*

Arianna

I woke up first. Judging by the darkness outside it was most likely the middle of the night. We decided to nap after four hours of lovemaking. My head rested on Tajel's breast while my arm snaked around her waist. Tajel's change in breathing let me know that she was awake.

"I love this," I whispered.

"Hmm?"

"Just...being like this." I lifted my head up, gazing into her eyes. "With you."

We kissed slowly, Tajel's hand cupping my cheek.

"My body still hasn't recovered," I admitted.

"Hungry?"

I shrugged. "Maybe a little."

Tajel rubbed her eyes. "Let's get something to eat."

We got dressed in the dark, fumbling around for our clothes and still feeling a bit sleepy. When we opened the door, we found Sasha and Danielle sitting on the couch together watching a movie. *Awkward.* I was only able to find my underwear and tank top in the dark. Tajel was wearing her shirt and her briefs.

"Cute," Sasha snickered.

"You guys couldn't send us a text letting us know you were here?" Tajel asked, visibly irritated.

"Well," Danielle smiled, "you two seemed busy at the time—"

"Oh, my God," I gasped. "You heard us?"

"It's not like we listened by the door," Danielle argued.

"Sure."

Sasha's phone rang, and she answered it. "Hello? She's right here..." Sasha was clearly talking to either Tajel's uncle or aunt. "Damn... when?"

Everyone was focused on Sasha's conversation.

"We'll be there soon...okay." When she hung up she turned to Tajel with a serious look on her face, "Your brother tried to commit suicide. It doesn't sound good."

It looked as if all the blood in Tajel's face had disappeared. She went completely still and there was a blank look in her eyes.

"Come on, let's get dressed," I told Tajel.

"I can't go."

I used my hands to grab her face to force her to look at me. "Hey, look at me. This is not your fault."

"Yes, it is."

"No. Your brother let his addiction control him. You tried. I know how hard you pleaded with him." I ran my fingers through her curly hair. "What matters is that when he wakes up he will know you still love him. If you decide to be there."

"Were you there for your brother?"

"I gave up on him." I stifled the tears that were forming in the corners of my eyes. This wasn't about me. "You don't have to let him into your life. Just show up when he needs you. And he needs you now."

Tajel covered her face with her hands. "I told him I hated him."

I kissed her cheek. "That won't be the last thing he hears from you."

Tajel nodded.

"Here." Sasha brought the rest of Tajel's clothes out to her.

"We should hurry," Tajel said.

We both dressed quickly and made our way to the hospital.

Chapter Twenty-Four
Tajel

I was terrified. It was only last night that the birthday dinner in which my uncle found out the truth about my secret relationship with Arianna became a disaster.

"You can talk to me." Arianna kissed my shoulder as we sat together on a bench right outside the hospital. "We should go inside. It's cold."

The icy air made me shiver. I was sure we'd both get sick if we stayed another minute outside.

I was about to get up to go inside when Arianna stopped me, holding my hand tightly. "Sit."

I became even more aware of the temperature when I felt the heat of her hand. I was wearing a jacket and scarf, and Arianna wore the same. I knew the sooner I stopped resisting her the faster we could go inside. I sat back down.

She smiled sweetly. "This is not your fault."

"You say that but—"

"This is not your fault," she repeated. "Your brother cannot blame you for your parents' death any more than you can blame a woman for being raped because she looked too pretty."

I frowned. "That's not the same thing."

"The situation is not the same, that's true. You were a child who simply wanted to go to the movies. You convinced your parents to take you and they were killed in a car accident. You were not the drunk driver in the other car. You are not to blame."

Arianna was right. I'd always known it wasn't really my fault, but I felt guilty anyway. My brother helped to make sure I continued to blame myself.

"You did not hand your brother that needle. You did not pressure him to take drugs or to drink his life away. All you've done is try to fight for your brother's future."

I agreed, but I was so nervous that I wanted to turn around and leave. My hands shook, and my heart was racing as we walked inside and waited for the elevator. Inside the elevator, it felt as if it was taking hours to reach the fourth floor. Arianna stepped out first when the doors opened and offered her hand to me. I took it without hesitation. I wasn't ashamed of our relationship. My uncle would have to accept this.

As we turned the corner heading to my brother's room, I heard someone call my name.

I turned to find myself in the arms of my sister, Brooklyn.

"Hello, again." She smiled at Arianna and then faced me. "So, our brother overdid it this time."

"Something like that." I didn't really feel chatty.

The three of us continued toward the room and I took Arianna's hand in mine again.

"You two look cute together," Brooklyn complimented.

Standing outside the door to my brother's room, I could hear my aunt and uncle arguing. Probably about us. I felt the urge to retreat, but I remained in place.

"Come on. You know Tyler will be happy—"

"You go in first," I insisted.

Brooklyn left Arianna and me alone in the hallway together. She turned to me and squeezed my hand. "Hey. "

"Hmm?"

"You are the fiercest woman I've ever known." Arianna knew what was making me hesitate at that door. "I know you don't feel ashamed about our relationship."

"Of course not," I swiftly responded. "I'm so in love with you."

"I will never doubt you."

Arianna kissed me, and I welcomed it openly. Only the sound of my uncle clearing his throat broke the spell of our moment together. I winced.

"Your sister said you were here."

Arianna reached for my hand again and squeezed it to show her support.

"I see what your brother said at dinner was true." Under my uncle's calm tone, I could detect anger inside of him. "Can I speak to you, privately?"

"Am I breaking any rules?" I asked. "Is being with Arianna violating any policies at work?"

I already knew the answer. We weren't doing anything wrong. I knew I would only be breaking my uncle's rules. He did not care about anyone else's relationship but mine. If Arianna had chosen to be with someone else at our station then he would simply remind her of keeping her relationship outside of work, but she was with me.

"Tajel..." My uncle started to say something, but he looked at Arianna and kept quiet instead.

"I came to see if he was okay." I was referring to Tyler, of course. "No matter what I say or feel at that moment...I don't know how not to care for him."

He was blocking my path to my brother's room. "Your aunt is emotional right now."

"I think I'll go see her." I didn't bother saying anything else. I pushed past my uncle and led Arianna into the room where my aunt waited beside the bed.

She rushed over to embrace me. "I am so glad you came."

"Thank Arianna, not me. I almost stayed away," I admitted.

She reached out for Arianna next, kissing her on the cheek. "Thank you for being here."

"She has definitely tamed my sister," Brooklyn teased, patting my head like I was still the little baby sister she remembered as a child.

"Did you know that these two were dating?" he asked Brooklyn in an accusatory tone.

"Uh...yeah. They came to my club." Brooklyn looked at me and received a hostile stare from our uncle. "What am I missing here?"

I spoke first, "Arianna's not only my girlfriend... she's also my partner at the station."

Brooklyn's eyes widened. "Oh. I see."

"Why can't you be happy for them?" my aunt asked, taking note of my uncle's anger.

"Because," my uncle growled, "I do not care if she is gay so long as she keeps it outside of my station."

It felt as if he had slapped me across my face. But his words did more than sting. I knew he would not like me dating Arianna, but I couldn't have imagined this would be his reason. My aunt's face drained of color, but that did not deter my uncle from continuing his argument.

"Don't think I haven't realized that you've known this entire time." He pointed a finger at his wife.

"Uncle, you need to stop now." Brooklyn was trying to defend me.

"Don't bother," I told her.

"Perhaps, I should go," Arianna whispered to me.

Aunt Laura shook her head. "My husband can leave."

I kissed my aunt's cheek and then stole a quick glance at my brother lying unconscious on the hospital bed. "Tell him that I hope that one day we can be brother and sister again."

She only nodded and narrowed her eyes at my uncle. When we walked out I took a deep breath, not realizing I had been holding it in for so long.

"I'm sorry." I cupped Arianna's face with the palm of my hand. I opened my mouth then closed it. I thought I would know what to say. I was wrong.

No other words were spoken. We walked together in silence knowing that this would not be the last of my uncle's distasteful attitude toward our relationship.

Chapter Twenty-Five
Tajel

"Seems I'll be working with Ms. Castaldi tonight." Manny, our field supervisor, approached Arianna and me with a smirk stretched across his face.

"What are you talking about?" I nearly growled.

He pointed back toward my uncle's office. "Talk to Chief."

"I'll do that." I smiled reassuringly at Arianna and then headed to my uncle's office.

I knocked on the door twice and loudly. I inhaled deeply and reminded myself to remain calm. He was still my boss.

"Come in," he said from the other side of the door.

I entered my uncle's office and found him sitting casually at his desk shuffling through a stack of paperwork.

"If you came in here thinking you can change my mind, you're dead wrong."

Relax. Breathe. "Can you tell me why?"

He lifted his head up from his papers to look at me. "I don't have to explain anything."

Was he trying to piss me off? I crossed my arms. "Actually, you do."

The blank expression on his face quickly morphed into a scowl. "Excuse me?"

"You do not have a valid, work-related reason to split us up. We've worked side by side together for the last four months without any problems."

"You will not be working with her tonight and that will be the end of this discussion."

"Then will I be working with her on our next shift?" I was not letting this go.

"We'll see."

"What the fuck do you mean we'll see?" I snapped.

My uncle rose from his chair, his normally large frame appearing even more threatening as his anger became more apparent. "Do you want a write-up?"

"Do you?" I shot back. "The moment you fucking knew Arianna and I were dating your attitude toward us changed. And let's not forget the comment you made at the hospital."

"Well..."

My uncle straightened his posture, keeping his anger stifled as much as he could.

"You will continue your partnership with her. One mistake...and I will separate you two." I was about to leave when he continued, "For tonight, you will have a two-day suspension. You came in here with a hostile and unprofessional attitude. Take the suspension. Or do you want to gamble and see if you can get out of marking your record?"

I really needed to work on my outbursts. "Can you switch Arianna with another partner? Manny has made inappropriate remarks to her before."

"There is no negative report on Manny."

I was disappointed in my uncle's inability to see Manny for what he was. "I told you about the things he said. You are both Chief and my uncle. Why are you acting as if you do not know what I'm talking about?"

My uncle's expression was uncaring. I knew what he was doing, but I couldn't believe he would sink this low in order to separate Arianna and me. There was no sense in commenting further on the subject. I already screwed myself for this shift. I headed for the door.

"I did not dismiss you." He watched as I turned to face him and then he added, "One mistake and I'll split you two up. Remember that."

My expression was grim, and I started biting the inside of my cheek. I had been telling myself that if I stayed silent I would win. He dismissed me, and I did not take my time leaving.

Arianna waited for me to draw near until she said anything. She noticed the look on my face. "Please tell me that I am not losing you as a partner?"

"You're not losing me as a partner." She relaxed, and I worried how she would feel after what I needed to tell her about Manny. "But, you will have to work with Manny for this shift."

It was as if I'd pulled the rug out from underneath her feet. "Oh."

"I think it might be my fault. I lost my cool."

"Don't do that. I'm proud of you." She used her fingers to raise my head to meet her gaze.

I was ashamed. "I got suspended."

"But, you accepted the suspension without argument. Would you have been about to do that a few months ago?"

I took a moment to consider her words. She was right.

"Come on, Ms. Castaldi. I don't have all day," Manny called to Arianna from across the station at the door of the ambulance bay.

"God, I really don't like that guy." I grabbed Arianna's hand. "If he does one thing, let me know and request to come back to the station."

Arianna eyed Manny. "I've dealt with men like Manny before, Tajel. I will be fine."

"One thing." I held my index finger up and stepped closer to her. "He does one thing, let me know."

I was happy when she nodded. I guess she could see the seriousness of my request. Manny strolled our way with a smug look on his face. I would not let him get to me.

I assured Arianna, "I'll pick you up."

"See you." She smiled and walked off with Manny.

Was it acceptable to think of the many ways I wanted to crush Manny's ego and balls? I pulled my phone from my pocket and sent a quick text to Sasha to let her know about my suspension. When I looked up from my phone I found my uncle watching me. I had no desire to talk to him. Instead, I left the station knowing our relationship would never be the same.

*

Arianna

I sat quietly while Manny drove us to our next call. For the last several hours all I heard was his lecturing on the station's policies. He thought he could use this shift to re-train me. It didn't matter that I was a medic in California for three years before moving to Oregon. I ignored him and sent texts to Tajel throughout our shift.

"I concluded weeks ago that the only reason Tajel hadn't dumped you as a partner is because you two were fucking each other." I scoffed, and he smirked. "Then, to find out I was right? No wonder you never ended up in my bed. You lesbos should realize what you're missing out on."

Tajel would flip out if I told her what Manny said. It was probably best to say nothing, even though my first impulse was to yell at him. Little did he know I was recording him. If the Chief wanted to pretend his field supervisor wasn't sexually harassing us, this would wouldn't allow him to pretend any longer.

"Medic 128."

I answered dispatch. I was not going to let Manny get away with his comment, but I had more important things to worry about right now. Manny turned on our sirens after we received our orders and it wasn't long before we arrived at the bar where dispatch said our patient would be. We approached our patient cautiously since he was leaning against the wall of the building with his back to us. I walked around to try to see his face. He was breathing. His skin was drenched in his own sweat and was flushed.

Manny used his boot to nudge the man's shoulder. It worked. The man awoke frightened. He swung his arms out erratically and defensively so I took a step back.

"Bro!" Manny waved his hand in the air as if he was trying to swat away a fly. "You smell like shit."

I glared at Manny and then I crouched down a few feet away from the man, placing my medic bag on the ground beside me. "Hey, I'm a paramedic. My name's Arianna. Can you tell me your name?"

His eyes were unable to focus, but he couldn't stop looking in Manny's direction, as if he were checking to make sure that Manny wasn't coming any closer to him. He shivered and kept scratching at his arm as if he had an itch that would not go away.

"Manny step over there, please." I needed this man to concentrate on me and Manny was not helping.

Manny looked at me defiantly and I spotted some people several feet away, watching both of us as I tried to help this man.

"We have an audience."

I knew that was enough for Manny to comply. He couldn't very well be a dick to our patient in front of them. And I wouldn't have let him.

"All I wanted was a drink. The bartender kicked me out," he ranted, now feeling a little safe.

"When was your last drink?"

He started crying, trying to lift himself off the ground, but he winced in pain and fell back to the ground.

"Where does it hurt?" I asked, keeping an eye on his breathing.

"I was so mad. I just want this feeling to stop. Please make him give me a drink."

It was obvious what he was suffering from, but I needed to treat his pain. "I can't give you alcohol, but I can help with the pain. Where does it hurt?"

"I don't care about the pain. I want a fucking drink." The man tried standing again but fell down a second time, cursing at anyone who would listen. "If you can't give me a drink then leave me the hell alone!"

"Fine by me," Manny muttered.

"Why did you bring him?" the man asked while pointing at Manny.

I looked up at Manny who was standing behind me and addressed our patient, "We always work in pairs—"

"I didn't do anything wrong." My patient's hands shot upward. "Why is he pointing a gun at me? Please don't let him shoot me!"

He was in a state of panic – paranoid and delusional. Our patient urinated on himself, crying hysterically.

"Sir, he does not have a gun." I knew I had to calm him down or someone would get hurt.

"Are you calling me a liar?"

"No," I replied quickly. "I believe you see him holding a gun. Manny, take a few steps back."

Manny did so without argument.

"Do you feel safer?" I asked the patient. I knew he was hallucinating.

He kept his eyes on Manny, not trusting any movement he made. I was glad we had a crowd around. Manny would have probably been responding to our patient in a much different manner otherwise.

"Sir, can you trust me enough to give me your name? I said earlier my name's Arianna."

It took him a few seconds, but he finally answered, "I'm Paul Brusky."

"All right, Paul. Now that we know each other's names, can you let me check and make sure you are okay?"

I watched as his fist slowly relaxed. He was beginning to trust me. "What are you going to do?"

"Check your blood pressure and your heart rate. And I would like to see where you're hurting."

He nodded. I pulled my stethoscope and cuff out of my bag and then moved closer to him as he held out his arm for me. He bit at his lip repetitively, unsure about everything and everyone around him. Both his heart rate and blood pressure were elevated. He was experiencing what was known as Delirium tremens.

"Where does it hurt?"

"My leg." He winced again, this time closing his eyes as he did.

I couldn't see a wound on his leg because it was wrapped up in a trench coat.

"I thought my leg had ants inside it."

His statement worried me. "I need to look."

Paul agreed to let me look and I began unwrapping the coat from around his leg while he continued to wince from the pain. I knew I would have to cut the leg of his jeans off and thankfully, he gave me permission to do so. The wound looked as if he slammed his leg into something hard repeatedly. The bone appeared to be broken. I reached in my bag for some gauze and applied pressure to it until I could wrap it.

"Manny, I need a leg stabilizer."

Manny walked back to the rig, retrieving the leg stabilizer. He did not attempt to make nice with our patient or to help. What was he even here for? He was like a spectator, only meant to watch. After a few minutes of convincing, Paul finally agreed to let me take him to the hospital. Manny rolled the gurney over and I helped Paul onto it.

"I can give you something for the pain," I offered.

"I only want a drink," he responded. "You can't try and convince them to let me have one beer? Just one?"

He grabbed my arm and fear stirred in me for a second until I managed to calm myself. "I can tell the nurses whatever you want me to tell them. For now, I can only help with the pain. Let me start an I.V.—"

Instantly, he started screaming, "No!"

"Okay. I won't."

He let go of my arm and I felt relieved as Manny loaded him into the back of our ambulance. I climbed in back with Paul and Manny shut the door then got into the driver's seat.

"Oh no!" Paul cried.

"What's wrong?"

"I feel one coming!" he shrieked.

Before I could say another word, Paul began seizing.

"You need help?" Manny asked.

Now he cares. "No. Just get us to the hospital."

I turned Paul to his side so he would not aspirate, then snatched a non-rebreather mask from the shelf. I let his seizure continue while I kept my drugs close to me in case he seized again. Once his seizure ended, I placed him on 15 liters of oxygen.

Again, I checked his blood pressure. He didn't want me to set up an I.V. so I would respect that. As long as he didn't have another seizure, I'd let the hospital handle starting an I.V. At least there, they would have more staff to help with the process.

We arrived at the hospital and rolled Paul inside.

When it was all over, I started my paperwork, not thinking of anything else. Manny strode over to where I sat inside the back of the rig, finishing my report. I frowned when I saw him. I felt as if he was invading my space.

He sat beside me. "Damn, I hate calls like that. Did you smell him?"

Is this what he usually did after calls? Belittle the patients he had? Paul was suffering and needed support not judgment. Manny was a medic. It bothered me that he was a supervisor with authority over other medics. That needed to change.

"You should clear the call," I suggested.

"But I want to sit with you." His hand patted my thigh while his gaze traveled over my body. Instinctively, my elbow slammed into his ribs. He winced and doubled-over, gasping for breath.

"What the fuck was that for?" He struggled to speak between breaths, hunched over next to the gurney.

"Clear the damn call," I ordered, not caring that he was my superior.

He hobbled out of the rig cursing under his breath. I didn't sit in the passenger seat on the drive back to the station. I decided it was best for me to stay in the back of the rig.

When we arrived back at the station, I hopped out of the rig and rushed to the front of the station where I found Felipe and Rogan sitting on the couch.

"How was your last call?" Felipe asked.

I ran for Chief's door, ignoring him. Felipe made a move to block my way, concerned about the angry expression on my face.

"What are you about to do?"

"I'm not working the rest of my shift with that moron." I pointed toward Manny who was walking into view.

"What did he do?" I've never seen Felipe angry before, but it seemed as if he was ready to attack Manny.

"She's just being a typical dyke," Manny said casually.

Felipe's body twisted, and he lunged at Manny, shoving him in the chest forcefully. "You watch your fucking mouth!"

"Come on now. You can't tell me you're not upset that as soon as we got another female here we find out she's another pussy-licker too?"

Chief chose to walk in at this moment. "What's going on in here?"

"Nothing, Chief. I was just reminding them of their duties," Manny said, puffing his chest out.

I could not help it. I lost control of myself.

"You are absolutely right." I slammed my knee into his genitals and he fell to the floor. "It was my privilege and duty to see you on the ground where you belong."

"Ms. Castaldi," Chief growled. "I could fire you!"

"Do it. I don't want to work at a station that thinks it's all right to employ people like Manny. Or discriminate." I glared at him. "My reputation speaks for itself. I thought you were a leader of integrity. That's why I chose this place over the other offers I got."

I didn't bother to pause and listen to anything he had to say. I no longer felt comfortable or safe. This was the first time I walked out on the job.

"I'll contact my Union rep."

I left the station without another word. The only person I wanted to see right now was Tajel.

Chapter Twenty-Six
Tajel

I flipped through the messages Arianna and I had been exchanging for the last day. I had become a giddy, love-sick woman. She had yet to respond to the message I sent her two hours ago, but that was normal for paramedics. We never knew when a call would come. I leaned on the bar counter hiding my changing expressions from strangers that stood nearby. If I could feel myself blushing I was sure others could see it.

"Yo, Tajel." I looked up from my phone to find Sandy, the best bartender I knew, smiling at me. She slid three drinks over to me. "You keep looking like that and people will start thinking you're in love."

I grinned, carefully picking up the drinks. "I am."

She smiled and started slicing lemons as I walked away.

"Took you long enough," Sasha complained as she took her drink from my hand.

"Where's Danielle?" I took a few sips of my drink as I awaited her answer.

"She had to take care of something first," Sasha said coolly, not looking at me. "I have something to tell you."

I straightened myself as I sat down. "Sure. What's up?"

"You know I've never been good at love." I snorted at her admission. She bit her lip nervously. "But I need to tell you this…I'm in love with Danielle and I think I want her to be my baby momma."

To say that I was caught off-guard was an understatement. "You're not trying to impregnate her already, are you?"

Sasha laughed. "Of course not. We've talked about the things we want – kids and stuff like that, but I've never declared my undying love for her or anything. I mean, I've told her I love her."

I had to ask. Sasha was my best friend. "Does she love you?"

Sasha nodded and grinned. "She tells me every chance she gets."

Then Sasha fell silent.

"What is it?"

She inhaled deeply. "What if I'm not healthy enough for her?"

I put my drink down on the table and asked, "Is there something wrong?"

"Oh, no," Sasha replied. "Nothing life-threatening anyway. It's just that a month ago, I went to get myself checked out. I was curious. Things with Danielle are great, and I want to be perfect for her."

"What did you find out?" I asked cautiously. I reached across the table to put my hand on hers.

Tears threatened to erupt from her eyes. "I will never be able to have children. I'm going through early menopause."

"Oh, Sasha." Instinctively, I rose from my seat and went over to hug her.

"I mean, my sex drive is still thriving, thank God, but I have begun feeling exhausted along with some other unpleasant symptoms." She cried in my arms despite being in a public place. "My mother had early menopause, so I was curious. I didn't think it would happen to me, too."

I held onto her as she cried. "Does Danielle know?"

Sasha shook her head. I handed her a napkin and she wiped her face. "I've been afraid to tell her."

"Sasha, you have to tell her. She loves you."

"I know," she replied. "I'm going to tell her tonight."

I smiled warmly at my friend. "I see the way she looks at you. Trust in that love you two have."

Sasha put her hand on my arm. "And I'm going to say the same for you. Arianna and you look so happy together."

I blushed. "Thanks."

"There's my girl! And she brought a friend." Danielle appeared and threw herself into my best friend's arms for a brief embrace. I watched for a moment as Danielle looked her girlfriend over.

Yep. Danielle was the woman for my friend. She could tell right away Sasha had been crying. I felt a tap on my shoulder and it made me freeze for a moment. I turned around to find Arianna standing behind me. I smiled and pulled her to me, hugging her tightly.

"I've missed you," Arianna whispered in my ear.

I was confused. "Don't you still have another 20 hours left on your shift?"

"I did."

I frowned. "What happened?"

She looked off to the side. "Nothing I couldn't handle."

I wasn't going to accept that answer. I asked more firmly this time, "What happened?"

"I think I might have quit or was fired. I'm not really sure." Arianna linked our fingers, seemingly unbothered.

"Wait—"

"I will explain later." Arianna snaked her arms around my lower back, slowly leaning in to kiss me.

It was so hard to resist her charms. "You do know we're in public, right?"

"Yes, I know." She rested her head on my shoulder for a moment, keeping her arms around me.

"All right." I smiled and kissed the top of her head. "No more hiding?"

She squeezed my ass and I gasped in surprise. "I'm sure they'll be fine on their own. Let's go."

We headed to my place where I supposed we would be doing a lot more than just kissing.

*

Arianna

"I want you to fuck me."

Tajel didn't understand my aggressiveness. I was pissed at her uncle and at Manny. I wanted to keep their behavior toward me to myself because I knew Tajel would probably do something reckless. What I wanted was to clear my mind. All this time I'd been worried about other people's views on our relationship. Being judged. I felt bad for keeping our relationship in the dark. I knew what Tajel wanted.

I was angry at myself and people like Manny. I'd never felt this kind of fury before. I wanted to take that energy and use it on Tajel's body.

I repeated, "I want you to fuck me."

My body hungered for it. I could already feel my clit throbbing so hard it was almost painful. I stifled a groan as Tajel's hand brushed over my thigh.

"Remove your clothes," Tajel ordered. Determination was in each movement as she stripped off her own clothes. "You want me to fuck you?"

I was already enjoying where this was going. My breath caught, and I nodded. I couldn't even form any damn words. My clit was swollen and tight, my juices ready to be guzzled up.

As she unbuttoned her shirt I watched admiringly, ready to see her naked body. I wanted to feel her on top of me.

"I want to hear you say it again." Tajel took off her sports bra, her nipples rigid.

"I..." I tried to talk and control my breathing at the same time. It was difficult. "I want you to fuck me."

I was completely naked when I laid on the bed, spreading my legs to invite Tajel in. She held one finger up and then disappeared into the bathroom. I didn't know what to expect, but when she reappeared in the doorway she was wearing briefs with a black harness and dildo strapped onto it. It hung a little to the left and was at least six inches long. I was intrigued. When I asked her to fuck me, the last thing I expected was this. But knowing she would be the one fucking me with that, I wanted it.

"Not too big, I hope," Tajel said, her smile was wide as she stood with confidence. I could tell she knew how to use it. "Just bought it last week."

"I trust you."

Tajel climbed onto the bed and straddled me. The foreplay was going to have to wait for later. Our lips touched, and an electric sensation shot through me, causing me to curl my toes. My hands explored Tajel's body, pressing into her flesh when our kiss deepened. I moaned as her teeth nipped on my earlobe, her hot breath making it hard for me to focus on where to touch her next. She was already devouring me.

"I'm going to start off slow," she whispered in my ear in a raspy tone that nearly made me cum. I shuddered. "Once I am completely inside you, I will fuck you as requested."

Tajel's fingers slipped in between my thighs and for all the restraint I normally had, I lost it. I groaned loudly, digging my fingers into her biceps as my orgasm slammed into me.

"God! What was that for?" My body was in shock.

"You were already very close," Tajel explained. "I want to have you starting from the beginning."

Her fingers slipped away from my clit and she repositioned herself so she could rub the tip of the dildo over my mound. My eyes shut tightly, and I bit my bottom lip.

"Look at me," Tajel demanded in such a tone that my nipples tightened.

I did as she ordered.

"Inside. Please. Now," I begged.

Tajel pressed the tip of the dildo directly over my center. Our eyes locked and my arms shot over my head and clenched the pillows. I tossed one of the pillows to the floor, feeling the need to lay my head flat. Tajel curled one arm under my shoulder to steady herself. Her other hand kept the dildo against my throbbing clit.

I opened my legs wider to allow her to enter me. I arched my chest upwards, shuddering from anxiety. Tajel kept her eyes on mine and eased inside of me. I tightened in reaction to the pain.

Tajel kissed my cheek softly. "Are you okay?"

I nodded. "I trust you. Don't stop."

Tajel grinned and continued to push her way inside of my pink, wet flesh slowly. Pain soon gave way to pleasure. It was what I wanted. Pivoting her hips a little, Tajel began to pump slowly inside me, and it was as if every nerve in my body came alive. My fingers gripped the sheets as Tajel quickened her pace. I begged for her to go harder. Tajel pumped harder and deeper inside me, our bodies now moving together.

"Oh...right fucking there!" I screamed when Tajel shifted to a slightly new position. "Don't stop, Tajel!"

Both of our bodies were in perfect sync. My mind swirled and I was in a sweet daze. I couldn't hold in my cries. The feeling of her fucking me like this was surreal. My clit drummed as the dildo pressed against it. My center swelled as my orgasm worked its way through my entire body. I pressed my hands into the skin of Tajel's back, my hands gradually making their way to her ass. I squeezed her harder, moaning almost breathlessly. My legs wrapped around her lower body. I saw rays of orange and yellow as I reached the peak of orgasm.

We came together, our screams of pleasure filling the empty space in the room. Everything in my mind went blank. All I felt was Tajel. All I could see was Tajel. All I could hear was Tajel.

Once my clit was done throbbing she slid off me and onto her back, breathing deeply with a smile on her face. "I'm not finished."

I laughed, and we took a momentary break, not yet done with each other for the night.

Chapter Twenty-Seven
Tajel

I woke first. Arianna was curled up against my side sleeping soundly. God, I loved this woman. I sighed contentedly. My phone buzzed on the nightstand and I decided to ignore it. There was no way I wanted to wake Arianna. I wanted to enjoy this moment.

Arianna's phone buzzed, and it was then that I considered waking her.

I whispered, "Babe?"

Arianna grumbled and then repositioned herself. I tried to reach over her to grab her phone and I heard her say, "Leave it."

"Sure." My fingers played with the ends of her thick, black hair.

"What time is it?" she asked.

I looked over at the nightstand. I didn't have a clock, and my watch and phone were too far to reach without disturbing her. Looking out my window, I observed that the sky was littered with gray clouds suggesting rain.

"I can take a guess. Eleven, maybe?" I thought it would be afternoon by now.

Arianna lifted her head and smiled. "You're cute."

I laughed. "Only cute?"

"Don't get cocky on me," she said and kissed me.

She tossed the covers to the side and leapt out of bed. Her nakedness caused a strong reaction in my body.

"Where you are going?"

"Bathroom."

I couldn't take my eyes off her ass. "Don't take too long."

"If I do you can always come and search for me."

I wiggled my eyebrows. "I might have to do that."

As Arianna escaped to the bathroom my phone began vibrating again. "Damn."

I took it from the nightstand. It was my brother's phone number. I guess he reactivated it and wanted to talk, but I wasn't ready to talk to him yet. I rolled my eyes and turned my phone to silent. I wanted no distractions and would ignore the whole world to keep it that way.

There was a loud knock at my door.

"Damn it, Tajel and Arianna!" It was Sasha outside my bedroom door. She had a key to my apartment. "The whole fucking world has been trying to reach you both!"

"What's wrong?"

"There is a multi-car collision on highway 99. One of the trucks involved was an oil rig. There's a huge fire spreading through the area. There are also multiple people injured."

My heart raced. "Give us a minute."

"Fine! We're waiting in the living room!" Sasha yelled.

We both dressed quickly. Luckily, Arianna came last night already in uniform. I

grabbed my own personal medic bag. We would need everything. No words were exchanged. In less than five minutes we both came out of the room ready to go.

"Where is my uncle?" I asked.

"Last your aunt checked he was running triage at the crash site. Then the fire started, and she hasn't heard anything since. Your station has already been called out."

Danielle was sitting on the couch. I said firmly, "You two...stay here."

Sasha shook her head. "We've already volunteered with your aunt to help in the safe zone."

"We need to get to the station," Arianna advised. I agreed.

*

Arianna

"How many O2 tanks can we fit in the rig?" Tajel shouted her question from the shop area next to the ambulance bay.

"Eight," I replied. I put a full tank on the back of the gurney and strapped it tightly. "I have ten burn blankets, 20 nasal airway respirators, and non-rebreathers."

Two blackboards, one scooper, a vehicle extrication device, limb stabilizers, and cervical stabilizers. I added four medic bags. I counted every bandage – exclusive bandages, pressure bandages, and triangle bandages. Everything was here. A cardiac monitor and I.V. bags. Saline fluid and airway bags rested in one of the cabinets in the overhead near where I always sat beside patients. I slung my stethoscope around my neck, my gloves already on with additional ones in my pocket. I also kept a pair of shears on me.

"We're good to go?" Tajel asked, sticking her head into the back of the rig.

I gave her a thumbs-up. We hopped in the front.

Tajel radioed dispatch, "Fire med nine... Medic 112 on air, ready to go."

"Medic 112...fire med nine, copy that. Be safe out there, ladies."

"Copy that," Tajel responded.

For the first five minutes of the drive Tajel's fingertips drummed on the steering wheel.

"Have you ever been a part of something so major like this?" I asked.

"I've seen it as a kid. That's what made me want to become a paramedic. My uncle answered a call like this right after picking me up from school. I was about 15." She scanned the streets and then turned onto the freeway. "My uncle did not have time to take me home, so I came with him. It was unlike anything I'd ever seen before. I helped to feed people and gave other updates. When I saw my uncle in action I was hooked."

I knew what Chief said was still bothering her. "Your uncle regrets his words, I'm sure."

"You don't know that."

I smiled. "You know your uncle better than me. What does your heart say?"

I could see flames and smoke filling the sky and my smile vanished. Our conversation would have to wait. We were a few miles away, but our minds were already focused on the many lives we would try our hardest to save. I couldn't think about those we would lose. Not today. I took a deep breath and reminded myself of why I became a paramedic, letting that guide me.

Chapter Twenty-Eight
Tajel

"Where's my uncle?" I walked over to Felipe.

He shrugged. "Law enforcement needed help."

We arrived on-scene, checked in with the incident commander, and then were directed toward our station supervisor, Manny. I was already in a bad mood. He was busy giving a presentation on how we should listen to him.

Manny was a terrible medic and in a situation like this, he did not deserve his position as a supervisor. This shit was not in his comfort zone. He'd do better leading people at small sporting events that had required multiple bandage usage for kids. Staying professional, I approached merely to get my assignment and start work.

Manny spotted me first.

"Aren't you still suspended?" he asked. He looked at Arianna. "And I think you quit."

"Sue me," I said. It was better than my other choice of words.

"I can also suspend you a second time for insubordination," he pointed out.

"File your complaint later. Right now, we have bigger things to worry about and we need to work together."

My stern look did not waver, and he quickly caved. After a few more minutes of his blabbing he gave us our assignments. I received my assignment and I frowned.

"Here we go," Felipe whispered as he saw the look on my face. "Talk later. Got to go."

I held the piece of paper up, waving it in his face. "You can send EMTs to do something like this. Give me a real assignment."

"Don't argue with me," Manny said smugly. "At this moment...I am your boss."

"I'm not doing this," I hissed through gritted teeth.

"Then go home," he retorted.

"Tajel!" Arianna called out to me. I looked around at a few other medics and firefighters who were watching. "Let's just go bandage up the ones that are tagged green or yellow. He'll need our help soon enough."

I blew through my nose like a bull ready to stampede all over his face. I stomped away following Arianna to the section people were already tagged as green or yellow. These people were merely suffering from cuts and other mild injuries. Nothing life-threatening. Sucking in my anger, I put on a smile as I began to treat people. Several minutes rolled by before I checked my watch. It had actually been an hour. Arianna was not too far away when one of the medics who worked at our station came rushing toward me.

"Yo, Tajel."

I turned around, finding him standing with a grim expression. His tone was calm, but I knew there was something wrong.

"What's up?" I asked him.

He shook his head. "Manny doesn't know I came for you. We were assigned to do triage where that festival was and he's fucking everything up. We have a patient—"

That was all I needed to hear. I yelled over to Arianna, telling her we needed to leave. I went over to the triage supervisor, telling her that we were needed elsewhere. The fire was still burning through the trees. The firefighters wouldn't be finished working for quite some time. It was mid-afternoon, and the heat of the sun was certainly not helping to diminish the fire. I winced under its glare.

We walked past some medics who were transporting patients away from the wreck. My medic bag hung from my shoulder and Arianna was carrying a stretcher and an airway bag. I noticed tire marks leading off the highway into the direction of where the festival was being held. Looking to the side of the road I saw three smashed up cars littering the grass. From a few dozen feet away, I could see Manny shouting at a few medics near the cars.

"What the hell are you—"

I frowned, cutting him off, "I'm taking over."

"The hell you are." He heaved his way out of the ditch. "Get your ass—"

"Anyone here agree that I outrank him?"

I looked to all the medics within earshot. Every said *yes*.

Manny looked from me to them and was about to argue, but Felipe spoke, "This isn't about you, Manny. So, either shut up and help, or leave."

I wasn't going to wait for Manny to figure out his answer. Dropping down to my knees, I peeked under the car. One side of the car was stuck in the ditch, and the driver was already at the hospital. Underneath the metal frame were two bodies, one of which was a young woman. She was unconscious. One of the wheels of the car was pinning her down. Fortunately, even though this car had landed on top of her, the incline of the ditch is what saved her life, not allowing the car to place a great amount of weight on her leg under the tire.

"How long has she been under here?" I asked to anyone who would answer.

"Nearly two hours," one medic responded.

We didn't have a lot of room to retrieve her. There was maybe two feet of space that I would have to work with.

"Shit," I mumbled.

I was sure that by now crush syndrome was kicking in. She was not getting blood and oxygen to her leg. Once this tire could be lifted, it could possibly kill her

"Arianna?"

She slid down into the ditch and opened her medic bag. She pulled out a small tank of oxygen and a non-rebreather. Arianna examined the SUV.

"Is this vehicle stable? Let's get some cribbing and wedging material over here," Arianna ordered.

"It's right here," an EMT replied.

"Let's start building it on the side closest to the patient," Arianna directed.

EMTs and some members of the fire crew brought a long, metal pipe and thick, wooden blocks, placing them under the vehicle and close to the patient.

"Only build enough to make sure it doesn't put more pressure on our patient's leg. We don't want to lift the vehicle just yet," I explained.

"Got it," one of the EMTs responded.

"Make sure you have a spotter and another watching our patient," I added.

"Copy," was the response I received.

Stepping back, I studied the angle of the vehicle. Our patient was fortunate to be stuck under the back end of the SUV rather than the front. As long as we stabilized the back of the SUV so it wouldn't collapse on our patient we would be able to help her.

"How is it going over there?" I asked a firefighter nearby.

He lifted his hand. "It's not moving anywhere unless the earth moves itself."

"Good to know." I put on my protective eyewear, slid on an extra pair of gloves, and cautiously scanned the car for any sharp edges.

"Here." Arianna offered me a helmet with a flashlight. I put it on as she hopped onto the back of the car.

"You check for any gas leak?" Arianna asked, setting out all the equipment she would need.

The firefighter nodded his head. "All clear."

I climbed out the ditch. "I need a spotter on both of us at all times. If this car shifts, let us know."

I laid flat on my abdomen just as rain began to fall. At least it would help take care of the fire.

"You can't go underneath," one of the fire crew said.

Arianna frowned. "You are right. Under normal circumstances this would be a big *no*. But, our patient's been under for a little over two hours. We can't lift the SUV off her right away without treating her first and it's raining. That means the dirt will turn into mud and then this vehicle will crush her completely. We take full responsibility. All we ask is that you cover us and have someone directly behind me if I need anything."

"I can help," Felipe said, standing directly behind Arianna.

"Are we good now?" I asked everyone. "Can we do this?"

They all took a second, then nodded.

"I got you," she assured me.

I smiled and crawled under the car slowly. Fortunately, the leg pinned was close to me. It took me a minute to reach her, crawling cautiously and trying to be wary of any hazards. I set up a few flashlights to see clearly. Arianna tossed the non-rebreather mask to me. The young woman had to be in her early 20s. She was unconscious but breathing. I observed her for a few seconds and watched her chest rise and fall.

I reached across her neck to check for a pulse.

After another ten seconds, I shouted, "She's breathing and has a pulse!"

Felipe acknowledged my shout and then I put the non-rebreather mask around our patient's face and used my portable pulse ox to check her saturation level.

"We need to figure out the best way to treat her," I told Arianna.

If we lifted the car off her leg she could form multiple blood clots that would kill her. My eyes caught my patient's head shifting to one side. She was regaining consciousness.

"Leave the mask on," I whispered to our patient.

"Everything all right?" Arianna asked.

"Yes. She's waking up."

I used my shears to cut away as much of her jeans as I could to get a clear view of the leg that was crushed. It was bent in an upward angle; an open wound indicated a broken bone. I heard one of the men talking on the phone and by the response it was obvious that he was talking to my uncle. The woman slipped back into unconsciousness. I tried to wake her, but she remained still. Her skin was pale. I looked over at her pinned leg and noticed severe bruising and gashes. Her ankle was dislocated. The patient groaned in agony, waking, and removing the mask from her mouth.

"My leg!" she cried.

"I'm Tajel. I'm a medic. I won't leave you down here."

She continued to sob and shifted her weight, becoming agitated and anxious. I couldn't blame her, it was a distressing situation to wake to.

"Hey, hey." I distracted her long enough for her stop moving. "I'm going to help you, I just need you to be still. Can you do that for me?"

She cried, tears mixing with the dirt on her face. "My leg. It feels like a thousand needles are stabbing into me. I can't feel my foot. Its numb."

If she couldn't feel her foot than that meant there was no blood in it.

I continued to work, doing a full body scan as I spoke to her, "I know you're scared. You have every right to be. I just need you to try your best to fight with me. Can you do that?"

She nodded.

"Good." I pointed to her abdomen. "I need to feel your belly."

She nodded again, putting the mask back over her mouth.

I tried my best to keep my head raised as I reached both arms out to palpate her abdomen. She showed no sign of distress and I felt relieved.

I called out to Arianna as calmly as possible.

"What's going on?"

I really didn't want to put Arianna's life at risk, but this was our job. "I need a I.V. set up."

"Here you go," she replied.

"Hey, Felipe!" I yelled.

"Yes?" he answered.

"Call the medical director of this region for an online control order. I have to perform a procedure and need the approval."

"What procedure?" he asked.

"A fasciotomy."

He did not respond, but I knew he was on his task.

"I don't want you to talk. Just informing my partner, Arianna, about what I need to help you."

Our patient breathed slowly. I wanted to keep her informed. It could help her feel safer or better. I put a rubber tourniquet around her arm, feeling carefully for a vein with the tip of my gloved finger. I quickly put an I.V. in her arm and set up the extension. I wanted to avoid our patient having severe kidney damage from the effects of crushing syndrome.

"Saline line," I requested.

Carefully, Arianna extended her arm out to pass me the saline line. I connected the line.

"Open up the drip. Let's also get some potassium fluid in her," I told her calmly.

I let the patient know I was going to give her some medication that would help.

I yelled for the firefighters. "Are you all confident in lifting this car up safely when the time comes?"

"Yes," one of the firefighters replied.

The patient removed the mask "They're going to move the car?"

"Yes." I held her hand, squeezing tightly. "I may have to perform a procedure and I won't lie to you, it's going to hurt like a bitch. But when it's over you will feel a lot better."

She dropped her head back into the dirt as more tears fell from her eyes. She was terrified. I couldn't blame her.

"Tajel," Felipe hollered, "you are clear to give her calcium chloride, 500mg for over two minutes. Our director is discussing the approval of the procedure."

That was better than nothing. "Let's do it."

"I need to slide in a little further," I told Arianna. I turned to face the patient and asked, "Can you move your other arm closer to me?"

She moved her arm shakily and slowly.

"What's going on?" Arianna asked.

"I need to set up a second I.V."

She reached under the car, handing me the second I.V. set. "I'll get the calcium chloride ready."

"Copy." I began a second I.V. line over her right hand. Thankfully, she had good veins. I looked at our patient. "Hey, I will not leave you. Take deep breaths for me."

Her body was trembling. "You promise?"

"I won't go. I promise."

"We're ready when you are," one of the firefighters said.

"Can you hand me a foil blanket?"

It was something normally used for burned victims to cover a patient's body from debris, but when this vehicle lifted, I wanted her injuries to be covered as quickly as possible. The less chance of contamination, the less chance for infection.

"I need that calcium line." Arianna handed it to me and I put it in the I.V. extension.

"The doctor said to give her all you can and just get her out. They will perform the procedure."

I bit my tongue knowing it was a procedure I could do. "Okay."

She was still trembling, but she was trying to be as still as possible.

"Before we lift this vehicle, I want to put her on the heart monitor and push some sodium bicarbonate through her I.V. line. And I need a combat tourniquet to put around her leg." I wanted to stabilize her as much as I could.

The moment we lifted the SUV all the toxins from her crushed injury would release.

"Do we have paramedic transport here?" I heard Arianna ask.

"Yes. Gurney and emergency ambulance are ready to go," Felipe said.

"Give them a quick report of all we've done so they can continue once she's out of there."

I put the tourniquet over the woman's leg, covering her up with foil blanket. "This will hurt but you can do it. I will get you out of here and the other paramedics will get you to the hospital."

She nodded, breathing heavily.

"Ready!" I shouted.

The firefighter started counting down as all three of us held still, wary of the SUV moving in the wrong direction. At any moment, it could drop back down and this time crush both the woman and me.

Instinctively, I reached for Arianna's hand and we felt the sun touch our backs as the car was being lifted by the cribbing. Once I knew it was safe, I pulled the woman out, Arianna helping me by coming to the side to slide the stretcher underneath her. Arianna stayed at the woman's side, holding her hand as Felipe brought extra bandages and a clean cloth to place under her deformed leg. I removed her shoe and her sock, and then Felipe cleaned her leg. We wanted to make it as sterile as possible. I felt for a pulse at her foot and found none.

"Follow how I breathe. When I tell you to...we breathe together," Arianna told the woman.

Thankfully, the rain stopped but it was a bit muddy. I didn't see any fires in my peripheral vision. Our patient groaned and then fell unconscious.

"Let's move," I said to Arianna.

We raised the stretcher, and then the paramedics atop the ditch helped to get her up and out. They lifted her onto the gurney and immediately took her to the ambulance.

I collapsed a few feet from the SUV, exhausted.

*

Arianna

We made it back to the site of the accident where the fire began on the other end of the highway. Another two hours had passed and most of our victims were at hospitals by now. It was early evening and the sun was low. Hues of orange and red filled the sky. Tajel and I were heading toward our rig when we suddenly heard screams followed by a crackling sound. We both turned, watching in slow motion as an enormous tree snapped, falling in our direction.

Emergency personal scattered to avoid its path. Tajel grabbed my arm, pulling me along with her as we ran out of the path of the tree. It fell on top of one of our ambulances. A few people screamed, and we knew there were new victims to treat. Some of our own were now hurt. Immediately, Tajel and I rushed over to the people we knew would be injured.

"We need chainsaws!" someone screamed.

There were a few of our own paramedics pinned down by their limbs and a few others were entirely under the tree and unmoving. From the corner of my eye I noticed a child, perhaps ten years of age, walking around lost and scared. I pointed to the kid and Tajel caught sight of him. Running on pure instinct, she rushed toward the him. He was near the ambulance that was almost crushed under the weight of the tree.

I screamed for Tajel to wait. She did not. She was within reach of him in a matter of seconds. I took a deep breath, relieved she was taking him away from danger. A massive explosion sent me reeling backward several feet. It was the ambulance. Fear slammed into my gut but I managed to jerk my body up from the ground, screaming for Tajel before I started running.

One of the firefighters grabbed me. "You have to wait!"

I didn't care. I could only think of Tajel.

Some of the firefighters worked at the fire and the one who held me loosened his grip as I calmed. It was all I needed to yank myself free. I skirted around the fire, watching as Tajel slowly stood.

"Tajel!"

Relief settled in me as she began to turn toward me. But my relief was short-lived. The light in her eyes extinguished and she fell forward, hitting the ground with a horrifying *thud.*

I didn't hear anything else. I didn't see anything else. I knew my legs were moving, though. I was running. Running for my life. Running for Tajel.

Chapter Twenty-Nine
Arianna

I ran to Tajel, yelling for a few other paramedics to assist me. I fell to the ground beside her while another medic raced over to the boy. I stole a quick glance at the boy as he regained consciousness. He was all right. Tajel, on the other hand, would not wake up. Carefully, one of my fellow medics and I rolled her on her back. I called out her name while doing a sternum rub. No response.

I inspected her from head to toe while slipping my hand under her head to feel for wounds. When I pulled my hand from underneath her head it was covered in blood. *Shit.* I checked her pulse. It was weak. I used my pin light to check her eyes. One pupil was a pinpoint while the other was dilated. There was also some dark coloration beginning to appear around her eyes. I did not like where this was leading. The medic I was working with put her on oxygen. Small sparks popped a few feet from the ambulance.

"We need to move her!" I barked.

It was loud among the echoes of other voices, a flaming ambulance, and vehicles still moving about. I placed a cervical stabilizer around her neck.

Felipe sprinted over to us, dismayed by what he saw. "What the hell?"

"She needs to get to the hospital now!"

I finished scanning the rest of her body and gave a thumbs-up to head out. We put Tajel on the stretcher and carried her to Felipe's ambulance. Once inside, I checked behind her ears. There was some bruising.

I closed my eyes, calling up to Felipe who was driving. "She has all the signs of a basil skull fracture."

I continued to search around her ears. Clear fluid and blood seeped from her ear canals and her nose. I started an I.V. line and put her on the ECG.

I watched the medic check Tajel's blood pressure. He frowned. "Her blood pressure is 188/100." She was hypertensive.

Tajel started seizing. I twisted her left lateral as she went into a full tonic seizure. Her body shook rapidly and was stiff.

"Push 2 mg of Versed," I told the medic.

He used the I.V. to give Tajel the medication. Her seizure lasted thirty seconds.

I squeezed Tajel's hand tightly and whispered in her ear, "I love you. Stay with me."

I checked her respirations. They were dimming and shallow.

"She needs assistance breathing."

The medic handed me his BVM. I placed the mask over her mouth and started squeezing air into her lungs.

It wasn't helping.

"She's losing her pulse," I said, pressing my fingers to her carotid. I shook my head and moved the BVM away. "I need to intubate."

I grabbed what I needed, opened Tajel's mouth, and slid the tube down her throat. My hands were steady, and I held my breath until it was secure.

"Got it." My heart raced as I got the BVM again and attached the intubating tube, giving her the oxygen she needed.

The coloration of her skin brightened but was still pale around her mouth.

The ambulance stopped, and Felipe opened the back doors. "How is she?"

"She can't breathe on her own." I continued squeezing air into her lungs.

I remained with her while we rolled her through the doors of the hospital and stayed to give a full report to the doctors.

"We got it from here," one of the RNs told me.

They transferred Tajel from our gurney to theirs. I was left behind as the nurses, doctors, and Tajel disappeared into the trauma room.

A nurse passing by took note of my frazzled appearance and said, "Our break room is down the hall. You can clean off in there."

I thanked her and walked off toward the break room. Once inside, I went straight to the sink to wash the dirt and blood away from my arms. I scrubbed my arms and hands so hard I almost started to scrape my skin. When I looked up from the sink and into the mirror, my face was blotchy, my eyes were red and glassy. I hadn't realized I was crying. I pooled water into my hands and splashed it on my face. There were a few paper towels placed on the counter beside the sink and I grabbed one to wipe my face.

She'll be okay. I wasn't going to leave Tajel, not now. I located the waiting room and sat in the first chair I found. We were kicked out and moved into the E.R. Chapel. It could barely fit 15 of us. The sound of my knuckles cracking was the only noise in an otherwise silent room. Felipe entered after a few minutes and sat beside me. Neither of us could speak. I don't know if we even wanted to. The minutes ticked away on a clock on the wall and I was lost in its monotonous rhythm until the trance was broken by a blurry figure in the doorway. The doctor. In unison, Felipe and I stood when the doctor walked over to us. Several of our coworkers looked up as well, wanting news of Tajel.

"I assume you are all here for—"

"Tajel, " I responded anxiously.

"I know Tajel personally. I am going to do my best to pull her out of this. Is her uncle...or another member of her family here?"

Everyone shook their heads.

My heart felt as if it were made of crust, cracking slowly from anticipation of his diagnosis and expectations. "Please..."

The doctor understood what I needed. "She has a basil skull fracture and she is already being prepped to go into the O.R."

"What else?" My voice was hoarse as if I'd been screaming all day.

"Her seizure was brought on by a slow bleed in the brain. With the seizure..."

I couldn't hear the rest. I refused to listen to the doctor talk about the possibility of Tajel never waking up. Of her being brain dead. Of me losing her. She was the woman I loved. We had just made love this morning. No one mattered except Tajel.

When the doctor was finished and gone, I was still standing in a trance. Soft hands brushed my arm. I turned with a smile, thinking it was Tajel, but it was Danielle. She held her arms open for me to fall into. Sasha stood beside Danielle, continually wiping the stream of tears away from her eyes. I let all my strength go and fell into my friend's arms sobbing and squeezing her. Maybe I hoped she could save me from this nightmare. This was a nightmare.

I cried, and my body trembled. "I can't lose her!"

"Hey...she loves you..." Danielle whispered in my ear. "She will fight to come back to you."

I cried for what felt like hours, standing in the middle of the waiting room. A few of our coworkers and firefighters started telling stories about their experiences working with Tajel and all the crazy things she did. Why was it that people always reminisced when someone they loved was near death? I didn't want to talk about Tajel as if she existed in the past. She was still here, and I wanted to create new memories with her.

Tajel's aunt and sister rushed through the doorway, running directly over to me for answers. I didn't know what was happening. My mind had left reality some time ago. Felipe volunteered to answer their questions. Tajel's aunt began crying fitfully while I finally stopped. I wiped my eyes and stared at the floor. I couldn't face her, or anyone for that matter. I wanted to disappear, to slip between the cracks in the wall and into nonexistence.

"You saved my baby's life!" Laura reached out for me.

How could I save Tajel if she may never wake up again? As Laura wailed in my arms I sensed my strength returning. It was the kind of strength used to comfort others. I wanted to take care of Tajel's family. As I wrapped my arms around Laura, Chief stormed into the room, scanning it until he saw his wife and me.

His face was blank and flushed, his uniform covered in dirt, ash, and blood. "They told me Tajel was hurt."

He did not know the seriousness of her injuries. One of our coworkers told him, and his gazed shifted to me.

"You were with her?" he asked.

I nodded.

He sighed heavily again. "She'll be okay. My niece is too stubborn."

I stood there for a moment watching the expression of his face change from a look of calm to a look of fear. Everyone had doubt in their eyes. I left the room, not caring if anyone would notice my absence. I needed to be alone.

I found myself in the cafeteria after wandering around the hospital aimlessly for 20 minutes. I didn't order anything, but I stood in line for five minutes looking at the options, trying to be normal. There was no use pretending. Every minute stretched until the concept of time seemed strange. I sat at a table alone for a while until Chief approached. His presence annoyed me, and I didn't care whether he knew it or not. Boss or no boss, he would have to deal with my attitude right now. All I cared about was Tajel.

Roosevelt shook his head, sensing my aggravation. "I deserve that. I know I'm the last person you want to sit next to you."

I said nothing. Made no reaction.

He rested his elbows on top of the table and interlaced his fingers. He looked over at the nurses and doctors chatting by the cafe line.

"I love my niece. And I know I haven't been showing that to her...but I do." He licked his cracked lips, sighing. "Did she ever tell you how she came to live with us?"

I would go along with this conversation. "Her parents were killed in a car accident. Both Tyler and she were in the car when it happened."

He popped his knuckles. "Well, when we first took them home, Tajel would not speak for months. We tried to get her into counseling, anything to get her living again.

Nearly a year past when I got a call on a day just like this. Chaos. She was in the car with me and I had no time to take her home, so she came with me."

I listened, but I kept staring at the table. Tajel shared a little of this story with me earlier.

"Her eyes lit up that night. It was the first time I'd seen any real reaction from her. She saw firsthand what I did." He took a sip of the coffee I hadn't realized was there. "Tajel was hardheaded and left my car to get closer to what was going on. Immediately, some of the staff had her helping.

She was giving people food to eat. Held their hands if they were scared. She did it all. There was this woman there..." Chief's eyes darkened. "She was six or seven months pregnant. I worked on her as if my life depended on it. This woman...the odds were against her. Tajel saw me and ran over to us. She kept staring at me, willing me to save this woman's life."

"Did you?" I asked. "Save her?"

"Her and her baby." He straightened in his seat. "And for the first time I heard Tajel speak in almost a year of silence. That was the first time I saw life in her eyes and the passion that brought her to be one of the best paramedics out here."

Hearing his version of that story made me smile. Then, I looked down at my hands and reminded myself that Tajel may never wake up.

"Why did you tell me that story?"

"Because...I forgot it. I forgot what that story represented. I mean, I worked hard to save that woman just to please Tajel. And I did. And for the last five years I have been limiting her. Keeping her from all she truly desires.

That spark was dimming because of me. And then you came along."

"I really don't want to hear how you feel about—"

"Please let me finish," he said. I frowned but waved him on. "I should have noticed that spark. I was blind. My niece truly loves you. And just like the spark I saw in her eyes that night many years ago, she worked hard every day to get where she is now. Without my help. She will work every moment now to recover fully just to have a future with you. That is my niece."

I sat quietly for a moment trying to absorb everything Chief had said. I was about to say something to him, but it was then that Felipe ran into the cafeteria, calling out to us. "The doctor's back!"

My heart started racing and I rushed out of the cafeteria hoping that good news awaited me.

Chapter Thirty
Arianna

For the next week, I remained at Tajel's bedside. I watched the machines continue to push oxygen into her lungs. Every time it beeped, I would jump up to read her vitals. I laced my fingers with Tajel's, hoping for just one squeeze of her hand. Any indication of life. My swollen eyes burned because I hadn't slept in days. I yawned every other minute and continually shifted in the chair at her bedside.

I missed Tajel. For the last week, I couldn't do anything except be here. Unable to focus on anything other than her, I put everything else to the side. My career, my apartment, my friend. I missed Danielle and I was thankful she was so understanding, but I needed to be here. A knock at the door caused me to panic momentarily. It was the doctor. His knocks were always soft.

"Ms. Castaldi?"

"Come in," I said flatly.

The doctor was carrying a folder that looked ominous. He gave me a sincere smile. I didn't look at him. My eyes were glued to the folder in his hand.

"It's time," he reported.

"It's only been a week!" I yelled, refusing to accept his words.

"Yes, ma'am. I understand—"

"No, you don't!" My hands were at my face, pressing into my skin. I seized Tajel's hand and begged, "Please wake up!"

"She got the documents legalized, Ms. Castaldi. If ever she was in a state such as this...in which she could not function—"

"She didn't have me then!" I shrieked. "She would change that fucking piece of paper! Rip it up if she knew this would happen!"

The doctor listened to me until I was finished. He motioned for the nurse beside him to check Tajel's vitals. The nurse walked past me, nodding apologetically.

"I'm sure if Ms. Pierce—"

"She goes by her first name, which is Tajel," I interjected as if what I said mattered to the doctor.

"Yes. Tajel," the doctor relented. "Nonetheless—"

Nonetheless. What did that mean? Fuck his sympathy. "Spare me the bullshit."

Two years ago, Tajel was hospitalized and decided to have a plan in place in case she was seriously injured and unable to function on her own. She gave herself a week. A week before removing life support. Tajel couldn't know at that time what that really meant. One week on a ventilator with brain activity, no matter how small, was worth giving herself more time. There was a chance. Her uncle and aunt wanted to respect Tajel's wishes, but I knew they also wanted her to live.

15 minutes passed, and the doctor ordered me to step out. He was doing a full examination to look for any changes. I scratched at my forearm absently while standing outside the room, desperate for him to come out with good news. Danielle and Sasha were with me, holding me in their

arms as I cried. Tajel's family arrived, and I was surprised to see Tyler with them. He was fidgeting but functional.

A few of our coworkers, including Felipe, were already here and waiting with me. So many people cared about Tajel. So many people loved her. All eyes were on the doctor as he stepped out of the room. His expression was grim. There was no change, I knew it.

"Tajel was very specific. In her will and DNR, it said to extubate and if she couldn't breathe on her own, to put her back on oxygen. She wants to give away her organs."

All I could think about was breathing as if Tajel's lungs and my own were connected. More than anything, I wanted her to breathe on her own. For her to prove that she was going to come out of this. Danielle squeezed my arm tightly.

"I can only allow Tajel's family—"

"Arianna *is* family," Roosevelt declared, catching me by surprise. "Her and my niece are more than friends, they are partners in every way you can imagine."

The doctor motioned for us to enter the room. There were two nurses waiting inside. The doctor put on new gloves and approached Tajel.

"Mr. Pierce."

"Call me Rosy," he requested.

Tajel's nickname for him. Now he was using it as if that name had always belonged to him. The doctor smiled and began his work.

"I'm going to extubate...starting off..." he explained.

Laura put her arm around me. "Tajel loves you."

"I know," I replied. "I love her so much."

"She knows."

A few alarms beeped, and the doctor ignored them, continuing to remove the tube in her throat.

"Watch her vitals," he instructed the nurses.

They nodded. He kept going, detaching the tape that was holding the intubating tube in place. I held my breath. Tears stung my eyes. The muscles in my body clenched as I studied every move the doctor made and how Tajel's vitals were reacting.

Slowly the doctor pulled the tube out of her throat and I watched as her oxygen saturation dropped from 98% to 91%. She wasn't getting enough oxygen into her lungs.

"Breathe," I pleaded. "Breathe."

"She's at 89%." The doctor glanced at the machines. Her vitals were dropping.

I moved closer to Tajel and the nurse motioned for me to back away. I yelled for her to back off and the doctor signaled for the nurse to leave me alone.

"Tajel," I knelt beside her bed, begging her to breathe, "please baby...breathe."

The doctor asked for another intubation kit. "I need to make this happen quickly to preserve her organs."

"Wake up!" I cried.

"Arianna." It was Roosevelt's voice.

Brooklyn and Tyler were crying in each other's arms and Laura was wrapped around Roosevelt's side. He held an arm out for me to fall into. I looked at Tajel and then Roosevelt. If I left her side now, I'd be giving up, letting go of the notion of her coming back to me. I didn't know how to do that. In meeting Tajel I didn't know she would change my life, but she did, and I couldn't give up on that. I saw our future. We never talked about it, but I saw it. It wasn't fictional or just a dream. It was real. I kissed her. My tears fell onto her face. I played with the curls of her hair as my breath coated her lips.

"I love you," I whispered in a melodic tone. "I love you. Don't make me wait anymore for you. You can't make me fall in love with you only to leave me so soon. So, wake up."

The doctor's hand touched my back gently, alerting me that I needed to move. More tears fell and with all the strength I had to give to Tajel, I gave it to her in another kiss.

My head popped up. A breath.

"She can breathe!" I shouted.

The doctor and the nurses gave me a sympathetic look. They thought I was making it up or was delusional. I didn't blame them. I would have thought the same thing if I was in their position.

"I'm not losing it or lying," I argued.

The doctor opened his mouth to speak when the nurse spoke first in astonishment, "Doctor...her vitals."

He looked at the monitor. Her saturation was back at 90%. In another few seconds, they were back at 91%, then 92%.

"Check her blood pressure," the doctor ordered, grabbing his stethoscope to check her lungs.

Everyone stood in stunned silence holding their breath. I chewed my fingernails, something I hadn't done since I lost my brother.

My gaze went from Tajel to the doctor. He smiled.

"Seems she's improving." He looked at me more than anyone else. "I'm going to run some tests. I need a moment to do another examination."

"She can breathe on her own," I said before falling into Danielle's arms outside of the room once again. I was exhausted, relieved, and emotional.

"Thank God!" someone in the group exclaimed.

It took the doctor ten minutes before he stepped out of the room to give us an update. "She appears to be responsive."

Cheers erupted from everyone in the hallway. Tajel would be fine. I knew she would come back.

"We are going to do a battery of tests to make sure everything is fine. She won't be awake for another few hours at least."

"You can breathe now," Danielle told me.

I smiled, taking in several deep breaths. Leaning my head against the wall I looked at everyone. Excitement was in all their eyes. The nurses and a tech rolled Tajel out of the room. I watched until I could no longer see her as they turned the hall, taking her off for testing. I went into her room and sat in the chair. I wanted to be the first person she saw when she opened her eyes.

I was left alone. Everyone knew that's what I wanted. I placed my elbow onto the cushioned armrest, laying the side of my head in the palm of my hand. My muscles relaxed and the only thing on my mind was seeing Tajel.

*

Tajel

My eyes felt dreadfully heavy. I could feel myself breathing. Gradually, I lifted my eyelids. A terrible burn, followed by my eyes watering, made me shut them. It was going to take me a little while to get myself together. A minute later I tried again, this time opening my eyes slowly.

My head turned to the side and I saw an obscure figure in the chair next to the bed. I squinted my eyes until my vision cleared. My heart raced seeing Arianna asleep sitting next to me. She looked utterly drained.

"She hasn't left your side." It was my brother. I was surprised to hear his voice. "I'll leave if you want. Aunt Laura wanted me to keep an eye on you both."

"How long have I been out?" My throat felt charred.

"Been out?" he asked, a bit too hysterically. "You were more than out. That damn DNR or whatever of yours almost made the doctor pronounce you dead."

The will. Right. I had forgotten about that. I must have been seriously injured.

"How are you feeling?" he asked nervously.

"How long have I been out?" I asked a second time.

"Oh...right..." he said. "A week."

The door swung open and my uncle and aunt walked in. Their eyes widened in surprise seeing me awake.

"Sweetie," Aunt Laura squeaked quietly enough not to wake Arianna.

My aunt gave me a big hug and a kiss on the cheek, trying not to hurt me at the same time.

"How do you feel?" My uncle put his hand on top of my feet.

"My legs," I complained in a hushed tone. "I can't feel my legs."

He shook his head. "Still have your humor."

"Of course. As long as I still have my job and Arianna without a confrontation."

"You just woke up. There is no need—"

"Honey," Roosevelt interrupted his wife. He looked at me. "No resistance. You've earned a spot on my SWAT team...if you still—"

"Yes!" I squealed, causing my vitals to increase.

"Would you like us to wake her?" my aunt asked. "She fought for you to stay alive and the moment we learned you were going to recover...she sunk in that chair and crashed."

I stared at Arianna. "No. I'll let her sleep."

The doctor walked in, looking first at Arianna then me. He did a quick examination and he told me that he believed with some physical therapy I'd make a full recovery. He and my family walked out of the room, leaving me alone with Arianna still asleep in the chair beside me. I watched her as she breathed. I was so thankful to have her in my life. I would be gone if not for her.

20 minutes had passed when Arianna's eyes finally opened. She stretched her limbs. I had missed her. Absently she looked my way, sleepily leaning back in her chair. A second later she popped her head up after realizing I was awake. Her breathing quickened, and tears welled in her eyes.

"You're awake," Arianna whispered, almost unbelieving.

Weakly, I reached for her.

She took my hand immediately, kissing my knuckles softly. "*Te amo. Siempre.*"

Arianna smiled, light dancing in her eyes. "I love you."

The space that was between us was now shattered. She kissed me passionately and deeply. We were closer than ever.

Kissing her like this, with not only my heart in it but also my soul, I couldn't stop myself from saying, "Move in with me."

Chapter Thirty-One
Tajel
Five months later…

Sweat dripped down my body. Arianna was by my side as we ran through one of our favorite hiking trails. I was wearing a sports bra and red running shorts. It was a good way to get Arianna to compliment my figure. I couldn't help myself.

Arianna lifted her water bottle to her lips, taking a few sips, and then handed it to me. "Here."

For the last five months Arianna helped nurse me back to health. I was going to start working again and training for the SWAT medic position.

As I took a sip of water, Arianna took advantage of my silence. "It's official. My parents are coming."

I saw the panic in Arianna's eyes as if saying it aloud made that fact far worse.

I put my hands around her waist. "Babe, you told them through a text that you're dating a woman and living with her. If I had told my aunt and uncle that over text they'd be at my doorstep in a heartbeat."

Arianna began biting her fingernails and I pulled her hands away from her mouth.

"I think we'll both survive a visit from your parents."

"Ha!" Arianna threw her arms up exaggeratedly. "*¡No bueno!*"

"Babe." I gave her a serious look.

"My family is crazy." Arianna shook her arms out, loosening the muscles. "It won't just be my parents. I have nosy aunts and cousins, too."

"Then we will figure something out, but they should still stay with us."

"No," Arianna dismissed my suggestion. "They can go to a hotel."

I knew I had to make her reconsider. "I think you're going overboard."

"Maybe a little." She rested her forehead against mine. "They weren't easy to live with. In a Hispanic family, there is always someone in your business. Babe, they would drive us crazy."

Instead of saying anything I kissed her on the lips and said, "Race you home."

*

Arianna

Time was passing quickly, and we were nearly finished with our shift. It was Tajel's first day back, and it was as if she never left. We were all standing in the kitchen of the station, and Felipe was making everyone his famous grilled cheese sandwiches. He called them famous and he had every right to do so. I bit into mine, wincing at the heat burning the inside of my mouth.

"Medic 112, you have a call out to Gresham... An unknown..." the dispatch called out to us over the intercom.

"Damn," I lamented.

Tajel was already walking to the rig.

I hopped in, putting on my gloves. "My favorite kind of call."

"Yep...can be walking into anything." Tajel pinched the bridge of her nose. "High alert."

I nodded. It took us ten minutes to get to the scene. It was a small neighborhood full of boxy, little houses. Tajel jumped out and ran around to the back, pulling out the gurney. Our eyes searched around the house we were approaching. There was a fence separating us from the front door. A dog came running toward the fence. The dog barked, and we stopped in our tracks.

"Damn it," Tajel growled.

A man with a scruffy face came out of the house, shouting at the dog. "Bulls! Get your fucking ass over here!"

"Can you secure your dog, sir?" Tajel asked in a sharp tone.

"This is my property!" he barked as loudly as his dog.

"Do you want our help?" Tajel was getting annoyed.

"I didn't call you paramedics for nothing," he retorted.

"Then put your dog up." Tajel's politeness had left the building.

"They send me pussies for paramedics," he grumbled. "What a fucking joke."

He walked his dog to the side of the gate and restrained him.

"Come in and get this bitch out my house."

Tajel muttered under her breath.

"Let's just grab our patient and go," I said. "I radioed dispatch, saying, "We are requesting officers."

Tajel questioned the man, "Sir, is the woman badly injured?"

"Sort of!" he shouted from inside the house.

"What the fuck is sort of?" Tajel frowned, asking me.

We both started moving back to our rig.

"Where the hell are you two going?" The guy's bulky arms were crossed over his chest.

"We left our medic bag in the ambulance," I lied. I did not want to alert him that we called the cops.

"I really hate unknown emergencies," Tajel whispered.

"Me, too. Our patient could really need us right now."

A police car pulled up a few minutes later.

"What do you know?" One of the officers Tajel never got along with approached us with a smug look. "Tajel finally needs help."

"Arianna requested you. You know me, Ron...if I ever requested an officer, it wouldn't be you or Sheriff Henry."

Officer Ron sneered. His partner interjected, "That's enough. Let's work together."

"Well, I have a bad vibe about this guy," I explained. "He just looks wrong."

The officers studied the house.

Ron's partner asked, "Is he in the house?"

Tajel nodded. "He had to see you guys approach. He was running his mouth more than you, Ron."

Ron spat on the grass. "We'll take a look."

Tajel and I waited by the ambulance and a while later, the officers returned.

"You sure he was here?" We nodded, and Ron continued, "There's a woman here who was locked in a room. She won't come out, Whoever the guy was beat her up. I see booze and dirty needles. My guess he was hoping you two were dumb enough to come inside so he could steal your drugs."

"Did he look high?" the other officer asked, scratching the tip of his nose.

"We didn't get close enough to find out," I answered. "He appeared very agitated and was sweating profusely. "

"All right," Ron said. "You two can come pick her up."

The officers walked back into the house with us following behind.

"Ron, duck!" Tajel shouted, and Ron ducked right as a bat was being swung at his head. The guy must have entered from the back of the house.

The other officer tackled the guy who kept fighting even as he was being pinned down. "Stop resisting, I'm a police officer!"

Eventually, they put him in handcuffs and escorted him to their vehicle. We headed to our patient. She was lying sideways crying.

"Please, no officers," she mumbled.

"We're not cops," Tajel told her.

"I'm Arianna." The young woman looked up at me. "This is my partner, Tajel. We are the paramedics."

"Where do you hurt most?" Tajel asked, moving to one side of the woman.

"My chest," the woman sobbed.

"Can I check you out?" Tajel crouched beside her.

The woman looked at both of us then nodded timidly.

I moved closer to her. "I would like to check your vitals while my partner makes an assessment. Is that fine?"

She nodded again. We began to work, both of us inspecting her body.

Tajel asked cautiously, "Did he do more?"

The woman shook her head rapidly. "No. He tried...but...he couldn't."

"Gotcha," Tajel said.

There was a lot of bruising around one side of her abdomen.

Tajel brought out her stethoscope. "Can you take a deep breath?"

The woman tried, wincing halfway through.

I grabbed some gauze and put a little saline on it. "I'm going to clean around your face."

"You appear to have a few ribs broken. Nothing that won't heal." Tajel looked up at the woman. "Do you want to press charges against him? We can tell the cops if you like. You don't have to speak to them right now."

She shook her head. "I just want to forget this night."

I sighed. "Can you stand?"

She nodded once more. It bothered me that so many women never pressed charges against their attackers. All I could think of was who his next victim was if not her again. And how unlucky the woman would be next time. I went to retrieve the gurney and maneuvered it into the room. Tajel helped the woman onto it. We buckled her in and transported her out.

"Pierce," Ron called to Tajel.

Tajel turned to him with a dangerous look on her face. She hated being called by her last name. "How can I help you?"

"I know we're always bitching at each other...but, you had my back tonight. So yeah...thanks."

He offered Tajel his hand. She smiled. "Are you getting sentimental on me, Ron?"

He frowned. "Fuck you."

And the peace was gone.

Halfway back to his vehicle, Tajel yelled over to him, "You'd have my back if things were in reverse!"

"Of course." He opened his car door, yelling at the assailant.

Tajel jogged over to me. "Can we switch?"

"Sure thing."

I waited for Tajel to climb into the back and then closed the door. It wasn't often she stayed in the back of the rig.

I asked after I was in the driver's seat, "You ready?"

Tajel said *yes* and we were off.

*

Tajel

Life in the back the of the rig had its ups and downs. There were a few reasons I didn't work in the back. It was exhausting and emotional. There were patients who were unconscious and then there were others who talked way too much. Some patients screamed the entire time. They became violent and needed to be restrained. Others were completely silent.

I noticed the look in our patient's eyes when we were inside that house. She sat upright, knees to her chest, with a pillow in between as a cushion for her broken ribs.

"Was the guy your boyfriend?"

"My husband," she said weakly, on the verge of tears.

I didn't say anything after that for a few minutes. This was her chance to talk freely. I saw Arianna looking through the rearview mirror at me. I twirled my index finger around and she understood what I was telling her. I wanted to prolong our trip to the hospital.

"I'm going to check your vitals again."

She rubbed her eyes. "We lost our son a year ago."

Finishing my assessment, I said, "That's a terrible thing to go through, for both you and your husband."

"He shut down. Six months ago, I found out he started taking drugs. Coke, meth, anything to make him forget the pain. He changed."

She was silent again.

"I lost my parents when I was a kid. I have a brother who never quite recovered and got hooked on drugs. Four years ago, he brought his buddies to my house uninvited. I came home to them lying unconscious on the floor. I slapped my brother awake. They got up like I wanted...but sometimes I wish I would have just left."

I was telling her my story because I wanted her to see that she could overcome. That we could be human together. It always seemed to work for situations like this. It made my patients feel comfortable enough to express themselves because they knew I understood pain and wouldn't judge.

"They were high on heroin. His friends thought it would be funny to give me a taste. That maybe I wouldn't be so uptight if I tried it for myself."

The woman seemed focused on my story.

"My brother watched as his friends held me down and injected me with heroin." I wasn't intending to cry in front of our patient. I wiped one tear away, smiling weakly." It took months to recover from one dose. My uncle sent me to rehab immediately. I had a craving like nothing anyone who hadn't tried heroin could imagine."

"Do you hate your brother for getting on drugs and hurting you like that?" she asked.

I thought about it and then said, "There are days I try not to. We have so much history. I love him. He's barely trying to get clean now, so every day will be a new day to try and forgive him."

"I hate him sometimes. And I hate myself for staying with him," she said.

I observed Arianna circle the block again and then head for the hospital. "Look, we are going to be at the hospital soon. You will have everyone surrounding you. You can't let this destroy you or make you think certain things. How long have you been cutting?"

Her eyes widened, surprised that I had noticed her scars, and then turned away. In a small voice she said, "A few months. I'm just...over it."

There were several old and fresh cuts over her arms and legs. She was a cutter. Being closed off and depressed would cause the doctors to put her on a 72-hour hold if she didn't communicate with him about her illness.

"Before we go inside, take this moment to let out whatever you're feeling. Scream, or say whatever. I promise you'll feel better."

She wiped her eyes and took a deep breath. She began crying harder. I understood. I just made her feel more vulnerable. She screamed at the top of her lungs. Then, she began ranting about how angry she was at her husband and that she wanted to punch him. She screamed how much she hated him. She screamed until we arrived at the hospital.

I handed her some tissue and she used it to clean her face.

After a moment, she sighed and started laughing. "That helped. No one's done that for me before."

"I'm glad it helped."

Arianna came around to the back and opened the doors. "You ready?"

The woman smiled, tears still in her eyes. "I am. Really...thanks."

I stepped down and pulled her out on the gurney. "Anytime."

*

Arianna

We made it home, and all I wanted to do for the last five hours of our shift was to make love to Tajel. She noticed the way I was looking at her and she winked at me. I loved her bravery in opening up to our patient. I loved that she gave the woman a chance to let her emotions out. You didn't see that every day. I was impressed and turned on. I wrapped my arms around her shoulders, kissing her heavily.

My breath hitched, my clit pulsed, and I was not able to slow anything down. Blindly, I pushed Tajel backward onto the couch. I yanked off my shirt and tossed it to the floor, and then climbed on top of her. Her fingers dug into the skin of my waist. I leaned over and caressed her cheeks with my lips.

"You know I love you like crazy?"

Tajel smiled and she said, "I'll always love you and want you. Every second."

I bent down low enough to feel her breath upon my lips as she gave me our defining kiss. The kiss that sealed our relationship. I groaned, tasting the warmth of her mouth as she opened it wider for me. She was sexy, and the smell of her enthralled me. I grazed my lips against hers teasingly. Tajel tried to kiss me, but I pulled back quickly enough to make her growl. Perhaps I wanted a little foreplay.

Being that she was slightly stronger, Tajel grabbed my waist and firmly held me in place. My skin prickled from the chills. She scraped her nails up my spine lightly, and I felt the heat coming from between my thighs.

"Take this off." Tajel pointed to my sports bra.

I obliged and smiled. "Your turn."

I unbuttoned her shirt, trailing kisses from her neck to her collarbone. I felt her tremble and went back up to her lips.

"Damn. You're so soft."

My head fell back as her mouth and tongue grazed my nipple. Tajel's fingers began playing with my other nipple between her fingers. Absentmindedly, I rotated my pelvis, grinding my clit against her knee. My skin flushed, and I was wet and hot between my thighs.

Tajel flipped me onto my back on the couch. I giggled. "What are you doing?"

"About to fuck my girlfriend."

I watched her pull down her pants to reveal the strap-on dildo. I gasped. "When did you put this on?"

She grinned. "I put it on back at the station."

My eyes widened in confusion.

"I don't keep it at the station. It was in my car and I brought it in discreetly and put it on." Tajel crouched over me, unbuckling my pants. "I saw the look you kept giving me."

She slid my pants and underwear down, tossing them to the floor. I groaned from mere anticipation. Excitedly, I snaked my hands around her neck, reeling Tajel in for a kiss. My breathing grew ragged as Tajel positioned herself in between my legs. Her hand went over my shoulder. I wrapped my arms and legs around her body as she slowly entered me with the extension.

I gasped. My mouth was agape, panting from the pleasure. My nails dug into her back. Tajel gripped my thigh, slowly rotating as she penetrated me deeper. My back arched, and my hips buckled.

"Mm," I moaned.

Tajel panted breathlessly in my ear, picking up speed. My body rose to the occasion, rocking my hips as Tajel pumped into me. I cried out loudly, squeezing my eyes shut.

"Gosh," Tajel said breathlessly. "You sound so sexy."

She pumped harder and my head smacked into the cushion of the couch.

"God. You're fucking me so good...ohm!"

Tajel kept the pace, breathing fast and loudly. Toes curling, I growled as my orgasm overtook me. I felt nothing but her body and my orgasm. She waited until my body relaxed before slipping out of me.

"You are amazing."

I heard a chuckle escape Tajel's lips.

"Anytime you want...I'll give it." She bent down to kiss me. "I love you."

"I love you too."

She sat up, stripping off the strap-on and tugging at me. "Come to bed. We have a week to prepare for your family. I can't fuck this up."

I frowned. "Wait, I thought my parents were no big deal to you?"

Tajel gave me a sheepish grin.

"Baby, this is new for me, too." I narrowed my eyes at her and she paused for a moment before saying, "I love you and your crazy side."

I lunged at Tajel. "Did you just call me crazy?"

Tajel held her hand up as if to ward against me. "Babe, I'm only saying you have a fiery side. And if you say your family's crazy...that makes them probably worse than you."

I laughed and chased her to our room where I would finish her off.

I jumped on top of Tajel, making the bed shake. She laughed as I pinned her down.

"What are you doing?"

I didn't respond. Instead, I began sucking on the flesh of her neck. Tajel moaned, shifting under me. I positioned myself at her feet, taking off the rest of her clothes. I wanted to see her completely naked. I moved back up, my body stretched over hers. Our breasts pressed together, and I moaned when my fingers dipped between her legs. She was wet.

"I need to make love to you."

"Need, huh?" Tajel asked.

I nodded. "Very badly."

I kissed her lips, the passion burning through my flesh. I could barely keep my composure. I kissed my way down her body, suckling on her breast. Her nipple hardened in my mouth as she moaned.

"Please," she panted.

Taking my time, I devoured every part of Tajel's body. She shivered when my lips made it to between her legs. The juices from her pink flesh were heavy. I flicked my tongue over her swollen center and she jerked. Instantly, I sucked lightly on her clit, causing her to squirm. I rotated my tongue over her wetness, until I found a rhythm that seemed to drive her mad. I moved my hand down to her inner thigh, grazing her flesh. My other hand was stretched out, twisting her nipple between my index finger and thumb.

Slipping two of my fingers inside of her, Tajel gasped, tightening as I curled my fingers inside her wet flesh. I picked up speed, both my tongue and fingers causing Tajel to squeal. She whimpered as an orgasm flooded her body.

I straddled her with the biggest grin on my face. "Now that's what I like to hear."

Chapter Thirty-Two
Arianna

I could openly admit seeing my family was going to be uncomfortable. My family reflected the sort of lifestyle you'd see on soap operas. They were dramatic, over the top, and everyone knew everyone's business. It wasn't all that bad. They loved you to the point of smothering, would give you anything you needed, and today their love would be put to the test. Would they accept a gay daughter?

Tajel convinced me to let them stay with us. Now here we were, standing near the baggage claim at the airport waiting for them to arrive. I kept cracking my knuckles, nervous and impatient. I was ready to get this over with.

"Will you stop fidgeting?" Tajel grabbed both my hands so I could stop moving them.

"I'm not—"

Tajel's look made me shut up.

"I can't help it."

"Yes, you can." Tajel knew me all too well. "We will pick them up and take them back to our place. Then we will go to my uncle's house in a couple of days. This will go smoothly."

"I still can't believe your uncle suggested to host a dinner at his house."

Tajel laughed. "My uncle can handle just about anyone. Plus, it's a few days away."

"*Chica!*" I heard someone calling out to me in a blissful chime. I cringed away from my cousin. "Arianna Castaldi. *Chica que extraño tu culo.*"

I felt her arms wrap around my waist and she squished me with her hug. I laughed, turning to hug her properly. I had to admit, I missed her and the rest my family.

"Hey, cousin." I kissed her on the cheek. I pointed to my cousin who was now facing Tajel. "This is my cousin, Mariana. Mariana, this is Tajel."

Tajel extended her hand and Mariana took it, scrutinizing her every movement. She nodded her approval to me. When my parents came into view, Tajel straightened herself. For the last week, she had been practicing her Spanish, wanting to make a good impression. I was very nervous. I wasn't ashamed of my relationship, only nervous exposing my sexuality to my family for the first time. I took hold of Tajel's hand as my parents and aunt approached.

Eyes only on me, my mom reached out to me first.

"*Cómo eres mi hija mi amor?*" My mom gave me a kiss on the cheek, hugging me tightly. "*Nos hemos perdido mucho.*"

Once my mom was done my dad hugged me next, planting a kiss on my forehead. The look in my aunt's eyes as my dad embraced me was heartwarming. It had been several months since I moved to Oregon, and I knew I had been missed.

I hugged my aunt next. She whispered in my ear, "*Ella es lindo si te vas a gustar las mujeres que tiene que lucir lindo como ella.*"

My Aunt Carmen looked over at my father for approval. He only shrugged. "*No lo entiendo.*"

I frowned. At least he was being honest without sounding so cruel about his ignorance toward my sexuality. Tajel had been standing patiently and quietly.

I reached over, holding my hand out.

"Stop trying to isolate my girlfriend."

I looked at my aunt knowing she was the start of this, *'we can't speak English,'* charade.

"You all can speak English." I looked at Tajel. "My aunt said—"

"Something about me being gorgeous," Tajel smirked.

She wasn't completely correct but knowing Tajel, she said what she wanted to hear from my Aunt Carmen.

"Close enough." I shook my head, smiling.

"She's funny." My cousin, Mariana, chuckled and tucked a few loose strands of her hair behind her ear.

"And she's right here," I added with a bit of attitude.

"Jeez, my bad, sparky," my cousin retorted.

She always called me that when I got upset or tried correcting her.

"Aunt Carmen. Mom. Dad."

I linked my fingers with Tajel's as my father eyes trailed down, staring at our hands. He seemed disbelieving and yet expressionless.

"This is Tajel Pierce..." I swallowed, adding, "my girlfriend."

"Holy shit," my cousin snickered. "I told you guys she'd actually say the words."

Mariana looked at me teasingly and I thought I might pass out.

"Just so you know...I always knew it. I was not surprised. You never wanted to go out with the boys I tried to set you up with and they were fine as hell."

I smiled shyly, more concerned about my parents' reactions.

"So," my mother waved to Tajel, "you two work together as paramedics and what? When did this happen?"

I bit the inside of my cheek. "A little over seven months ago."

"*Mija*, you are just now sharing this with us?"

"Yeah...well. I just wanted to..."

"You thought we'd disapprove?" my mother asked.

I frowned, unsure of where this conversation was going. "Yeah. I mean...you've both expressed how you see the world and me in it and I've seen how you've responded to gay people in our neighborhood. You said they corrupt our youth."

"Oh *mija.*" My mother sighed, regret was in her eyes.

"How about we get going?" my father suggested. "Not the place to do this."

"It would be an honor for you all to stay in our home." Tajel smiled charismatically as always. That was my charming girlfriend.

Mariana pursed her lips, impressed. She arched her brows at me.

"I like her," she whispered in my ear.

I shook my head as we headed back, happy to hear I had at least her support.

*

Tajel

If anyone ever said meeting your partner's family was easy, they were full of shit. Fortunately, the apartment I leased a few years back had three bedrooms. I excused myself from conversation to take a quick shower. I felt hot and sticky. Summer was here and honestly, being surrounded by Arianna's family made me sweat more than the weather.

After I was out of the shower and dressed in a new set of clothes, Arianna came into the room.

"You all right?"

I nodded.

Her arms slipped around my waist. "Babe, please tell me if this is too much."

"I'm fine." I kissed her to reassure her. "I'll be fine."

We walked back out into the living room and I hadn't yet sat on the couch before Arianna's father had a great deal of questions prepared for me. An hour passed before the questions finally slowed.

"You thought we would disown you?" Arianna's mother finally asked.

"If I had told you...tell me how you would have handled it?"

Her father said nothing.

"I admit, I had my suspicions watching you grow up." It was Arianna's Aunt Carmen who spoke. "I defended you all the time when people asked if you were gay. You're right. Back then, we wouldn't have accepted you."

"What are you saying?"

"We're saying we love you. And we support you," Arianna's father answered.

Tears fell from Arianna's eyes as she leaped into her parents' arms. I watched, happy to see the look in Arianna's eyes. Seeing her parents accept her was a beautiful sight.

"Don't ever lie to us like that again, *mija*." Her mom shook her head. "*Usted nos envía tales noticias a través de un texto*."

"Sorry, mom," Arianna replied.

She reached for my hand and squeezed it.

"*Mija*. Your aunt wants to make us all dinner tonight."

I looked over at Carmen excitedly after hearing that from her mother. Arianna could cook, but she told me about Aunt Carmen's cooking. Let's just say she'll always be welcome in our place.

"Can you take your aunt and cousin to the store?"

Arianna narrowed her eyes at her parents. They wanted to be left alone with me. As if them simply being here wasn't intimidating enough.

"Sooner you take them to the store the sooner I can enjoy your aunt's cooking." I kissed her on the lips, not considering the fact that her family was watching.

"See you in a bit." Arianna squeezed my thigh. She glanced at her parents.

"Come on, *mujer*," Mariana ordered. "I'm sure she will survive."

Arianna rolled her eyes and headed out.

"Can I offer you two another glass of sangria?"

"So Tajel, what are your plans for my daughter?"

It was Arianna's father who spoke first and was straight to the point. There was no time to waste. I guess physical space was all I'd get right now. I sighed, not interested in wasting time either. I returned with their wine and sat back down across from them.

"Our intention is not to be disrespectful in someone else's home." Arianna's father took his wife's hand and scooted to the edge of the couch. "I can accept Arianna being with another woman. We've learned to accept that long ago. For me, it does not change anything simply because you are a woman. I want to know your intentions for my daughter. Especially, since two are living together."

I understood and respected that. I smiled, happy that they would treat me the same way they would treat a man in a relationship with their daughter. I wanted to be equal to man if not greater.

"We also know you convinced my *mija* to tell us the truth," Arianna's mother added. "Thank you."

I didn't bother trying to take the credit. That's not what I wanted. I took a deep breath and said the thing that would give Arianna's parents a clear impression of my intentions for their daughter, feeling confident in my decision.

*

Arianna

I embraced Laura and Roosevelt the moment I walked into their home. Brooklyn was in the kitchen, putting the finishing touches on dinner. I wanted to introduce my cousin to her, so I pulled her into the kitchen with me.

"Hey, Arianna," Brooklyn greeted us first.

"Hey. This is my cousin, Mariana." I pointed to my cousin then over to Brooklyn. "This is Tajel's sister, Brooklyn."

Taking the lead, Tajel's sister offered her hand to Mariana. "Nice to meet you."

They said their pleasantries as I observed the unset dining table.

Brooklyn noticed what I was looking at. "It's beautiful outside and we have a lot of guests, so we thought we'd have dinner on the patio."

"Sounds perfect. Need any help?"

Brooklyn grinned. "Gosh, you're so amazing. My sister would wait until everything was done before asking if I needed help."

We all laughed and gathered the food. The patio was set up elegantly with fire lamps resting atop several tall posts. There was a bottle of wine centered with wine glasses, preset plates, and utensils wrapped in napkins on the table.

Tajel waved her arm toward the setup. "My aunt has been waiting for a moment like this to set out her favorite dishes."

"This is…" I shook my head, turning to Tajel. "Thank you. This is amazing. A bigger welcome than I envisioned."

"Knock, knock," Felipe said, Sasha and Danielle following right behind him.

I was surprised to see Felipe. Tajel greeted him with a high-five and he gave me a hug.

Mariana screeched, "Oh my God, where have you been?"

She leaped into Danielle's arms. We were all friends growing up.

Mariana spotted Sasha. "Oh, I see. Found yourself a lady, too. Arianna did tell me."

The doorbell rang as everyone was preparing to sit down.

"I'll get it," Tajel offered.

A few minutes passed and Tajel walked back in with Tyler beside her. She sat down beside me.

Leaning across to me, she whispered, "I invited him."

I was certainly surprised. The last few times I'd seen Tajel's brother I had tried to connect with him, slightly failing and succeeding all at once. To invite him here now was risky but a step in the right direction. Tajel needed to try and make him feel a part of her world again. He was clean and that was a big improvement. Everyone was seated, and I looked over to Tajel feeling thankful to have her around. Life couldn't get any better than this.

*

Tajel

"Are you excited about starting the SWAT training?" The question came from my sister.

I noticed Felipe was flirting with her throughout dinner. I took another bite of my eggplant lasagna.

Arianna supplied me with a napkin. "Babe, don't go overboard with the cheese."

"Okay." I noticed Arianna's parents observing us. I smiled shyly, clearing my throat to answer my sister's question. "I've been waiting for this chance since I first learned about it."

"I bet," Felipe joked. "You don't want Arianna coming after you if you don't act right."

I narrowed my eyes at Felipe playfully. "Just thank Arianna for saving you from the many times you ate my snacks at work."

Everyone laughed. Tyler was quiet almost the entire dinner, taking a bite of his lasagna and gradually warming up to everyone.

It was Arianna who brought Tyler into the conversation. "What was it like being a twin with Tajel?"

Tyler smiled, looking over to me as if to ask for permission to speak. I didn't want him to feel that way. He was trying, and I would give him the credit he deserved.

"I wasn't that bad, right?" I asked jokingly.

I wanted to make sure he was comfortable. I trusted him enough to know he wouldn't say anything inappropriate.

275

His smile widened. "Unbelievably, Tajel was always the one getting us in trouble."

Brooklyn laughed. "That's true. Mom and dad used to flip at the stunts Tajel pulled. Tyler always said nothing and took the blame, but our parents always knew it was you."

My uncle smirked. "I'm proud of all three of you."

My aunt grabbed my uncle's hand. "All three of you have overcome so much and are succeeding in your own ways."

"I am happy that my daughter is around a loving family," Arianna's mom spoke emotionally, capturing everyone's attention. "Makes me want to move closer to my little girl."

Arianna's face flushed, and I couldn't help but to laugh.

I cleared my throat, grabbing my glass of wine. I held it high and signaled for the everyone to listen. This was a perfect time to express my thanks and love. I pushed my chair back and stood.

Arianna touched my thigh. I was nervous. "Obviously, there's much to be thankful for."

I looked around the table.

"Truth is...today is more than about welcoming Arianna's family." I pointed my glass toward Felipe. "You're here because you're my closest friend...second to Sasha, of course."

Sasha nodded her head in agreement. "Damn straight."

"My big sis. I know I've been stubborn toward you—"

"Just her?" my uncle asked sarcastically.

I rolled my eyes and my aunt said, "Leave her alone."

"Anyway," I continued, "being here tonight. I want to leave here tonight...different."

I'd never been this nervous before.

"We've been through a lot and I'm glad to have you here."

I looked down at my brother who was taking a sip of his water.

I spoke directly to him now, "You always promised you'd have my back for a night like this."

I shook my hand that was hanging to my side. I took another sip of my wine and then placed it on the table.

"You okay?" Arianna asked, thinking I was about to deliver bad news. She was always assuming the opposite of what I did or said.

I nodded. I relaxed enough to breathe normally again. I slid my hands into my pockets. My chest tightened a little.

" You look like you're about to have a heart attack." Felipe had a concerned look on his face.

I needed to express myself in a way that made it easy for me. "You still have my keyboard, uncle?"

He nodded with a smile. "Still in great shape."

He got up to get it as I looked down at Arianna. "I did promise that you'd hear my voice eventually."

A blush covered Arianna's cheeks. "Babe."

"I leaned down to kiss her lips as my uncle came back and set up my keyboard to the side of the table. I moved over to it.

Sasha grabbed her phone. "I'm recording this."

I laughed, knowing she would. It has been four years since I last played.

"Our dad was a pianist. Our mother was a jazz singer. That's how I fell in love with music." I stood over the keyboard, wiggling my fingers. "They used to tell us that music isn't just art."

In unison, my brother and sister joined in with me to say, "It's a way to have someone fall in love with you...one way or another."

We all laughed.

I placed my fingers comfortably against the keys. "My mom sang this song to my father every year for their anniversary. She said it was a song every woman should sing to the person they loved."

I looked down at Arianna, who now had tears falling from her eyes. I only saw her.

"Teena Marie was one of the greatest artists out there. Her voice was mesmerizing. I hope to do my mom justice in singing her favorite song called Hypnotized."

I began to play the song, moving my fingers lightly over the keys. When my time came, I began to sing. I went through the whole song at a soothing, non-rushed pace, making sure every word expressed what I felt. I finished the song perfectly, adding a few of my own notes at the end. When I was done, my gaze returned to Arianna. Everyone else sat speechless and emotional.

Arianna stood up to embrace me. "That was...perfect."

"There is no doubt in what I want. I thought my life was as good as it was going to get before meeting you. We're not here to only welcome your family. We're here...because I want us to be a unity of one whole family."

More tears fell from Arianna's eyes. "I want that, too."

"Then you'll have no problem marrying me," I said with tears streaming down my face. "Because I got your parents' approval."

"This is real?" She looked over to her parents for confirmation.

They nodded.

Arianna turned back to me and I held out two engagement rings. "These are for both you and me. The beginning of our new lives. I don't need to be with you for years to know how madly in love I am with you."

"This is happening!"

"If you don't hurry and answer her question, I will," Danielle said. "I have my Pinterest already set up for my maid of honor role."

Everyone laughed.

"I was so defiant against what I felt from the moment I met you." Arianna turned to everyone who wasn't there that night. "She was so arrogant and smooth. I told myself I would just... I would just entertain her flirtation. Then I found out we'd be partners at work and I freaked out."

"Understatement," I said. "You were in denial."

"You set me straight." She took a deep breath, looking at me with those beautiful, brown eyes. "I love you and I'd be as stupid as I was in the first few weeks we knew each other, if I denied us...this...if I didn't say *yes*."

I smiled, waiting for her to answer clearly. I was holding my breath.

"Yes. I will marry you. And I can't wait to be your wife and have babies with you."

I reached for her suddenly, my breath knocked out of me by her words as I embraced her lovingly. This was it! Our new start. Something I never thought I'd find. Falling in love with Arianna was more than I could ask for.

*

Arianna

There was nothing that could ruin this day. For the rest of the night I clung to Tajel's side like an additional limb. Danielle and Sasha were already going over wedding ideas.

"You know you two are next," Tajel teased.

"Oh, yeah!" Sasha winked at Danielle, causing my best friend to blush.

My parents squished me into a hug, my aunt behind them. "We're so happy for you two, *mija*."

"Thanks," I blushed.

"Welcome to the family!" My mom kissed Tajel's cheek. "I'm so happy."

I know you'll be good for each other," my dad added.

We commenced conversation regarding our future, everyone eventually scattering. Finally alone for the first time since we got engaged, I pressed my fingers into the skin of Tajel's shoulders. She sighed, relaxed and tranquil from my hands massaging her. I leaned to Tajel's side, kissing her cheek. I held my hand stretched out in front of hers where my engagement ring rested on my finger.

Tajel reached up to my other hand that was still at her shoulder. She squeezed it firmly. "These rings belonged to my mother."

I moved to the front of her, sitting on her lap. I stared back at the ring on my finger. "She had two engagement rings?"

Tajel laughed.

"Funny story. My dad proposed twice. Once, he gave her the ring on my finger." Tajel admired it for a moment. "They were engaged for two years...nearly broke up, and when he was finally serious and ready to marry her, he bought her a second engagement ring. These rings were left for me. My mom's wedding ring is for my sis and my dad's ring is for my brother."

"Well...this is us." I looked at Tajel. "I love you and I promise to always cherish this moment and this ring."

Tajel smirked. "Relax, babe. No need to be working on your vows right now."

"I have a lot more where that came from." I leaned in, stealing a kiss. "For now, I'll start with something simple and right to the point."

Tajel put her arms around me. There was no greater feeling than this. My heart was overwhelmed, and I rejoiced. I only wanted her.

"Let's ditch them. Go home and make love."

Tajel sighed when my lips brushed her neck. "Wait..."

"You really want to stay here?" I asked, disbelieving.

"Of course not." She looked off to the house. "What about your parents?"

"Really?" I shook my head. "They're adults. They'll figure out how to get back. Besides, if they're smart they know not to come back tonight and Laura and Rosy will invite them to stay the night."

"True." I knew I had convinced her. "Let's go home."

"Let's make this wedding happen soon," Tajel said. "The sooner the better. And we'll be able to get everyone off our backs."

I laughed knowing that was so true. "Agreed."

We snuck away from the house, escaping to our place for the rest of the night. No distractions, only us, to plan for a life we both desired.

About the Author

Domina Alexandra is a native of Southern California who has recently transplanted to Salem, Oregon. She is an author of stories with strong female protagonists, authentic emotions and thrilling action scenes that mirror her career as an EMT on the way to becoming a SWAT Medic. She grew up writing poetry as an outlet and, in 2006, joined a Live Theater program, where she played many roles in productions of plays and musicals. During her four years of acting, she fell in love with writing monologues, screenplays, and all things story. When she's not saving lives as an EMT, she advocates for LGBT Youth with a vision of growing a stronger community of care, acceptance, and compassion. Her books include *Her Endure*. She gets her imaginative ideas from her life as a EMT as well as being stuck in her head too long as a child.

Other Titles Available From Triplicity Publishing

Awakened by Fate by Lynn Lawler. Jackie is a woman living life according to her own rules. She's married, but it's the unspoken, open kind. She can have as many female lovers as she likes; she just can't talk about them. After a bizarre encounter turns her world upside down, things slowly begin to change. She finds herself in desperation as she searches for answers. What she discovers is nothing is delivered in a neatly wrapped box. Now that everything has been brought out into the open, she finds she can't run away from her truth anymore. With her new life, comes new responsibilities and a different outcome than what she was expecting. Jackie isn't alone in the story. She meets several new people who help her along her journey.

Nautical Delights by S. L. Gape. Lady Elizabeth Barrington has spent her entire life trying to please her family; constantly opting for a quiet life, she utilises her profession as a doctor to keep out of her families' clutches; bar the annual two-week Caribbean private cruise, where there is simply no budge. Confined to two weeks on board the Iconica super yacht, she intends on keeping her head down and enjoying as much of the holiday as she can, whilst keeping her family at arm's length. Until a crew member catches her eye.

Whispers of the Heart by KA Moll. Days after completing her fellowship in pediatric ophthalmology, thirty-five-year-old Aki Williams travels from her home in Los Angeles to a small town in Illinois, interviewing for a job that she doesn't want. What she does want is to meet her biological sister, Jack Camdon, a sister whom she didn't know existed until she dreamt of her. Three years ago on Sunday, forty-three-year-old professor of archaeology, Carsyn Lyndon, lost her parents and her wife in a tragic accident. Since then, she's suffered from PTSD and loneliness. She's kind-hearted and handsome but dates no one. When she meets Aki at her four-year-old Godson's birthday party, they're incredibly attracted to one another, and those feelings intensify during a family camping trip— a particularly interesting development for Aki since prior to that she'd never considered that she might be a lesbian.

Worlds Apart by S.L. Gape. Hollywood A-lister Heidi Spencer-Brady is everything you'd expect of an Idol. Loved by all, the British Beauty is graceful, talented, humble and so far removed from the 'typical' LA scene. When her husband's infidelity with his new 'leading lady' is leaked, Dawn, Heidi's best friend and manager, goes all out to protect her. She arranges for Heidi to go back to the UK and stay on her cousins farm they had visited as children, much to the disappointment of the animal fearing Heidi.

Castor Valley (Law & Order Series Book 2) by Graysen Morgen. Jessie Henry is torn when she reads about the capture of the Doyle brothers, two young men who were part of her old gang. Unable to let them hang for a crime she's sure they didn't commit, Jessie leaves her wife and the Town of Boone Creek behind, and sets out on a journey back to the one place she thought she'd never see again, *Castor Valley*. Ellie Henry watches the love of her life leave, not knowing if she will ever return. When she gets an odd telegram, nearly a week later, she fears Jessie is in trouble. With no other choice, she goes to the one person who can help her.

Close Enough to Touch by Cade Brogan. Joanna Grey injects the deadly poison into the chamber of the syringe—time after time. She's murdered before and she'll do it again. She's intelligent, educated, and beautiful. Rylee Hayes is a respected homicide detective. Her best friends are her grandparents, her coonhound, and her partner—in that order. Kenzie Bigham is the single mom of a thirteen-year-old, a church secretary, and a woman who's struggled much of her adult life with her own sexuality. Their paths will cross when Rylee's new investigation involves members of Kenzie's congregation. Will Rylee have what it takes to meet the challenge of a serial killer who's proven herself to be a more than worthy opponent?

Fight to the Top by S. L. Gape. Georgia is a forty year old, single, Area Director from Manchester, UK who is all work and definitely no play. Having no time to socialise or spend time with her family she prides herself on being fit and well-polished. Erika is an Area Director for the same company, but in the United States. Whilst she is concentrating so heavily on the promotion she has been fighting for, she's starting to feel like her life outside of work is falling apart. The two women are exceptionally different, and worlds apart. Both of their lives are turned upside down when their jobs are snatched from under their noses, and they are suddenly faced with being thrown together by their bosses for one last major project...in Texas.

Boone Creek (Law & Order Series book 1) by Graysen Morgen. Jessie Henry is looking for a new life. She's unknown in the town of Boone Creek when she arrives, and wants to keep it that way. When she's offered the job of Town Marshal, she takes it, believing that protecting others and upholding the law is the penance for her past. Ellie Fray is a widowed, shopkeeper. She generally keeps to herself, but the mysterious new Town Marshal both intrigues and infuriates her. She believes the last thing the town needs is someone stirring up trouble with the outlaws who have taken over.

Witness by Joan L. Anderson. Becca and Kate have lived together for eight years, and have always spent their vacation in a tropical paradise, lying on a beach. This year, Becca wanted to try something different: a seven day, 65-mile hike in the beautiful Cascade Mountains of Washington state. Their peaceful vacation turns to horror when they stumble upon a brutal murder taking place in the back country.

Too Soon by S.L. Gape. Brooke is a twenty-nine year old detective from Oxford, who has her life pretty much planned out until her boss and partner of nine years, Maria, tells her their relationship is over. When Brooke finds out the truth, that Maria cheated on her with their best friend Paula, she decides to get her life back on track by getting away for six weeks in Anglesey, North Wales. Chloe, a thirty three year old artist and art director, owns a log cabin on Anglesey where she spends each weekend painting and surfing. After returning from a surf, she stumbles upon the somewhat uptight and enigmatic Brooke.

Blue Ice Landing by KA Moll. Coy is a beautiful blonde with a southern accent and a successful practice as a physician assistant. She has a comfortable home, good friends, and a loving family. She's also a widow, carrying a burden of responsibility for her wife's untimely death. Coby is a woman with secrets. She's estranged from her family, a recovering alcoholic, and alone because she's convinced that she's unlovable. When she loses her job as a heavy equipment operator, she'll accept one that'll force her to step way outside her comfort zone. When Coy quits her job to accept a position in Antarctica, her path will cross with Coby's. Their attraction to one another will be immediate, and despite their differences, it won't be long before they fall in love. But for these two, with all their baggage, will love be enough?

Never Quit (Never Series book 2) by Graysen Morgen. Two years after stepping away from the action as a Coast Guard Rescue Swimmer to become an instructor, Finley finds herself in charge of the most difficult class of cadets she's ever faced, while also juggling the taxing demands of having a home life with her partner Nicole, and their fifteen year old daughter. Jordy Ross gave up everything, dropping out of college, and leaving her family behind, to join the Coast Guard and become a rescue swimmer cadet. The extreme training tests her fitness level, pushing her mentally and physically further than she's ever been in her life, but it's the aggressive competition between her and another female cadet that proves to be the most challenging.

For a Moment's Indiscretion by KA Moll. With ten years of marriage under their belt, Zane and Jaina are coasting. The little things they used to do for one another have fallen by the wayside. They've gotten busy with life. They've forgotten to nurture their love and relationship. Even soul mates can stumble on hard times and have marital difficulties. Enter Amelia, a new faculty member in Jaina's building. She's new in town, young, and very pretty. When an argument with Zane causes Jaina to storm out angry, she reaches out to Amelia. Of course, she seizes the opportunity. And for a moment of indiscretion, Jaina could lose everything.

Never Let Go (Never Series book 1) by Graysen Morgen. For Coast Guard Rescue Swimmer, Finley Morris, life is good. She loves her job, is well respected by her peers, and has been given an opportunity to take her career to the next level. The only thing missing is the love of her life, who walked out, taking their daughter with her, seven years earlier. When Finley gets a call from her ex, saying their teenage daughter is coming to spend the summer with her, she's floored. While spending more time with her daughter, whom she doesn't get to see often, and learning to be a full-time parent, Finley quickly realizes she has not, and will never, let go of what is important.

Pursuit by Joan L. Anderson. Claire is a workaholic attorney who flies to Paris to lick her wounds after being dumped by her girlfriend of seventeen years. On the plane she chats with the young woman sitting next to her, and when they land the woman is inexplicably detained in Customs. Claire is surprised when she later runs into the woman in the city. They agree to meet for breakfast the next morning, but when the woman doesn't show up Claire goes to her hotel and makes a horrifying discovery. She soon finds herself ensnared in a web of intrigue and international terrorism, becoming the target of a high stakes game of cat and mouse through the streets of Paris.

Wrecked by Sydney Canyon. To most people, the *Duchess* is a myth formed by old pirates tales, but to Reid Cavanaugh, a Caribbean island bum and one of the best divers and treasure hunters in the world, it's a real, seventeenth century pirate ship—the holy grail of underwater treasure hunting. Reid uses the same cunning tactics she always has before setting out to find the lost ship. However, she is forced to bring her business partner's daughter along as collateral this time because he doesn't trust her. Neither woman is thrilled, but being cooped up on a small dive boat for days, forces them to get know each other quickly.

Arson by Austen Thorne. Madison Drake is a detective for the Stetson Beach Police Department. The last thing she wants to do is show a new detective the ropes, especially when a fire investigation becomes arson to cover up a murder. Madison butts heads with Tara, her trainee, deals with sarcasm from Nic, her ex-girlfriend who is a patrol officer, and finds calm in the chaos of police work with Jamie, her best friend who is the county medical examiner. Arson is the first of many in a series of novella episodes surrounding the fictional Stetson Beach Police Department and Detective Madison Drake.

Change of Heart by KA Moll. Courtney Holloman is a woman at the top of her game. She's successful, wealthy, and a highly sought after Washington lobbyist. She has money, her job, booze, and nothing else. In quiet moments, against her will, her mind drifts back to her days in high school and to all that she gave up. Jack Camdon is a complex woman, and yet not at all. She is also a woman who has never moved beyond the sudden and unexplained departure of her high school sweetheart, her lover, and her soul mate. When circumstances bring Courtney back to town two decades later, their paths will cross. Will it be too late?

Mommies (Bridal Series book 3) by Graysen Morgen. Britton and her wife Daphne have been married for a year and a half and are happy with their life, until Britton's mother hounds her to find out why her sister Bridget hasn't decided to have children yet. This prompts Daphne to bring up the big subject of having kids of their own with Britton. Britton hadn't really thought much about having kids, but her love for Daphne makes her see life and their future together in a whole new way when they decide to become mommies.

Haunting *Love* by K.A. Moll. Anna Crestwood was raised in the strict beliefs of a religious sect nestled in the foothills of the Smoky Mountains. She's a lesbian with a ton of baggage—fearful, guilty, and alone. Very few things would compel her to leave the familiar. The job offer of a lifetime is one of them. Gabe Garst is a police officer. She's also a powerful medium. Her work with juvenile delinquents and ghosts is all that keeps her going. Inside she's dead, certain that her capacity to love is buried six feet under. Anna and Gabe's paths cross. Their attraction is immediate, but they hold back until all hope seems lost.

Rapture & Rogue by Sydney Canyon. Taren Rauley is happy and in a good relationship, until the one person she thought she'd never see again comes back into her life. She struggles to keep the past from colliding with the present as old feelings she thought were dead and gone, begin to haunt her. In college, Gianna Revisi was a mastermind, ring-leading, crime boss. Now, she has a great life and spends her time running Rapture and Rogue, the two establishments she built from the ground up. The last person she ever expects to see walk into one of them, is the girl who walked out on her, breaking her heart five years ago.

Second Chance by Sydney Canyon. After an attack on her convoy, Marine Corps Staff Sergeant, Darien Hollister, must learn to live without her sight. When an experimental procedure allows her to see again, Darien is torn, knowing someone had to die in order for this to happen.

She embarks on a journey to personally thank the donor's family, but is too stunned to tell them the truth. Mixed emotions stir inside of her as she slowly gets to the know the people that feel like so much more than strangers to her. When the truth finally comes out, Darien walks away, taking the second chance that she's been given to go back to the only life she's ever known, but she's not the only one with a second chance at life.

Meant to Be by Graysen Morgen. Brandt is about to walk down the aisle with her girlfriend, when an unexpected chain of events turns her world upside down, causing her to question the last three years of her life. A chance encounter sparks a mix of rage and excitement that she has never felt before. Summer is living life and following her dreams, all the while, harboring a huge secret that could ruin her career. She believes that some things are better kept in the dark, until she has her third run-in with a woman she had hoped to never see again, and gives into temptation. Brandt and Summer start believing everything happens for a reason as they learn the true meaning of meant to be.

Coming Home by Graysen Morgen. After tragedy derails TJ Abernathy's life, she packs up her three year old son and heads back to Pennsylvania to live with her grandmother on the family farm. TJ picks back up where she left off eight years earlier, tending to the fruit and nut tree orchard, while learning her grandmother's secret trade. Soon, TJ's high school sweetheart and the same girl who broke her heart, comes back into her life, threatening to steal it away once again. As the weeks turn into months and tragedy strikes again, TJ realizes coming home was the best thing she could've ever done.

Special Assignment by Austen Thorne. Secret Service Agent Parker Meeks has her hands full when she gets her new assignment, protecting a Congressman's teenage daughter, who has had threats made on her life and been whisked away to a Christian boarding school under an alias to finish out her senior year. Parker is fine with the assignment, until she finds out she has to go undercover as a Canon Priest. The last thing Parker expects to find is a beautiful, art history teacher, who is intrigued by her in more ways than one.

Miracle at Christmas by Sydney Canyon. A Modern Twist on the Classic Scrooge Story. Dylan is a power-hungry lawyer who pushed away everything good in her life to become the best defense attorney in the, often winning the worst cases and keeping anyone with enough money out of jail. She's visited on Christmas Eve by her deceased law partner, who threatens her with a life in hell like his own, if she doesn't change her path. During the course of the night, she is taken on a journey through her past, present, and future with three very different spirits.

Bella Vita by Sydney Canyon. Brady is the First Officer of the crew on the Bella Vita, a luxury charter yacht in the Caribbean. She enjoys the laidback island lifestyle, and is accustomed to high profile guests, but when a U.S. Senator charters the yacht as a gift to his beautiful twin daughters who have just graduated from college and a few of their friends, she literally has her hands full.

Brides (Bridal Series book 2) by Graysen Morgen. Britton Prescott is dating the love of her life, Daphne Attwood, after a few tumultuous events that happened to unravel at her sister's wedding reception, seven months earlier. She's happy with the way things are, but immense pressure from her family and friends to take the next step, nearly sends her back to the single life. The idea of a long engagement and simple wedding are thrown out the window, as both families take over, rushing Britton and Daphne to the altar in a matter of weeks.

Cypress Lake by Graysen Morgen. The small town of Cypress Lake is rocked when one murder after another happens. Dani Ricketts, the Chief Deputy for the Cypress Lake Sheriff's Office, realizes the murders are linked. She's surprised when the girl that broke her heart in high school has not only returned home, but she's also Dani's only suspect. Kristen Malone has come back to Cypress Lake to put the past behind her so that she can move on with her life. Seeing Dani Ricketts again throws her off-guard, nearly derailing her plans to finally rid herself and her family of Cypress Lake.

Crashing Waves by Graysen Morgen. After a tragic accident, Pro Surfer, Rory Eden, spends her days hiding in the surf and snowboard manufacturing company that she built from the ground up, while living her life as a shell of the person that she once was. Rory's world is turned upside down when a young surfer pursues her, asking for the one thing she can't do. Adler Troy and Dr. Cason Macauley from Graysen Morgen's bestselling novel: *Falling Snow*, make an appearance in this romantic adventure about life, love, and letting go.

Bridesmaid of Honor (Bridal Series book 1) by Graysen Morgen. Britton Prescott's best friend is getting married and she's the maid of honor. As if that isn't enough to deal with, Britton's sister announces she's getting married in the same month and her maid of honor is her best friend Daphne, the same woman who has tormented Britton for years. Britton has to suck it up and play nice, instead of scratching her eyes out, because she and Daphne are in both weddings. Everyone is counting on them to behave like adults.

Falling Snow by Graysen Morgen. Dr. Cason Macauley, a high-speed trauma surgeon from Denver meets Adler Troy, a professional snowboarder and sparks fly. The last thing Cason wants is a relationship and Adler doesn't realize what's right in front of her until it's gone, but will it be too late?

Fate vs. Destiny by Graysen Morgen. Logan Greer devotes her life to investigating plane crashes for the National Transportation Safety Board. Brooke McCabe is an investigator with the Federal Aviation Association who literally flies by the seat of her pants. When Logan gets tangled in head games with both women will she choose fate or destiny?

Just Me by Graysen Morgen. Wild child Ian Wiley has to grow up and take the reins of the hundred year old family business when tragedy strikes. Cassidy Harland is a little surprised that she came within an inch of picking up a gorgeous stranger in a bar and is shocked to find out that stranger is the new head of her company.

Love Loss Revenge by Graysen Morgen. Rian Casey is an FBI Agent working the biggest case of her career and madly in love with her girlfriend. Her world is turned upside when tragedy strikes. Heartbroken, she tries to rebuild her life. When she discovers the truth behind what really happened that awful night she decides justice isn't good enough, and vows revenge on everyone involved.

Natural Instinct by Graysen Morgen. Chandler Scott is a Marine Biologist who keeps her private life private. Corey Joslen is intrigued by Chandler from the moment she meets her. Chandler is forced to finally open her life up to Corey. It backfires in Corey's face and sends her running. Will either woman learn to trust her natural instinct?

Secluded Heart by Graysen Morgen. Chase Leery is an overworked cardiac surgeon with a group of best friends that have an opinion and a reason for everything. When she meets a new artist named Remy Sheridan at her best friend's art gallery she is captivated by the reclusive woman. When Chase finds out why Remy is so sheltered will she put her career on the line to help her or is it too difficult to love someone with a secluded heart?

In Love, at War by Graysen Morgen. Charley Hayes is in the Army Air Force and stationed at Ford Island in Pearl Harbor. She is the commanding officer of her own female-only service squadron and doing the one thing she loves most, repairing airplanes. Life is good for Charley, until the day she finds herself falling in love while fighting for her life as her country is thrown haphazardly into World War II. Can she survive being in love and at war?

Fast Pitch by Graysen Morgen. Graham Cahill is a senior in college and the catcher and captain of the softball team. Despite being an all-star pitcher, Bailey Michaels is young and arrogant. Graham and Bailey are forced to get to know each other off the field in order to learn to work together on the field. Will the extra time pay off or will it drive a nail through the team?

Submerged by Graysen Morgen. Assistant District Attorney Layne Carmichael had no idea that the sexy woman she took home from a local bar for a one night stand would turn out to be someone she would be prosecuting months later. Scooter is a Naval Officer on a submarine who changes women like she changes uniforms. When she is accused of a heinous crime she is shocked to see her latest conquest sitting across from her as the prosecuting attorney.

Vow of Solitude by Austen Thorne. Detective Jordan Denali is in a fight for her life against the ghosts from her past and a Serial Killer taunting her with his every move. She lives a life of solitude and plans to keep it that way. When Callie Marceau, a curious Medical Examiner, decides she wants in on the biggest case of her career, as well as, Jordan's life, Jordan is powerless to stop her.

Igniting Temptation by Sydney Canyon. Mackenzie Trotter is the Head of Pediatrics at the local hospital. Her life takes a rather unexpected turn when she meets a flirtatious, beautiful fire fighter. Both women soon discover it doesn't take much to ignite temptation.

One Night by Sydney Canyon. While on a business trip, Caylen Jarrett spends an amazing night with a beautiful stripper. Months later, she is shocked and confused when that same woman re-enters her life. The fact that this stranger could destroy her career doesn't bother her. C.J. is more terrified of the feelings this woman stirs in her. Could she have fallen in love in one night and not even known it?

Fine by Sydney Canyon. Collin Anderson hides behind a façade, pretending everything is fine. Her workaholic wife and best friend are both oblivious as she goes on an emotional journey, battling a potentially hereditary disease that her mother has been diagnosed with. The only person who knows what is really going on, is Collin's doctor. The same doctor, who is an acquaintance that she's always been attracted to, and who has a partner of her own.

Shadow's Eyes by Sydney Canyon. Tyler McCain is the owner of a large ranch that breeds and sells different types of horses. She isn't exactly thrilled when a Hollywood movie producer shows up wanting to film his latest movie on her property. Reegan Delsol is an up and coming actress who has everything going for her when she lands the lead role in a new film, but there one small problem that could blow the entire picture.

Light Reading: A Collection of Novellas by Sydney Canyon. Four of Sydney Canyon's novellas together in one book, including the bestsellers Shadow's Eyes and One Night.

Visit us at www.tri-pub.com